With thunder, with thunder, you'll come
Undreamed of battles to be won!
She'll know at once your spirit strong,
Discover, sing, the earth's wild song.
And when you've taught her all you know
With thunder, with thunder, with thunder
You'll go.

Thunderwith

Thunderwith

Libby Hathorn

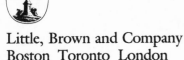

Little, Brown and Company
Boston Toronto London

First U.S. Edition 1991

The characters and events in this book are fictitious. Any similarity to real persons, living or dead, is coincidental and not intended by the author.

First published in Australia by William Heinemann Australia, 1989

Library of Congress Cataloging-in-Publication Data

Hathorn, Elizabeth.
   Thunderwith / by Libby Hathorn. — 1st U.S. ed.
     p. cm.
   "First published in Australia by William Heinemann Australia, 1989" — T.p. verso.
   Summary: After she moves to the Australian outback following her mother's death, fifteen-year-old Laura's friendship with a strange and beautiful dog helps her adjust to a new life with an unfamiliar father and unfriendly stepfamily.
   ISBN 0-316-35034-6
   [1. Dingo — Fiction. 2. Dogs — Fiction. 3. Stepfamilies — Fiction. 4. Australia — Fiction.] I. Title.
PZ7.H2843Th   1991
[Fic] — dc20   90-19410

10 9 8 7 6 5 4 3 2 1

HC

Printed in the United States of America

Dedication

This story was begun one night on a farm in the Wallingat, a spectacular rain forest on the coast of New South Wales, Australia. Around midnight I was awakened by thunder and lightning and looking out the window of the simple corrugated homestead where I was staying, I saw the shadow of a dog pass across a clearing. That holiday was memorable for the experience of the beauty of the surrounding bush and nearby wild beaches, for the strength and intensity of the storm and for the story. But it was on the return home that holiday I was to learn a friend of mine was gravely ill.

I dedicate this story to her, a blithe spirit, Cheryl Blois.

Thunderwith

1

Lara ran out of the neat little house by the school when at last she heard the sound of the motor. She'd been waiting over three quarters of an hour now, unable to settle down, her bags packed ready in the hall. She recognized the driver of the battered four-wheel-drive at once. It was her father, she was sure. He jumped out of the car.

"Lara. It is Lara, isn't it?"

She stood silently, leaning on the verandah post regarding the man she did not know at all and yet knew so well from the few old photographs her mother had kept.

He hesitated a moment. "It is you, Lara?" She nodded.

"Well it's me then," he said unnecessarily. "It's your father."

"I know."

When he hugged her to him she couldn't respond for a storm of tears was inside her and her mother seemed so close now. He smelled exactly as she'd imagined — of the bush, of fire and wood and sweat and also faintly of tobacco. She wished she could hug him back but she drew away when Mrs. Robinson pushed open the wire screen door and greeted him.

"Mr. Ritchie," she said warmly.

"Larry Ritchie," he said, awkward now. "Call me Larry, please."

"Lara has been more or less ready since the crack of dawn.

She moved all her things into the hall about an hour ago. She was expecting you from noon on," she smiled and then, putting an arm around Lara's thin shoulders, said, "We're glad we finally found you, aren't we, Lara?"

Lara found it difficult to know just what to say. Here they were in the hot sun on the verandah of the school principal's house — her long-lost father, this tall angular man with his piercing blue eyes, and her beloved teacher. Both of them standing and looking at her and expecting a reply of some kind. But she could only stare dumbly at this total stranger, who was nevertheless her only family now. Her father.

Mrs. Robinson had spared no effort to find Larry Ritchie, a stranger for more than eleven years to Lara. All the while during her mother's illness there had been the specter of the home for Lara if her father could not be traced. Mrs. Robinson had been as firm and as positive as Mom. "We're getting closer all the time to finding him. I'm sure of it. They'll find the man," her mother had told Lara over and over during those last few weeks of her illness. "No child of mine will go to any home. I know Larry will come for you, Lara."

And he had. But too late for Cheryl Ritchie, Lara's mother, to know. She died unaware that Mrs. Robinson had tracked Larry and his new family to a remote farm north of Newcastle just beyond the Bulahdelah Mountains in the Wallingat Forest. Cheryl Ritchie was never to know that only a few hundred kilometers separated Idle Hours Trailer Park from Larry Ritchie, the man in the crumpled photographs.

"Well, let's not stand around here all day. I believe Albert has the kettle on. We'll have a cup of tea before you're on your way." It was Mrs. Robinson who interrupted the prolonged silence. Larry seemed ill at ease inside the house though both Marjorie and Albert Robinson spoke warmly.

"Bit of a job tracking you down, mate," Albert said, handing him a steaming mug of tea and one for Lara too. "We heard you'd settled in Queensland."

"We did for a while," Larry said, "but Gladwyn — that's the wife — well, she couldn't take the heat up there."

Lara saw the color surge into his tanned face when he men-

4

tioned the word "wife" and she glanced away, embarrassed for him and for her Mom who once, long ago, had been "the wife." Larry's first wife.

"You see, we had this offer of a bit of land over the back of Bulahdelah Mountains on the forest road. A couple of hundred acres, so we came there to live for a while and see if we liked it. The wife had her fourth there, young Jasper." He blushed again as he mentioned the unknown family, but then looked straight at Marjorie and said, "And now thanks to you, we have Lara, too." There was that open friendly smile again for Lara.

She decided then and there that the Man, as Mom had always called him, was a really nice man.

The minute they'd pulled out of the driveway of the Lakeside School principal's house, Marjorie and Albert Robinson waving furiously, all awkwardness seemed to slip away. Lara found herself talking a great deal as they headed north towards the city of Newcastle and beyond. To the turn-off her Dad had told her about at the small town of Bulahdelah that would lead finally to the forest road and her new home. The Man seemed to like to listen. He asked just the right questions, made just the right responses, so that she found herself recounting the last few months in great detail. She found herself telling him things she didn't think she'd tell anyone.

She told him of the night her mother had said they would not have much longer together. She told him of her mother's concern for her daughter, the unsparing efforts she'd made to find Larry before the illness became too dreadful and laid her low, her energy completely sapped. She told him of her mother's cheerfulness and bravery right up until the last. Of how, just a few days before she'd died, they'd been laughing together in the hospital at some joke or other.

"Just like Cheryl," Larry said quietly.

"Mom said that her going would be a new beginning for me. She said it lots of times. But I can't help it. It feels like the end to me," Lara told her father.

"She was right you know, kiddo. This is all new," he said. "You'll have a brand new family, Lara. A baby brother and three little sisters and a new mom. I'm not pretending it'll be easy — but it's a fresh start and if we all try hard it's bound to work out okay."

She liked the way he spoke so quietly and cheerfully. Perhaps Mom was right. It would be a new beginning with the Man. If only Mom had been here to share it.

She stared out the window at the scenery that was unfamiliar to her now that they'd left the sprawling outskirts of Newcastle behind them. It was *really* the country here, she thought. Those rolling fields and glimpses of occasional farmhouses. And all the stationary cows that looked like cardboard cutouts, they were so still. Lara liked the sound of the Man's farm in the forest, too. Living on a farm would be good. Perhaps there'd be horses and she could learn to ride with the kids who were her new family. There were magnificent beaches nearby, the Man told her. They'd all go surfing together. Yes, perhaps it'd be okay in the end.

Lara felt sleepy. The sun was riding high and the motion of the car and all her talking made her tired. She closed her eyes. The Man didn't seem to mind that Lara didn't want to talk anymore. She wondered now as she'd wondered before why her Mom and the Man hadn't stayed together. He seemed so comfortable, so strong, so nice.

Lara could only vaguely remember the Man. Mom had left him when Lara had only been three and she'd met the musician from Melbourne, Walter. She distinctly remembered Walter, for all his unkindnesses to her as a small child. Mom had stuck it out in Melbourne with Walter for almost three years but finally, when their fights became too bad, she'd left him and taken Lara back to live near Sydney. They went to Mom's only friend, Narelle, who lived at St. Marys, not far from the Blue Mountains.

You could actually see the mountains from Narelle's back doorstep, a wavy line on the horizon. They changed with the weather from smokey blue to gray-green. But she and Mom had never been up there the whole time they stayed at St. Marys. Mom always said they'd go. "We'll see the Three Sisters, Lara, and have a picnic in Megalong Valley one weekend soon," but somehow Mom was always too tired. She'd recite

her bush poems to Lara often enough, though, when they sat
on Narelle's back step.

> By channels of coolness the echoes are calling,
> And down the dim gorges I hear the creek falling;
> It lives in the mountain, where moss and the sedges
> Touch with their beauty the banks and the ledges;
> Through breaks of the cedar and sycamore bowers
> Struggles the light that is love to the flowers,
> And softer than slumber, and sweeter than singing,
> The notes of the bell-birds are running and ringing.

leaving Lara to dream of the magic places that might be up
there.

They lived with Narelle and her two small kids for quite a
while. But one day Mom said she'd had enough of St. Marys.
She decided to move closer into the city. Mom said work
would be easier to find.

There'd been the series of apartments and rooms in broken-
down houses for them then, each one worse than the last. Mom
tried to stay cheerful but one day in the middle of winter when
the hot water broke down, Mom yelled at the stubborn heater,
"Enough! You've done it this time! I've had enough of you!
You stinking rotten thing!"

That night, after a cold water wash for both of them in their
freezing room, Mom decided that they should head north to
the Lakes area. Just like that. It was the way Mom did things.
She'd been told that living was cheaper up north, a few
hundred kilometers from Sydney, and warmer too. So that's
where they'd go.

"We're going to live in a trailer," she announced to Lara as
if it were the most exciting prospect in the world. Like going
to live in a wonderful mansion or castle or something. "We'll
be by a lake and you can go swimming. And maybe we can
even have a little boat, Lara! It'll be wonderful, you'd better
believe it!"

Yes, they would live in a trailer beside Lake Munmorah and
Mom would find a job and save up and then eventually they'd

7

buy a house! "It'll be like being on vacation all the time!" Mom said enthusiastically. Mom usually managed to see the bright side of things. "So you won't feel one bit sorry about leaving the city, will you, Lara?"

Lara wasn't sorry to be leaving the city and her school where she had been at the bottom of her class and people had constantly talked about her "learning problems."

They'd lived in a trailer at Idle Hours Trailer Park for two years. Mom had worried at first about it not being a proper house, but it had turned out to be the happiest time in their life, Lara reflected. Things seemed to go so well for them once they came to live in the large trailer that even had its own front garden. "How pretty! A garden right by our door, Lara," Mom had said the first day, noticing a wild clump of nasturtiums, the only thing in bloom in the dusty, ragged garden, "and my favorite flowers in all the world, Lara — well, after roses, that is." She'd picked a nasturtium and worn it in her crinkly red hair.

Mom had got a job right away at the local garage doing typing and bookkeeping. Mom had planted a rose tree and it had bloomed twice right by the front door among the nasturtiums. And Lara had learned to read properly at last! A miracle had happened with the help of her teacher, Mrs. Robinson.

It had been hell being so old, knowing you could hardly read at all and thinking you'd never ever learn. Lara was sure she was stupid because she just couldn't seem to get it together. So many people had tried to help her in the past. But no one had tried quite like Mrs. Robinson.

"But I don't want to read *kids'* books," Mom had complained. She was staggering to the car with a dozen or more books piled in her arms. Mrs. Robinson and Lara followed with more books in their hands. "Tell me that after you've tried these," Mrs. Robinson insisted. "I'll help Lara here at school. And you help her at home, okay?" She was so bossy about it that Mom had dutifully pored over the titles and said, "I suppose this one looks okay, love. Do you mind if I read it to you, Lara? She said to read every day."

Lara hadn't minded at all. They usually read in the long

summer twilights after the dishes were done. They'd lie on Mom's double bed, leaving the trailer door open so that they could glimpse trees and the lake, and Mom would read to her for hours on end. And a world beyond Idle Hours Trailer Park and Lakeside Public School, that neither of them had ever dreamed of, opened up to them. They traveled through forests and mountains, in cities of the past and future, to civilizations beyond Earth. They'd found places with the weirdest of names ("Listen to this one, Lara: *Loth-lor-ien*. I can hardly pronounce it but it's so, so beautiful this place, I think we should visit, don't you? After tea?") And they'd wandered through them together. Lara even dreamed about them sometimes.

And as heroes sought rings or maps or treasures and dealt with triumphs or sudden mishaps, Lara and her Mom had laughed and cried together. And they'd talked about the stories when they finished reading. Talked and talked, the way they used to talk about the TV shows they no longer had time to watch.

"I guess that stranger who came into the village is going to be bad news for Will, don't you, Mom?" Lara asked as she spread peanut butter thickly on her toast.

"Mmmm," Mom agreed, jabbing her fried egg thoughtfully with a fork. "He's a real bad egg, Lara!" They were sometimes still talking about stories when Mom dropped Lara at school. And afternoons Mom would spend ages in the library looking for the next book in the series and the next. Mrs. Robinson didn't say, "I told you so" but she looked kind of pleased when Mom would say, "Can we borrow this stack for the weekend?"

And then the miracle of Lara's reading had taken place, almost overnight. After years of struggling and fear, and despair and tears, the jumbled mass of sticks and circles on the page, that so often held no meaning for her, kaleidoscoped together. And suddenly it said something in her head. Lara could recall the exact day this happened. It was a Friday. The day her Mom and Mrs. Robinson drove to Newcastle where they were both doing a computer course. Lara had a new book from the library but she simply couldn't wait for Mom to come home. She had flung herself on Mom's bed, with the book in her hands.

It wasn't until about page twenty that Lara realized what was happening. She'd never really read more than a few pages at a time and only when she had to, with an adult beside encouraging her as she stumbled over the words. And now she'd plunged headlong into the story. Twenty pages had flown by and she hadn't even realized. Sure, she'd skipped plenty of big words, but the story made sense and she was reading by herself. "Hey," she cried out across the trailer to no one and to everyone, "hey, I can read! I'm reading!"

When Mom came in, rather tired as she always was after evening classes, there was no tea ready. Lara was waiting for her, book in hand. "Guess what, Mom?" she'd shouted. "Guess what?"

Then when she'd told her the news, Mom had dropped her folder to the floor in surprise. She'd grabbed Lara and they'd done an excited, awkward, wonderful dance around the tiny trailer. Both of them were shrieking and laughing and crying a bit, too.

"I knew you could do it, Lara." Mom hugged her yet again. "I knew it. Mrs. Robinson was right. She knows exactly what she's doing. We'll cook a special celebration cake for her in the morning."

Then Mom had stuck her head out of the trailer door and yelled at the top of her voice, "Lara's a very smart kid. My smart kid!"

Bonnie Sudovitch, Mom's friend who lived a few trailers down, had yelled back, "I know," and then came down to find out exactly why Lara was so smart this time. Bonnie had hugged Lara but it was really Mrs. Robinson Lara was longing to see.

Saturday morning they'd disturbed Albert in the vegetable garden at the back of the school principal's house. He'd rushed inside to call Mrs. Robinson, who was out visiting. "Come home," he'd said as if it were the most urgent thing in the world. "Lara Ritchie's here to tell you something very important."

Mom said Lara's learning to read was a turning point in their lives. "I thought I'd hate living in this trailer park, you know,

Lara. I hated leaving Melbourne. I hated leaving Sydney. But we've had the best time here. In next to no time you've learned to read properly. And now Mrs. Robinson is helping me get a better job. In about another year we'll look for that house outside Newcastle and you can go to high school there. It's going to be all right! Amazing how things can change so quickly."

Lara was glad to see her mother so happy, so enthused. "Something good always turns up, Lara," she'd told her daughter. "You'd better believe it!" And then the illness had turned up and for a few awful weeks Mom was in turmoil. It had come silently, voraciously, almost painlessly.

Mom had had backaches for three or four days. When the X rays came back the doctors suggested tests. When the test results came back they mentioned the awful word she dreaded and yet insisted on hearing: they told her cancer. They told Mom everything because she demanded everything. The X rays, the reports, the whole story. Mom had read her medical reports as eagerly as she'd read the children's books and explained what she could to Lara.

"Now listen to me, Lara. I'm not going to give up easily. There's a chance. Not much of one. But I'm going for it. I'm trying everything. And I mean everything." It was so like Mom to be enthusiastic. "But just in case the old liver decides to pack it in — we're going to make special plans for you." They'd talked a lot in the following months about Lara's father, Larry Ritchie, or the Man, as she called him. "Just in case, Lara. I want you to know all about him." Lara listened but she wasn't really interested. She didn't really want to know about the Man. She just wanted Mom to get well again.

And Lara was sure her mother would get well. She kept going to work and she stayed positive and cheerful. It was just after every treatment at the hospital she was very, very tired. Sometimes even too tired to talk. That was when Lara had read to her, sometimes for hours on end, so pleased to be able to do it. Yes, Mom would pull through, she was sure. They needed each other. Mom wouldn't go and leave her.

But one afternoon when she came home from school, Mom had bad news for her daughter. "I'm sorry, love. I can't seem to go on anymore," Mom apologized. "I'll only be in the hospital for a few weeks. Just to get me over this bit. You're to stay with Albert and Marjorie Robinson for a while. They'll bring you to see me every day. I'll be home in a week or two."

But Mom had never come home again. In the hospital ward, cheerful with chintz, Lara spent hours talking or reading to her. Sometimes she'd read out some of Mom's favorite poems, the ones about the Australian bush. But the familiar lines about bell-birds or the "Man from Snowy River" made Lara feel all choked up. It made her think of Mom reciting them in her dramatic stage voice out the trailer door and across the lake — and already this seemed a memory of the past. Lara preferred to read some of their favorite parts out of the many books they had shared.

"In a few weeks, or maybe months, Lara, we're going to have to say good-bye," Mom finally conceded one day. "You might think it'll be forever, love — it won't be forever. I can assure you we'll be meeting again. Let's make a meeting place, Lara, right now. How about the secret garden with all the rose trees? Or Tom's midnight garden — remember that place, Lara? — oh, it was so lovely!"

"That's only books, Mom," Lara had burst out, "It's fantasy!"

"It isn't fantasy that we've been to those places together, now is it?" That was the only time that Lara had cried. She'd put her head down on the bright floral hospital cover and wept bitterly.

"Don't be like that," Mom had comforted her. "You mustn't be afraid. Look at me, Lara," and she'd taken her hand. "You remember the dark bird I told you about that used to come fluttering into my life every so often. Made me feel so miserable and down. And remember how I'd make it fly off and leave me alone. Well, there's a dark bird hovering over you right now — but you'll send it on its way, I know it. Not now, Lara, but later on. I know it. Try not to be afraid, Lara. You've got to look your fear full in the face, love. And then things won't seem so bad."

Mom had said this kind of thing many times in the past. It

had often helped her. But with so much to fear, now and up ahead, Mom's words didn't seem to help at all.

"Now about this cancer thing. I must admit there've been times when I've been angry. Good and angry. And times when I've been scared too, Lara. Mostly, lying here in the hospital thinking about it, I've been puzzled. I couldn't work out why it should be that I won't see you grow up to be the lovely young woman I know you'll be.

"And then, Lara, I thought about the Man. I've wanted so much for you to know the Man, Larry, your Dad. And after I left him for that Walter and our time in Melbourne, well, I've never been able to find him. We'll find him now, I'm sure of it. Mrs. Robinson has people in the Police Department working on it right now. You won't just meet the Man. You'll be living with him again. You'll get to love him, be his daughter. He's a beautiful person, Lara."

But they hadn't found Larry Ritchie easily. And when Narelle said she couldn't possibly cope with another child in her house at St. Marys, the home loomed dangerously close for Lara. Lying alone in the unfamiliar space of a large bedroom in Mrs. Robinson's house, Lara thought about the home a lot. She'd read about orphanages in books. They always seemed cruel, awful places where children picked on each other and adults were generally unsympathetic.

Mrs. Robinson assured her that this wasn't so any more. That you'd have a House Mother and House Father. You'd live like a great big family in a pleasant home and go to a regular school. She said if she and Albert hadn't been going away overseas to her daughter's, Lara could have stayed with them a while. She promised Lara that when they came back she could come to them for school vacations. "Don't think about that home too much, Lara. They're still searching for your Dad and I've got the feeling they'll find him."

Lara hoped against hope that her Mom would see the Man and know that Lara was safe. But she'd been gone almost two weeks when news came through to the Robinsons' that a Larry Ritchie and family were living on a remote farm in the Wallingat Forest area. There was no phone, but the local post office had given a message to his wife. Ritchie was away working up north, it seemed. She wasn't sure where he was or when he'd be back.

Three days later on a long distance call, Larry Ritchie had announced himself to his daughter. "Of course you won't be going to any home in Sydney, Lara. The only home you'll be going to is ours. Now just hold on there, kiddo, and I'll be down in about a week to get you." She liked the Man's quiet voice at once. She'd liked the way he'd called her kiddo as if he'd known her for ages. She longed to see him and to tell him all about Mom. She knew at once that she wanted to go home with him, wherever home might be.

2

The slender woman in the dark cotton blouse and faded jeans paused a moment at the table on the back verandah where the children were playing.

"Show me what you're doing." She wiped her hands on the towel she was holding and then picked up the pencil sketch her eldest daughter had just finished. It was of the dirt road edged with straggly gum trees and teetering bottlebrush that led windingly to the front gate. Her daughter gave up the drawing unwillingly.

"It's good," she said, "very good, Pearl!" and the girl flushed with pleasure at her mother's praise.

"Can we hang it up inside?" one of the younger children asked. The woman nodded absently, still regarding the pleasing detail of her daughter's drawing.

"And she's got one of Dad, too," they told her, as Pearl tried unsuccessfully to cover one of the sheets.

When the mother looked down at the crude drawing so clearly her husband, so clearly Larry, a shadow seemed to pass across her face. Pearl saw it, recognized the longing and the loneliness, understood the deep frown lines that so changed her mother's face.

"There's still a lot of work to be done inside," the mother

said, her tone changing. "You can't fool around here all after-noon, you know," and she disappeared inside the house.

Wordlessly Pearl began clearing the table of her colors and the litter of paper. "I get that picture of Dad. I want it!" They fought over the piece of paper with her father's lean angular features so roughly outlined. But Pearl snatched it from their eager hands and crumpled it into a fierce ball.

"It wasn't any good," she told them, "so no one's having it!"

"Aw Pearl —"

"Anyway we gotta go and help Mom right now."

Lara woke up with a start. The truck was lurching along a rocky dirt road. This must be the forest, all right. There were hugely tall white-trunked trees and clumps of robust green ferns and palms crowding right up to the road. It was story-book country here, all right — a thick fluttery curtain of dense, beautiful bush to either side.

"Are we nearly there?" she asked.

"This is the forest I told you about, Lara. This is Wallingat! And our farm's right in the middle of it. About ten kilometers on," her father told her.

"It's lovely," she said, gazing out of the window again, and breathing in the cold freshness of the eucalypt-scented air.

"I'm glad you like it." He sounded genuinely pleased. "Pret-tiest place in the world bar none," he boasted.

"Now about the farm, Lara. You must understand it's pretty rough. There's a lot to be done. It's not much of a homestead. The bathroom's outside. Not a nice modern one like you had at the trailer park either. You see, we rely on tank water, when the dam's low. So you can't take long baths or anything like that. And the toilet — well, it's a little wooden shack down the back. Nothing fancy at all at Willy Nilly Farm. We called it Willy Nilly as a joke but it's kind of stuck. I plan to build a nice bedroom, all wood, for Pearl. She's the eldest and you can share it with her. Nice for her to have an older sister, Lara."

Lara nodded, wondering how Pearl might feel about the prospect of sharing her new bedroom.

"It's all a bit of a mess still at Willy Nilly. But beautiful

16

country and good rain, mostly. It'll be a showplace one day, I'm sure of it. I've already started a garden. We've had a long, dry spell but we're heading into a stormy season just now."

"Tell me the children's names again," Lara asked him. She couldn't bring herself to say "brother and sisters" or even "half-brother and half-sisters." For so long — well, all her life really — she'd thought that she was an only child.

"Afraid there's no one your age, kiddo. There's Pearl the eldest and she's twelve this year. And then there's Garnet, who's six. And Opal, she's five. And the baby Jasper. He must be twenty months old now. So quite a handful for Gladwyn, looking after them and helping run the farm. I'm away a lot. I used to follow seasonal work but now I plan to get lots of young palm trees from up north. We're building up a nice little palm plantation at Willy Nilly. Nice and close to Sydney. It'll be lovely some day, Lara. Lot of work to do, though.

"Gladwyn has to battle on alone a lot of the time. It'll be good for her having a big grown girl like you to help. And it's good you've got a few weeks of vacation before you go to the new high school. Time to help you settle in."

She was longing to see the children. It seemed a miracle to Lara, the prospect of a large family, no matter how young they were.

"And your . . . your," it was too difficult to say "wife" some-how, "and Gladwyn, is she pleased I'm coming?"

Larry hesitated before he answered. "Look Lara, I think I should explain a little about Gladwyn. She's had a hard life, you know. Sometimes she may seem a bit too quiet — even a bit cross — but you'll soon get to understand her. She works too damn hard — that's her trouble. Has all her life. But she's a good mother. A wonderful woman."

All at once Lara felt quite cold. She thought of her own mother and a terrible pain tore through her. "Wonderful woman." They'd said those words quite a number of times at the funeral. And of course it was true of Cheryl. She was — had been — the most wonderful woman in the world.

When Larry turned off the main road through the forest, the track narrowed. "It's really more a fire trail that leads to the farm," he explained. It was wild and dense and secret here. Squatter trees and thicker ferns were close and a rich, moist, dank smell rose up. Huge fronds brushed the truck lightly as they passed. And the piercing shrillness of cicadas carried them on waves of unbearably bright sound into the heart of the forest.

"The river," he told her. Lara could just glimpse the dark glint of water through a thousand shimmering leaves. "You'll be able to swim there on hot days." She peered ahead now, anxious to catch the first sight of the homestead. In her mind's eye she saw a simple wooden structure with wide verandahs all around such as old country houses often had. There'd be lattice, perhaps, with rambling roses entwined. Probably there'd be a tank stand or two at the edge of the house and an orchard to one side as well. It would all be very neat and pretty, she was sure, because Mom had told her lots of times how the Man enjoyed gardening. Mom had said he'd won prizes for roses and dahlias and things all those years ago when they'd lived in a little house in Maroubra. It'd be a lovely country house, she was sure, like the ones they'd passed on the way.

But the first thing she saw at the end of the track and beyond the gatepost, where a small ragged-looking child with a long single braid was perched, was a large tin shed. It was made of corrugated iron with a kind of lean-to verandah thrown up across the front. It was painted bright blue and it seemed to leap out at them, squat and harsh in the soft landscape of the countryside. She peered beyond the shed, seeking the farmhouse. But there was nothing else except open fields and, behind them, the densely wooded hills.

The Man pulled up beside the shed.

"This is it, Lara. Simple as it is, this is home."

Other children had run out of the house at the sound of the truck: a thin little girl with dark pigtails and large brown eyes; and a sturdy baby boy with jet black hair, milky white skin, and surprisingly blue eyes. They had greeted their Dad and now stood silently regarding Lara.

"This is her. This is the sister I've been telling you about.

Your big sister Lara. Now say hello." But they hung back and it was only when the girl who'd been perched on the gatepost joined them, calling as she ran towards them, "Hello Lara, I'm Garnet," that any of them spoke. The tall girl, obviously Pearl, the eldest, spoke at last. "H'lo . . . lo Lara," very quietly, very unenthusiastically, Lara thought. Pearl was thin and tall, almost as tall as Lara, though she was a few years younger. Lara would have said that she was pretty, with her cascade of dark hair, except for the way she held her mouth in a hard little line.

They trailed behind the Man and Lara as they crossed the back verandah. "We always go in the back way," he explained, smiling at the hesitant girl. The big old wooden back verandah seemed to Lara an amazing jumble of ill-assorted furniture. She glimpsed a small bed down at one end, a sagging sofa at the other, a large wooden table and a clutter of broken toys. The Man swept aside the brightly colored strips of plastic across the doorway that protected the dark interior from the ever-present bush flies, and plunged inside.

"Gladwyn, Lara's here. Gladwyn!"

Lara stood nervously on the wooden verandah, unable to see beyond the plastic strips. Her heart beat very fast and she felt the sickish feeling she always felt whenever she'd had to start at a new school. Only this was home, she reminded herself.

Gladwyn stepped out to greet her, a youngish woman, very handsome, with black hair brushed back severely off her face and tied with a ribbon. Her face was as thin as Mom's had been round. She was slender like Pearl, with great dark brooding eyes. An unsmiling face. She stared at Lara for what seemed a long time, taking in her tangle of golden-reddish hair, her hot thin face and her blue blue eyes everyone said were so much like Cheryl's.

"So this is the child," she finally said, and the Man who'd appeared behind her agreed.

"This is Lara, love."

Lara, finding it difficult to smile, managed to mumble some sort of greeting, and then looked back to the Man in appeal.

"Well, don't just stand there. Come inside and we'll get you a drink. You must be thirsty after all that driving." Gladwyn spoke firmly but not kindly, Lara thought. She followed meekly inside.

The house, it seemed to Lara as she glanced quickly about her, consisted of one large room with a painted concrete floor. At one end was a partitioned-off part where she glimpsed a double bed — must be Dad and Gladwyn's bedroom, Lara thought. At the other end there was a dark handsome table with an assortment of old wooden chairs around it. In one corner there was a kitchen section with laden shelves, a dresser and a pale blue enamel sink. Then in the middle there was a great wood stove on which stood unfamiliar large pots and kettles, that seemed to Lara to be from another age. Other blackened pans and utensils hung neatly from one of the beams that crisscrossed the house.

Seated at the huge table, which distanced her from Gladwyn, sipping the bittersweet drink she'd had thrust into her hand, Lara gazed about her in a more leisurely way. There seemed to be beds everywhere and in between them chests of drawers. Everything was very neat and very clean. It was cool and dim in here and, after Lara had got over the shock of the big single room, she thought it was rather pretty. She liked its white-washed hessian walls and framed pictures of what seemed a foreign countryside, or streets of a thoroughly foreign place, interspersed with kids' drawings and colorful posters of bush animals.

"It's not exactly deluxe," Gladwyn spoke almost trium-phantly, "like you've been used to. We're lucky to find you a space. But there it is. That's your bed," and she indicated a bed in one corner, "unless of course you'd rather sleep outdoors on the verandah."

"Lara's not exactly used to luxury. Are you, love? I saw the trailer where she and . . . her Mom lived and I explained about this place. Didn't I, Lara? She wasn't expecting the Ritz."

Lara nodded and tried to smile. She had expected a bed-room, even a shared bedroom. The bed Gladwyn had pointed out, shoved in among a jumble of others, was not a pleasant prospect. Not in here so close to this unwelcoming person. She glanced at her father. She could sense a change in the Man since they'd got here, too. He seemed more tentative, apologetic, around Gladwyn, almost as if he were being careful of what he said. Lara was frightened of her. There was a lack of softness in her face, around her eyes. From time to time, one or other of the children came to the door and pushed aside the plastic strips to peer inside at Lara. Then they'd giggle and run off, bare feet slapping across the wooden boards of the back verandah. "Either come right in or stay out there," Gladwyn called.

"I think I'd prefer to sleep on the verandah — if that's all right," she said. "Suit yourself," Gladwyn said shortly, gathering up the teapot and clanging it down on the enamel sink so that it struck a bleak note through the long room.

"Give it a try, love, if you like," the Man said, trying to be cheerful. "It might be a bit more peaceful out there away from all the little kids — and if it rains real bad, you can always come inside. Later on, like I said, I'm building a really nice room for you and Pearl over there in the clearing," but Gladwyn interrupted.

"Where are her things?" she asked the Man and then, turning to Lara, "I hope there's not too much. We don't have too much space, as you can see. Pearl's cleared a few drawers in her dresser for you."

"Only two suitcases, love. The schoolteacher has boxes of household things and books. She'll send them up by train to Taree — or she'll store them until we want them."

"I don't want them," Gladwyn said, fiercely now, her dark eyes flashing in the gloom. "Let her keep that stuff. Two suitcases and a teenage kid is enough of a burden for me."

She approached the stove then, turning her back on both of them, excluding them completely.

"Come on out and we'll get your things." The Man slipped his arm around her shoulders as they crossed the yard. She knew she mustn't cry — knew somehow that Gladwyn would despise her even more if she cried — so she hoped the Man would not say anything too kind to her. He called to the kids to come and help their new sister settle in. The children stood and gaped as she attempted to unpack her suitcase, piling the freshly ironed clothes into an inadequate drawer. Only Jasper, the baby, exhibited any friendliness at all — climbing inside the case and soiling the clothes with his black, dusty feet.

"My Mom doesn't iron," Pearl said, gazing with envy at three or four perfectly smooth dresses Lara had placed on the bed while she searched unsuccessfully for anything approximating a closet. "She says it's a waste of time with so much else to do."

"Yes," Opal agreed, running grubby hands down the white dress on top of the pile.

"You could put this up with Dad's suit. There's a hanging place," Garnet suggested helpfully, "in the corner, and he's got three good shirts there and Mom's good dress." She smiled at Lara, but then, seeing Pearl's frown, withdrew.

"My Mom didn't want you to come here," Pearl said. "She and my Dad had a big fight. They yelled and all."

"But I did," Opal said. "I wanted you to come. I said so, didn't I, Gar?"

Lara clicked the locks closed and stood the shabby case against the wall. She stood up, facing Pearl. "And what about you, Pearl?" Lara asked quietly. "Did you want me to come here?"

Pearl gazed at the pile of clothes in the bureau drawer, the dresses on the bed, the little boxes with trinkets and odds and ends, then at Lara. "No," she said fiercely. "I didn't want you coming here neither. Mom said you weren't really our family at all and you're not." She turned on her heel and, followed by the other three children, left the room. Lara heard them shouting and running around outside.

Left alone by the small chest of drawers, Lara didn't know what to do or where to go next. If she didn't have a bed inside the house, she didn't really have a place there, either. And if she went outside to sit on her bed on the verandah, there would be Pearl's hostile eyes, and the inquisitive eyes of the others. She glanced to the other end of the room and knew she couldn't sit uselessly at the table while Gladwyn, who was moving things in quick, savage movements, worked in the kitchen. There was nowhere to go. She sat heavily on the bed and fumbled with the trinket box full of Mom's precious things. When Mom's special keepsake, a silver American dollar, fell into her hand there was that hot familiar ache of unshed tears behind her eyes.

It was the Man who saved her at this moment, as he was to do a number of times over the next few days. "Come and see Willy Nilly Farm, Lara," he called in a cheery voice through the flapping plastic strips at the door. "You can finish your unpacking later." Again the kids trailed behind them, all except Pearl, that is, whom she could see now working spade in hand by herself far across the field. They passed the bathhouse that was attached to the house outside. "It's got hot running water now and everything," Garnet told her proudly. They visited the hens and the ducks in their wire-netted run as they made for the dam.

"You can help look after those fellas, Lara, that'd be a real help. Pearl'll show you how," he said.

"She won't," Garnet said quietly from behind.

"I will," Opal said.

Lara felt afraid of the tall horses with their shaggy red coats that galloped towards them when they went into the adjoining paddock. "Can you ride bareback?" Opal asked. "Garnet and me and Pearl can."

They reached the dam with its dazzling white-baked mud edges. Lara gazed across the muddy water at the little island in the middle. "It's only been dug these last few months," Dad explained.

"Henk — he's our neighbor — he helped. And men came on real big tractors," Opal told her.

"Going to put up a big greenhouse for plants right along here," the Man told her. "Palms! There'll be palms everywhere. Willy Nilly Palm Plantation — the best in New South Wales! No kidding! With the water here like this we can do just about anything we like now."

"My Mom and Dad already did all this," Garnet said with a sweep of her hand, as they approached Pearl. The older girl did not stop to look up at them but continued, solidly intent

23

on her job. Lara stared around the scrubby field, trying to see just what it was they'd done. At last she noticed some small plants in rows at one end. "Those?" she asked uncertainly.

"They're young palms," said the Man, stooping to loosen the soil where Pearl was digging, around the indistinguishable knots of green sprouting from the hard earth.

"Palms?" Lara asked. She only knew palms with trunks as obvious as elephants' legs, and with great showers of tough, thick waving fronds on top.

"*Livistona australis,*" Pearl said disparagingly as Dad walked off. "Any fool can see that."

Day after day the Man would have to rescue Lara from the house. "Can I help?" she'd ask, watching Gladwyn and Pearl busy inside with the housework.

"No, thanks," Gladwyn would usually say, and Lara, feeling useless, would walk outside. If she played a game with any of the smaller children out there, Pearl would appear as if by magic. "Opal, Garnet, Mom says you've got to come and clear up your toys. Right now! Jasper, you should go and wash your hands. Quick sticks."

"Come and help me in the veggie garden, Lara?" Dad would say, appearing at the house from time to time.

"Do you want to come and check the horses in the back pasture? You should have a ride, love."

"Have you ever been on a tractor? Have you driven a tractor? Pearly can. You c'mon and have a try, too." She would go gladly.

Over the next few days she walked the full length of the property with her father and explored the untamed parts of the creek. She worked in the fields with him, planting and fertilizing and watering the strange little plants she soon learned to recognize from their young bunched leaves. And she drove up and down the fields on the tractor. The Man even taught her to drive the truck up the uneven surface of the driveway. The smaller children had shrieked with laughter as the truck swung around the corner. Even Pearl had smiled as the truck lurched and leaped drunkenly towards the home gate the first time she'd taken the wheel. But Gladwyn, who was in the truck with the baby Jasper on her knee, did not smile. "Careful — be careful," she'd said. She never seemed to smile much.

There had been the hint of a smile on the first night when Lara had been handed an unfamiliar meal, steaming hot on a chipped plate.

"If you don't like it — well, there's nothing else," Gladwyn told her, noticing Lara's hesitation over the food.

"It's a sort of stew," Larry explained. "Polish dish. You'll love it. Eat up." She hadn't wanted to offend Larry or annoy Gladwyn so she dipped her fork into the messy steaming plate of scrappy-looking meat and indistinguishable vegetables. The food was hot and delicious and comforting and she ate every bit.

"Would you like more, love?" Larry asked, and when Gladwyn had ladled more of the delicious stuff onto her plate, Lara was sure there was a ghost of a smile on her face. A triumphant look, anyway, but she hadn't smiled again. She always seemed so grim to Lara. The only time she had really softened seemed to be with the baby, Jasper. When he climbed on to her lap in the evening or when he clung to her skirt until she lifted him into her arms, a look of softness came into her eyes. For a while her face seemed kinder, gentler.

Lara was glad of her bed on the verandah. At night the Man would roll a canvas blind where the bed was tucked into the corner against the wall. This made her feel secure and private, for the time being anyway. Sometimes he'd stay and talk to her for a little while. "Tomorrow I'll take you kids to a wonderful lookout. Other end of the forest. You can see the whole coastline. You'll soon get to know this little part of the world, Lara. And love it!" She loved these moments, Dad's kind eyes smiling down at her as he talked. The only thing was that he never stayed long enough. "Goodnight, love. Go straight to sleep, now," he'd say as he went. But she never did.

She'd look out at the tall gum trees, stark, white and mysterious against the vast curve of an often star-studded sky. And then she'd watch for the tiny possum, Oscar, to scuttle down the big tree closest to the house. "That's Oscar, the baby. And there's a Momma and a Poppa possum too," Opal had told

Lara one night on one of her trips from the outside toilet. "Oscar's my possum," she said, "but you can share him if you like, Lara. You can. Only don't tell the others."

When Oscar finished eating the scraps that Gladwyn always left out for him, then she'd be left alone to think of Idle Hours and Mom. It was a way of shutting out the present and the future.

Mom had said she'd always be there. "Just reach out, love, talk to me, I'll be around. I'll be watching over you. You'd better believe it!"

But it was hard to believe when the words you wanted to speak froze on your lips and you wanted to cry so badly you knew your raging sobs would wake the whole family inside the house. So she bit her lip and concentrated on Mom-of-the-past. Mom healthy and happy, as they walked beside the lake together; Mom arriving home excited by all the new things she'd learned at her course. Lying for hours on Mom's bed with all the wonderful books they'd shared. Mom's loud embarrassing poetry recitations:

It was the man from Ironbark who struck the Sydney town
He wandered over street and park
He wandered up and down

and all the rest. The dance of joy in the little trailer the night Lara knew she'd actually got the reading thing together. It was good to think about those times. It gave Lara something to hang on to. When she thought about now, the bleakness and emptiness grabbed hold and the longing for Mom seemed insurmountable. Mom didn't seem to be there, but Mom's big black bird of despair surely seemed to hover.

"Come for a drive, love. Got to take these cans over to Henk's place. He's gone away for a few days, but Arlie's there, and the kids. We can say hello. See if she needs anything. And we need milk. Gar and Opal want you to take the truck down the driveway. They say your driving's really good now."

It was after breakfast, and dishes had been dealt with by Lara and Pearl and stood sparkling now on the old dresser. Everyone had attended to chores this morning — bed-making, sweeping, dusting, watering the vegetable and then flower gardens with the heavy black hoses Dad had rigged up at the front of the house. Even Jasper took part in the general clean-up. Gladwyn had the whole place shipshape early every morning before she began the difficult task of attending to the washing with no machine and limited water, and then going out into the dry scrubby fields.

Lara loved going with the Man in his truck, especially when they were alone. It was the only time she felt easy. The only time she could smile. He always let her drive a little distance on the dirt road. She'd been very quick at getting the hang of it and even Pearl had grudgingly admitted she could drive okay.

"The way you came around that corner," Dad had said admiringly. "You handle this truck like a pro." This morning he let her take it right up to the main road, close to Henk's gate.

"You could drive to Newcastle, I bet," he'd said.

"Nah, she's not allowed," Pearl said from the back seat.

"Not allowed," Opal echoed.

"But she *could* if she *was* allowed," Garnet insisted.

"I'd say we've got a Nigel Mansell on our hands — she's that cool with the gears," Dad said, and although she had no idea who Nigel Mansell was, Lara glowed with pride at his unstinting praise. And when he let Pearl take the wheel and the truck teetered at the edges of the road and stalled so many times she finally gave up, Lara couldn't help feeling extra pleased with herself. "Better than Pearl any day," Garnet had whispered to her.

They collected milk from Henk's wife, Arlie, who greeted Lara warmly. Her small son with his halo of golden ringlets came out from behind her shyly. "Say hello to Lara, Louis," she said.

"No." He hid his face again but Opal came to tempt him with a baby lizard she'd found.

"Can see you're a Ritchie a mile off. You look just like your Dad, you do," Arlie said cheerfully. "Welcome to the Wallingat, Lara." Then she broke off a flower from the big bed by the back door for Lara — a great joyous canna, bright yellow with splashes of red on it. Lara took the shivering bloom, touched by the woman's kindness. "We hope you're very happy here," Arlie said, then she turned to the others. "Bring your Mom when you come next time. And little Jasper." She stood at the gate with the baby boy in her arms and one or two other little kids, who seemed to have appeared from nowhere and waved. And Lara had the feeling she would have liked to have gone back to the cheerful house with Arlie. There was something comfortable and easy, something welcoming here that she had recognized at once. The something that seemed so lacking in her new home.

On the way back to the truck, Pearl said, "Mom says cannas are real untidy flowers. She doesn't like them at all."

"But I like them," Garnet said. Pearl ignored her little sister and went on, "And they're real messy too. All that sap," as she watched Lara dab at the inside of her arm where the thick substance from the stem had trickled. "Last time Arlie gave Mom a bunch of cannas, she threw them away in the river. On the way home. Quick as she could."

"She kept the vegetables Arlie gave her, though. Henk has the best veggie garden in the world, bar none," Opal boasted. "Well, that's what Dad said."

"And Mom gets real cranky and says ours'd be just as good one day. And then she goes: 'Why she grows those awful pesky cannas, I don't know. Call them flowers. I call them weeds.' Doesn't she, Pearl?" Garnet said.

"Oh, shut up, Garnet," Pearl ordered. "You are full of nonsense."

Lara held on to the canna Arlie had given her. She placed it carefully on her lap when they got back into the truck. The untidy radiance of the thing reminded her sharply of her own mother. Mom in a swirly dress that had once belonged to Narelle. A bright yellow silky thing with slashes and splotches of red on it. Throwing back her wild curly hair, affixing a glittery earring, then looking at herself critically in the little bit of mirror on the cupboard door. "Do I look okay, Lara? Now tell me honest to God."

"You look fantastic, Mom," Lara had said with conviction.

She'd gone to the Talent Quest at the local TV station where she'd sung *You Made Me Love You* in a husky Billie Holiday voice, and won second prize.

"It was the dress that made the difference," she told Lara later. "I'm sure of it."

"I want to tell you something, kiddo," Dad said as he drove back from Arlie and Henk's place. His tone was so serious that a shiver of fear passed right through Lara. It was about the home, she was sure. Gladwyn wanted to get rid of her at once. Larry was about to tell her they would send her away. She slumped down in the seat feeling weak and sick to her stomach at the thought.

"Hey," the Man said, glancing down at her as he steered the precipitous road, "it's not all that bad. I've got to go away for a while, that's all. It could be quite some time. A few weeks' work up north. I'm trying to track down Cooper, the man we're buying from. We've sunk what money we had into the farm and now the final papers have to be signed. And we don't quite know where Cooper is. We want to get a move on with it. And I want to take a look at some palm plantations, too."

"How long will you be gone?" Lara asked, bleakly. Days and days loomed up ahead without him. She felt frightened.

"Don't know. Could take a little while to find Cooper, I guess. You can hang on for a few weeks, can't you?" he asked, squeezing her hand affectionately. She nodded dumbly. She knew she would have to.

"And Gladwyn can really use your help with me gone."

When the Man left, they all went through the front yard to the gate, a solemn little group, except for the squawking Jasper, to wave good-bye. Lara felt that old familiar heaviness of heart, as if any shred of feeling of safety or belonging was going with Dad. As they watched the battered four-wheel-drive lurch down the hill with the customary cloud of dust in its wake, she felt she could sob like a little child. Except Gladwyn would scorn her if she did that.

Pearl etched a neat little square in the dust with her bare toe and stood staring at it.

"Daddy's gone," Garnet said.

"Daddy's gone." Opal always copied.

"Dadda gone," the baby crooned, too.

Mom would have made a joke of it, Lara reflected. Sung a little song "Dadda's gone a hunting," and fooled around to distract them. But Gladwyn stood stock still staring out at the forest road, the truck long since out of sight. Her eyes didn't look sad or tear-filled. They had their customary brightness, but Lara sensed Gladwyn was dispirited by his leaving, too.

"Well then," she said finally, as if the words cost her great effort, "let's go back to get lunch. Plenty to do. Can't stand here all day."

3

The chores of the next few days seemed backbreaking to Lara. Gladwyn was intent on finishing the planting the Man had begun. The summer vacation was all but at an end and once Lara and Pearl went to school there'd be less possibility of clearing the overgrown field of its ragweed. They all labored in the mulchy soft ground beside the creek. Gladwyn and the children worked in rubber boots but Lara's sandals were wet and sodden in no time. Her legs were bitten by mosquitoes and there was the attack by the hateful leeches where she'd made such a fool of herself.

"Look, Lara. On the back of your legs. You got bloodsuckers," Garnet said, poking at something black and small and clinging. She looked down and saw two — no, three, four or more — of the slimy writhing creatures firmly attached to her lower legs. She let out a scream of horror at the thought of the squirming black things sucking her blood. She pulled at them with feverish movements, but the leeches wouldn't dislodge. She ran in a circle then, dancing and calling, "Get them off! Oh, get them off!"

Garnet was amazed. "You only gotta salt them and they curl up dead," she said.

"What's the fuss?" Gladwyn had called from across the field.

When she heard "leeches," she merely said, "Get the salt for her, Garnet," and then went on with her work.

"No use running around like that," Pearl had come up to investigate the cries of distress. Lara stopped her dance, then, and shamefacedly waited for Garnet's return. With a trembling hand she sprinkled the salt on the loathsome swelling bodies. The small children watched fascinated as each one shrivelled and fell, forming a little pool of blood that was bright red on the gray soil for a moment before sinking darkly into the earth.

"You must be unlucky," Pearl observed. "Only get lots of 'em straight after rain. And it hasn't rained or anything. Anyway, you should work in rubber boots like us."

"Imagine all those shoes you brought," Gladwyn observed later as she worked down the row of palms, passing Lara, "and not one pair useful."

Garnet and Opal gave up after an hour or so and returned to the creek to paddle with Jasper. They carried the salt shaker hopeful for leeches. But Pearl and her mother, with Lara beside, battled on hour after hour. Lara was determined not be first to give in. But at midday, when the sun shone its fiercest, she realized that Gladwyn would go on until she dropped. Lara's breath rasped in her throat and burst in her chest. She flopped under a tree, red in the face with exertion, wiping the sweat from her face with one hand and shooing the flies with the other. Gladwyn glanced up briefly. "Given up," she observed.

That night was the first of a series of thunderstorms that shook the tin shack. At first it terrified Lara to the core of her being. She was sure the wind had never blown so fiercely at the trailer park or the lightning been so brightly alive, or the thunderclaps so close. She and Mom had always welcomed storms. But this one seemed too near. And this one reminded her that Mom was no longer nearby. When the first rain swept across the verandah, making a mockery of the old canvas blind, Lara was forced to take shelter inside the house. She was amazed to find all the children still sleeping soundly. Her heart was fluttering wildly and she wanted very much to speak to someone to say: "Hey, this is wild, isn't it?" Anything. But all was quiet within.

Then she saw the shadowy figure of Gladwyn, and her fear subsided. Gladwyn was securing all the windows and hardly acknowledged her as she sat shivering on the spare bed, staring out through the streaming glass at the storm. As she watched the wild sky and lashing treetops, safe inside the sturdy corrugated iron walls, Lara felt a sudden strange calm. It seemed all the pain and despair and longing was snatched up in the storm's fury, leaving her empty and still, almost peaceful. When Gladwyn told her to lie down and go to sleep or she'd never work next morning, she obeyed at once, and fell into a deep and refreshing sleep.

Lara wasn't exactly looking forward to Palm Grove High School. Dad had stopped the truck one day by the school to look over the wire fence on one of their trips back from the town.

"This is it, kiddo. Right beside the lake." She looked at the sprawling set of concrete buildings set among cabbage tree palms, sitting so close to the large pale expanse of lake, and remembered. It was always so hard at new schools. She'd been to plenty of them.

"It's hu-mungus!" Garnet said.

"I don't like it," Opal offered.

"Don't be silly," Dad said. "It's practically brand new. Bit of a showpiece, the high school. And the primary school where you two will be going one day soon. Right next door. I think you'll like it, Lara."

"It looks okay," Lara said uncertainly, as she took in the large clumps of shaggy trees and the huge expanses of grass. But what would the place be like filled with all the terrifying kids from around here, all laughing and talking together, she wondered. There'd be hundreds of kids in a school this size. She wished it wasn't so big.

"You'll get lost," Garnet said as if reading her thoughts, "it's so bloody big!"

"This is the place where they make all the wooden toys," Opal announced as they resumed their trip home. She pointed out the large wooden house with its long, cool verandah that sat all alone in a large field at the head of Old Creek Road.

"And this is where you catch the school bus, mornings. Around about here. You just flag him down," Dad had explained. "Gladwyn or me'll drive you to the bus stop most mornings. But afternoons Pearl walks home through the forest. It's a pretty walk," Dad went on.

"Can we go inside the Toymaker's house to show Lara?" Opal begged, taking advantage of the fact that her mother and Pearl weren't with them to say no.

"Not today," Dad said. "We've gone right past it anyhow."

"It's not fair!" Opal complained. "You always say that." But she cheered up when Dad found her some chewing gum.

"We saw Lara's school," the two little girls began to chant as they came through the front gate, making Jasper cry, because he hadn't. "Who wants to see a stupid school?" Pearl flashed at them, picking up the small boy to comfort him and giving Lara a look of hatred. As they went inside with the bags of groceries in their hands, Dad had said to Lara again, "You're going to like your new school, Lara, I'll bet."

But the new school proved to be another disappointment.

On the morning of Lara's first day at school, Dad was still away up north. Gladwyn said she'd drive them to the bus stop. But she discovered a flat tire on the old Land Rover.

"The spare's still at the garage. I'll have to ask Henk to get it for me later on today," she told them. "You'll just have to walk to the main road this morning. It's only half an hour or so, and the bus doesn't come past until ten to eight. Good exercise."

Of course, there was no argument.

They might have enjoyed the walk along the leafy road. It took them deep into the forest with its green abundance of lushly growing things reaching out to them and its soft ethereal light — a place Mom would have said was enchanted, Lara thought. And then, minutes later, it opened into the avenue of surely the biggest trees Lara had ever seen. Massive sheets of dangling bark showed expanses of white, white trunks — so smooth that Lara longed to stop and touch them. Immersed in the early morning hum and the gentle filtered sunlight of the bush they might have enjoyed that walk. But Pearl walked apart. She didn't speak to the older girl, obviously resenting her presence.

When they finally reached the smooth paved road that led past the Toymaker's house that Dad had pointed out, Lara knew they were at the right turn-off. But there was no bus stop sign to tell her where to wait, and she couldn't remember where Dad had said to stand. Pearl had galloped off into the ditch at the other side of the road, leaving her. She threw down her schoolbag near the wire fence and pulled handfuls of green grass along the roadside.

"Pearl, is this the bus stop?" Lara called anxiously, but the girl strutted on. "Pearl!" Lara yelled. Pearl stopped and faced her.

"Find out for yourself." Then she ducked under the barbed wire fence and darted across the field, disappearing behind a clump of trees. Lara saw the foals Pearl had gone to feed at once. They followed Pearl back out into the sunlight, feeding on juicy tidbits of grass. Lara was under the wire in an instant. When she was halfway across the field, she heard the roar of the bus. Pearl broke away from the foals and began running madly towards Lara, waving wildly.

"Hey, hey!" she called. "Stop! Stop!" But the bus had roared by, the driver unaware of the two now face to face in the field.

"You silly bloody idiot," Pearl raged. "I said wait there, didn't I? He couldn't see us in the field. He couldn't see us!" she shrieked.

"You didn't say wait there," Lara flashed, "you said . . ."

"Silly bitch." The younger girl stomped about and Lara could see she was in a terrible state. She began to cry. Lara waited until the sobs subsided.

"Pearl, when does the next bus come?" she asked quietly.

"There aren't any more buses," Pearl said scornfully. "No more. And it's too far to walk to school. Mom says if ever I miss the bus I've got to go home," she said, her voice harsh. "We'll have to go home, that's all."

The walk home seemed twice as long. The skies clouded over and the forest was dark and cool, but Lara felt hot. She was stumbling with tiredness when they left the main road and turned for home. Gladwyn glanced up in amazement from the warehouse where she was laboring over piles of clothes. Pearl did not pretend.

"We missed the bus," she said. "I was feeding Roache's horses and the bus went past." Gladwyn's face went dark with anger.

"You silly girl," she said and poked Pearl's shoulder angrily. "I've told you before about fooling around with those horses. Now look what's happened. Missed your first day. Missed your class. And the high school won't even know she's coming." She glared at Lara. "Too bad. Well, you can help me here, Pearl. You won't be sitting about all day. You can miss the entire day, the entire week, for all I care." She turned back to her washing. "Well, get changed and come here and help me," she said to Pearl, who dashed off obediently.

Lara stood by awkwardly. She was about to speak, to apologize, to offer help, but Gladwyn spoke first, turning to her, eyes narrowed. "You're a great dumbcluck, you are. A big girl like you. Can't even get on a bus. Don't want you bothering me." She put her head down and went on with the washing.

"I'm sorry — I didn't know — I . . ."

Gladwyn turned from the tubs. "Just go away!" she yelled full into Lara's face. "Go on. Go away!"

Lara was running through the grasses of the freshly planted field and the reeds beyond, and up over the creek. She was running up the hill and her breath seemed to be going in and in and the pain in her chest was swelling and growing. She was running as if something fearsome were at her heels. And then she was falling, falling in a heap at the foot of a massive tree. She was banging her head again and again and again on the hard ground. Then she was still. She was lying quietly as the storm broke over her.

It was the same fitful lightning and thunder, the same hot mad wind and the same intermittent large cold splashes of rain as the storm of a few days ago. And it was good. When she raised her head from the ground the smell of the earth and the gum trees was in her nostrils. She longed for another immense roar of thunder to shake the earth. But it held back for the moment and she raised her head expectantly.

It was at this moment she saw the dog. She gave a gasp of surprise to see a dark silhouette against a gray skyline. The dog stood stock still, face to the wind, almost as if it were part of the landscape. It looked so splendid there, standing resolute with the backdrop of the storm — almost as if it had dropped from the heavens or emerged from the earth itself. Magic, powerful, wonderful.

She wasn't sure if it were real until it moved. There was a clash of thunder at last and that was when the dog turned towards Lara. She knew somehow that it recognized her at once. She wasn't afraid at all as the handsome beast began its loping descent towards her. She stood to meet it with the lightning darting furiously around her. There was an almighty clap of thunder as the dog reached the foot of the hill.

"With thunder you'll come and with thunder you'll go," she chanted suddenly, as if it were the line of a familiar poem. Only she didn't know a poem about dogs or thunder. The words had simply fallen out of her mouth unthinkingly. "With thunder," she chanted again. And then the dog was in her arms.

She fell back with the force of its body and rolled about on the damp grass and leaves, laughing wildly as the dog nuzzled her, licking her face. The sound of her own laughter seemed so unfamiliar it shocked her for a moment. She sat up and looked more closely at her unexpected friend. It was a handsome dog, part dingo, she thought. Hadn't Narelle's brother had a dog just like this on his farm at Nowra? Yes, a lovely dingo dog. And it had come out of the storm.

"My Thunderdog," she crooned, smoothing the short glossy hair on its strong neck, having to touch the thing in case it melted away before her eyes. She took the large head in her hands and stared into the dark eyes. "With thunder. With thunder. You came with thunder. I'll call you Withthunder. I'll call you Thunderwith. Is that it, dog? Is that your name? Tell me, beautiful one. Thunderdog, Thunderwith, yes that's it, all right. You're Thunderwith. You're my Thunderwith." It stood quite still as she addressed it, staring up at her solemnly.

"This is my magic of magic days," she said to the dog, to the trees, to the hillside, still strange in the storm. "Out of the storm, out of the earth, a dog bursts forth. And it's mine. A dingo dog and it's for me. You've been sent for me. Thunderwith. I know it. Just as I know your name." And she buried her face in the dog's coat and the first real tears she had cried since Mom's death coursed down her cheeks and the relief was wonderful. The rain that had been holding back suddenly pelted down in a deluge. The dog stiffened, seemed to listen.

"What do you hear, boy? You've got to go, Thunderwith, haven't you?" she asked, anticipating its dash back up the hill, "and I suppose I have to go too. But I'll be back tomorrow. As soon as I can get away from down there, okay? And you'll be here, magic dog, won't you?" She stroked its head and then released it. "Go Thunderwith, go!" she said, watching it bound up the hill and disappear into sheets of rain. "But come back tomorrow. And so will I."

When she returned to the homestead soaked to the skin, though Gladwyn clicked her tongue disapprovingly, she made a hot drink for Lara at once.

"Get out of those wet clothes or there'll be no school for you this week," she said. Lara knew Gladwyn was somehow ashamed of revealing the depth of her feelings.

Lying on her bed on the verandah, warm and dry, watching the steady rain, Lara was glad when Garnet came out and cuddled up against her. "Read to me, Lara," she said. "This is my best book. Arlie gave it to me one time when we went for the milk."

Lara glanced down at the big green picture book. She could hardly believe her eyes. The child held out a tattered copy of a picture book called *Giant Devil Dingo*. She gave a little gasp. "Don't worry, Lara. It's not scary or anything. Well, not too much. The giant devil dingo looks real bad. But it's a friend by the end of this story. Honest," she soothed.

Lara read the story to the child, thinking of her own magic dingo dog waiting on the hillside. A calm and beautiful creature, hers. And then she lay stroking Garnet's back until Pearl came and stood at the door. "Oh Garnet, there you are," Pearl said heavily. "You'd better come inside here now. We're playing dominoes." The child slid off the bed with an apologetic smile to Lara.

It didn't matter. She didn't care about being by herself. She lay on the bed, not really alone at all — Thunderwith was in her thoughts.

4

When the first confusing school day was over Lara looked anxiously for Pearl among the jostling children at the bus stop. She caught sight of her at last, surprised to see the usually sullen face bright with laughter as Pearl talked to two of her friends.

"Pearl," she called out.

But Pearl's face froze with displeasure when she saw Lara. And with her lips downturned, Pearl moved away from her companions. She trailed down the road. Even her bulging back-pack slung across her shoulders seemed a kind of accusing burden to Lara's eyes. Lara followed, humiliated by the muffled laughter of the knot of girls she was forced to pass.

On the bus Pearl moved swiftly to the middle section, where she threw her bag on the seat beside her. She sat staring sullenly out the window. She didn't look up again and Lara knew there was no sense in following her. Down the back she saw the older boy who had made himself known to her in such an unpleasant way today. He was laughing now with some of his friends. No, she wouldn't go down there. She sat as close to the driver's broad and friendly back as she could manage, knowing it was the only place she could avoid hostile eyes. Everyone seemed to be talking or calling out to each other. It was terrible, this bus of jostling, noisily cheerful kids. Pearl was terrible, ignoring her like this. School was terrible. And her first day had been terrible.

After a bewildering number of new teachers had been introduced in the morning, Lara had been put into a small group of new kids. They were assigned senior students, who were to show them around. But the school buildings and grounds had seemed so big and so confusing to Lara that she was seized with the kind of panic she'd known on so many other occasions in so many other schools. A dryness of throat that made it difficult to speak. A feeling of dread that she might be asked to say something to a group — or worse still, to read something aloud. Everything would go blank if that happened, she was sure, and she'd be embarrassed in front of teachers and kids alike.

She didn't take in much of what was being shown to her but trailed behind the group, white-faced and miserable, not talking to anyone. She wouldn't even be able to remember how to get back to the cafeteria to order her lunch, she thought. Then during the tour of the gym, one of the senior students, a tall, pale-faced boy with pale, almost colorless eyes, had spoken to her, causing her to jump in fright when he said her name in a kind of accusing way: "Lara Ritchie. Am I right?" She nodded dumbly, instinctively afraid of the tone of voice.

"So you're the surprise sister, eh? Hope you're not such a little trouble-maker as Miss Pearl," he laughed unpleasantly. She couldn't speak, but merely swallowed hard and stared at him.

"You're from the city, aren't you?"

She didn't know how to answer him. Idle Hours Trailer Park certainly wasn't the city. And yet she'd lived in cities for most of her life. Somehow she knew he wanted her to say yes, she was from the city. She cleared her throat nervously but he interrupted impatiently.

"Cat got your tongue? Or don't little city slickers like you talk to country bumpkins like us?" he asked.

"Aw, give her a break, Gowd," another curly-headed boy standing nearby cut in. The tall boy, the one he'd called Gowd, had turned at once to him and said smoothly, but unpleasantly all the same, "You seem to have a friend here, Lara Ritchie.

This is Stan Redmond. He's not a class officer." He indicated his own officer badge to her. "But he thinks he's champion of all the newcomers apparently. And he appears to like stuck-up city kids, too." He turned a dazzling smile in Lara's direction. "Not that I'm suggesting that you're stuck-up of course, Lara Ritchie, it probably only *looks* that way. I'll leave you to Stan's tender mercies. I have to round up the other new brats before the bell. But I do believe we share the same bus stop. We're neighbors, you know."

"Don't pay too much attention to Gadrey," Stan said, attempting comfort. "He likes to impress one way or another. He can be a bit of a dickhead sometimes." But Lara turned away from Stan, too confused to answer. She hadn't liked the way the Gadrey boy had talked to her any more than she liked the way his mocking tone turned to one of concern when he addressed the other kids. "The brats," as he called them. He spoke so pleasantly and smiled so kindly it was hard to believe it was the same person.

". . . and we hope it will be a really good year for all of you here at Palm Grove High. We're a friendly school and we'll all do our best to help you. Just come and ask if there's anything that worries you. Anything at all. Class officers and senior students are here to help you. Just remember that." It all sounded so reasonable Lara didn't know why it frightened her so much. It was just that she knew he didn't like her, the senior boy who was a class officer. For some reason she couldn't fathom at all, he'd taken an instant dislike to her.

"And if any of you are interested in rugby please see me after. We have some of the best teams in the district at this school." Again the friendly smile. "I'll let Debra Bartleson talk to you now," Gowd went on, turning to the senior girl by his side, "about the library and the computer club. Then we'd better report back to the principal so that those of you who are new today," and here he seemed to stare directly at Lara, "can be assigned to your classes."

While Lara waited with her new noisy classmates for the history teacher, she saw the Gadrey boy again. Lara stared down at her desk the whole time he was in the room joking with the younger kids. "That's Gowd Gadrey," Dieuwer, the girl sitting next to her, explained when he'd finally gone. "He really thinks he's something special now he's been made a class officer. Talk about two-faced. Really picks on some kids. Gets them terrified and then does the big brother act! Don't like him. Never have."

"If you want to see him freak out, just you call him Horse!" the smallish boy on the other side told Lara.

Lara looked puzzled.

"Gowd Gadrey. GG. Get it? Neeiiigh. He doesn't like it one bit."

"I wouldn't risk it," Dieuwer said, "specially if you're new around here. Keep out of his way."

"Jeez. I saw him go bananas in the playground when a few kids teased him once," Reg told them. "Not a pretty sight."

"Put it this way," Dieuwer said, "he's not the kind of person you'd want as an enemy."

"Oh, I don't know." The curly-headed girl from behind leaned over the desk. "He can act tough sometimes. But I feel kind of sorry for Gowd, you know, Reg."

"You must be joking, Shelley," Dieuwer laughed, and Reg made a kind of snorting sound. "That's like being sorry for a viper."

"His Dad told my Mom that when he was little he had a real rough time."

"My heart bleeds," Reg said.

"His Mom died when he was a little kid."

"So?" Reg intervened. "Lots of kids don't have — "

"Let me finish, stupid. His Dad took him down to stay with relatives in the city. He went to this school there. They teased the hell out of him. He was really small in those days. Anyway, he went a bit strange for a while. Didn't talk to anyone for about a year. So his Dad brought him back to the country again. Hard to believe he was a little squirt then, isn't it?" Shelley said, staring at Reg. "All of a sudden he got real tall. Country air, I s'pose! And his Dad said he got better then. Stood up for himself. Got tough. Well, look how good he is at soccer and things."

"I'd keep away from Gadrey," Dieuwer said to Lara again as the teacher appeared.

"He's a schizo," Reg agreed.

"You're the bloody schizo," Shelley teased, rumpling Reg's hair.

Lara was only vaguely aware of the high-spirited chatter of the kids around her now. Lost in thought, she was mostly unheeding, unseeing, all the long trip around the shores of the glittering lake and then through the thick palm forests. But when they reached the now familiar turn-off with the sign she knew was Old Creek Road, she recognized it at once. She was the first off the bus, surprised to find Pearl suddenly quite close beside her.

As the bus roared off she heard the sneering voice that she dreaded. It was Gowd Gadrey again, and he was right behind them.

"Ritchie girls. Missed you yesterday," he called, when the bus had rumbled off and they had turned up the forest road. Pearl moved instinctively closer to the taller girl for his voice had a definite taunt in it. They both struck out at a fair pace to walk the few kilometers into the heart of the forest. He remained close at their heels.

And then it began.

"Too stuck-up to talk, eh? Ritchie bitches. Not rich bitches, though. Dirt poor, you Ritchie lot." Lara, like Pearl, sped up her pace, frightened by the mockery in his voice. They had reached the end of the paved road already and now had to pick their way more carefully over the rough stones of the dirt road. Pearl glanced anxiously behind her.

"How many more coming to live in your little tin hut then, Pearl-of-a-girl? Your old man's got kids all over New South Wales, I'll bet. Ritchie many big fella tribe, ha ha."

Lara glanced down at Pearl's pursed lips. She could smell the fear of the younger girl filling the dappled road, quenching the eucalyptus fragrance of late afternoon and the rotting mulch of the still-wet dripping forest, an infectious fear. She didn't know why the unpleasant voice of the pursuing boy frightened her so much. But it did. It filled her with dread. She'd heard of *mighty dread* in a Christmas carol or in the Bible or somewhere. Well, she had it, this mighty dread, and it hit her chest violently. Just as if the pale-faced boy were punching her as hard as he possibly could with closed fists. Pearl was almost running now down the other side of the steep hill, stumbling on its rocky surface, her breath coming and going loudly.

"More where this stuck-up bitch came from?" he began again, gaining on Lara and poking her shoulder so savagely that she gasped with the surprise and pain of it.

"Shuddup, Gadrey," Pearl yelled over her shoulder but there was no conviction in her voice. It was then that Gowd Gadrey grasped Lara, digging into the soft muscle of her upper arm with his strong farmhand fingers until she cried out with the pain of it.

"Let go!" She wrenched her arm in terror but he held her effortlessly as a farmer might hold a rabbit or a hen destined for slaughter.

"I don't like you," he said, smiling into her frightened eyes. "I don't like you one little bit. Looking down your nose at everyone this morning. Well, we don't like stuck-up city kids at Palm Grove. Me especially. So you'd better keep out of my way. See."

Then he dropped her arm and disappeared, swallowed miraculously by the forest, it seemed to Lara. She expelled her intaken breath in the extreme relief of seeing his disappearing back.

"Short-cut. Fire-trail that leads to his place. His farm, runs along ours." Pearl gave out her staccato information without expression, but it was clear to Lara what she felt about him.

"He's an idiot. And he's crazy with a gun. Had a fight with him once over shooting on our place. Dad gave him trouble. He hates us. And he hates me, specially." Pearl's explanation completed, she put her head down again and they made for home swiftly. "Why does he hate you specially, Pearl?" Lara asked, trying to keep up with her, but Pearl just nodded her head and got that closed-in look again and wouldn't say another word. "And why should he hate me?" Lara thought bitterly.

As she walked silently beside the young girl Lara couldn't blot out the memory of the boy's pasty face and pale cruel eyes or his feeling of undisguised violence towards her. Her arm ached with the gathering of the dark blood cells that would leave the stain of Gowd's hatred with her for some weeks, making her sick each time she caught sight of it. But most painful of all for Lara was the realization that she had quaked before him. She knew she had *allowed* herself to be bullied.

"Kick him, scratch him, bite him, knee him if you have to," Mom had once said of a frightening boy who had lurked in the shadows of the trailer park for some weeks, terrifying everyone. She knew that bullies would always come off second-best with Mom. Even bullies as frightening as Gowd. But she, Lara, had quaked before him. She'd shrunk back from him just as he'd wanted her to. She hadn't been able to face his hatred because she was weak and silly and a coward. And he'd sniffed her out from a hundred kids at school knowing that. How she despised her weakness and fear! As he did.

"Face your fear," Mom had said so many times in the past that she could remember every word that was to come. "Look it full in the face, Lara. It's painful. But it's always better in the long run."

And she hadn't been able to face anything. Not Gladwyn, not Pearl, not the lurking Gadrey boy, not her loneliness. Not the dreadfulness of school. Not anything. They turned in at the gate and she caught the first glimpse of the brave blue corrugated iron homestead. Her feet felt heavy with the exertion of the walk over the rough ground and her heart with dark brooding thoughts.

Pearl came to life all at once, darting ahead down the car tracks. Lara could hear the joyful greetings of the little ones at the first sight of their schoolgirl sister. It was at that moment, with the hubbub of cries loud on the air, that Lara suddenly remembered Thunderwith. She knew that the big dog would be waiting for her this afternoon, perhaps right now, at the top of the hill beyond the house and the creek. Waiting for *her* as the sisters and little brother waited for Pearl. All at once her feet felt lighter as she walked the last little way to the back of the house. Her magic dog. She must get through her afternoon chores so that she could find him.

On the verandah the young children were swarming over Pearl. Only Garnet turned away from the feast of new pencils and exercise books that Pearl was scattering proudly before them on the wooden floor. "Lo, Lara," Garnet's eyes said, although she did not speak. Lara was grateful for the silent greeting and smiled back at her.

"This for me, Pearly," she heard Opal cry.

"Me, me, me," Opal and Jasper joined in.

Inside the large cool room Lara found their afternoon tea, sliced bread and great thick slabs of Gladwyn's heavy carrot cake, a tub of butter and a bottle of milk, waiting on the table. Her heart gave a strange little start to see it all set out so neatly. Two places and two knives, two mugs and two napkins arranged just so on the great expanse of table. It was the fold of the napkins she stared at, unable somehow to think of the scowling Gladwyn actually standing there creasing the paper napkins carefully, for them. And placing them neatly on the cracked plates with the knife resting so as to trap the flimsy thing from occasional gusts of wind that blew from front to back door. For them. One for Pearl and one for her. She touched the napkin.

Garnet had followed Lara inside. "Ma said when you and Pearl have finished, there's things to be done in the back field before dark."

Lara and Pearl chewed silently on the bread, listening to Garnet's strict division of the precious colored pencils keeping the three little ones quiet outside. "And some paper, too," they heard her say, "if you sit there and shut up."

When she'd finished eating Lara picked up the napkin and wiped her mouth delicately in the way Mom used to on those unusual occasions when they ate out. At Mrs. Robinson's, for instance. Or sometimes at the fancy café down the road where a friend of Mom's had worked. A friend. She crushed the paper napkin in her hand, thinking again of the dog.

They worked quite late up and down the rows of tiny palms, freeing them of weeds and turning the whitish clay-like soil where it wasn't packed too hard, so that her fingers ached with the toil of it. Pearl, of course, was uncomplaining and kept up with her mother row by row. But Lara fell further and further behind them. She was feeling more and more anxious. Maybe the dog was a dream-dog. Fantasy, like in a story. Maybe Thunderwith wouldn't be there at all. She must get up there soon. She must find out. "Oh, please be there for me, dog. Please be there."

When Gladwyn finally called a halt, standing and stretching and actually indicating some tenderness in the small of her back by a vigorous rubbing with one hand, Lara felt ill with tiredness. The afternoon sunlight was making long, golden slashes across the field and already the creek bed was in full shadow. When she made her fumbling explanation about a walk on the hill, Gladwyn simply shrugged and left the field for the house, with Pearl close behind her.

Lara passed by the bald white clay humped around the dam and then crossed the rough log bridge over the creek. She knew full well that Pearl's inquisitive eyes were upon her. "Thunderwith, be there. Oh, please, be there," she prayed, over and over again. A few minutes later she heard the ringing sound of water in the pail, indicating that Pearl and her Mom had already reached the big old tank outside the bathroom. They would be freeing themselves of the clinging soil that smeared her own hands and arms so thickly.

She cut through the reeds quickly. Once out of sight of the house her spirits lifted as if by magic. Of course her dog would be there! She began to run through the long grass between the great pink trunks of the trees that studded the hillside. Dad had told her they were not gum trees; they had a fancy name she couldn't remember. But they smelled like gum trees and the leaves hung down dead straight like gum leaves. She knew at this time if she moved quietly she'd see the gray forms of wallabies and perhaps larger kangaroos against the skyline. Dad had shown her how to get quite close to the nervous creatures who sat, noses and ears twitching for anything unfamiliar. But she couldn't be quiet, crashing eagerly through the undergrowth in her hurry to get up the hill in what was left of the daylight.

On the crest of the hill she saw him, a dark sleek form springing up from the grass like a bird startled from its nest. But the dog was not startled. It came towards her with sureness and speed, leaping up at her as she called its name. "Thunderwith, my beauty." She welcomed it with open arms. "My magic dog. You're here. You're not a dream at all. You're here waiting for me." She buried her face in its coat and stood quietly for a minute. Presently she raised her head and stared into the beast's eyes. "You know, don't you? You know everything. You know about this dreadful school and that bully of a boy. You *do* know, because you're my magic beast."

The dog licked her face and she laughed. "Your tongue's sloppy wet, dog, even if you are magic."

They ran together right along the ridge that formed the back field. Lara looked out over the patchwork of countryside. Great bushy palm trees poked up their shaggy manes here and there, flaunting a weighty beauty against the darkening skyline.

"One day soon, Thunderwith, we'll go there. Right into that secret forest," she told the dog. "Over the hills and far away." And when she said that there was a strange little jolt inside her all at once, for she thought of Mom. *Over the hills and far away*. It was a line from a poem Mom had read her from the old gray poetry book, she was sure. The book Mom had kept beside her bed in the trailer and read to Lara sometimes. Just before they'd gone to sleep. Mom's book. Mom's poem. Mom.

Mom lying on the bed reading to her, Mom looking up, laughing or crying sometimes, at the latest adventure they'd shared. Mom reciting the old bush poems:

> *The stark white ring-barked forests,*
> *All tragic to the moon.*
> *The sapphire-misted mountains,*

The hot gold hush of noon.
Green tangle of the brushes,
Where lithe lianas coil,
And orchids deck the tree-tops
And ferns the warm dark soil.

Over and over the same sweet, familiar words. Mom hugging her. Mom telling her over and over how wonderful it was, the two of them together as they were. Mom talking softly, seriously to her when she told her some of her worries at school. Mom singing and dancing and being crazy. Mom noisy and embarrassing at some of the get-togethers they'd had at Idle Hours.

She wanted Mom so badly at this moment that a great hot pain seared her whole body as if a bolt of lightning had struck and burned her to her heart. She looked up at the great black line of gums they had reached at the end of the field. And what had been soft and beautiful a minute ago became harsh and blank and lonely. Everywhere, everything, empty of her mother.

Tears were not possible for the sorrow for it all had frozen her. Lara stood motionless for some time as the sun slid out of sight behind the trees. The dog stood beside her, silent and still too. Then Thunderwith stirred and licked her hand. All at once, Lara's eyes were drawn from the bleak evening sky to the dog waiting so patiently beside her. She patted its head, grateful for its silent companionship. Then she knelt and hugged it to her fiercely. Oh, Thunderwith!

She knew the children would be sent to find her soon and she did not want them to know about the dog. Thunderwith was hers alone. She knew that. It had been sent to her. Mom had sent it to her somehow. She was sure of that. And she would not share her precious secret with anyone else.

"I've got to go, dog." She knelt and hugged it to her once again. "But I'll be back again. Wait for me, won't you?"

The dog walked beside her across the top field. But when she said, "Stay, boy, stay, Thunderwith, stay," it seemed to understand, for it did not attempt to follow her as she plunged down the hill. She glanced back and saw the swish of a tail as the dog darted back along the ridge, disappearing among the grasses to its secret bush home.

"Like out of a book," she thought. "My own magic dog." Leaving the hill and the dog was like closing the pages of a book, she thought, as she sped downwards towards the house. If you close a book — well, all the characters are sort of hanging there, between the pages. Waiting for *you* to come back. And only you can make them come to life again. Maybe her magic dog didn't exist once she left the hillside, she thought. Maybe Thunderwith only "came to life" for her. All that mattered was that the dog was there waiting when she wanted it. She didn't try to understand why or how, as she had not tried to understand some of the magic places she and Mom had believed in. She simply accepted the gift of the dog and was glad of it.

As she caught sight of the glimmering lights that indicated the house and the difficult family, she had a brief moment of gladness. She had her dog now. It was part of Willy Nilly Farm, but it was entirely hers. And she knew that whatever had sent her through the storm to find the dog was surely a force for goodness. Perhaps, she thought, as she crossed the bridge and ran through the field where they'd worked earlier in the afternoon, it would help her face up to everything else that seemed so hard about her new life here.

It was quite dark by the time she reached the back door. She pushed it open and hesitated for a moment. Once again she felt an intruder on this quiet family scene. Jasper and Opal were playing with their tops on a mat in the corner. "You have that one and I'll have this," she could hear Opal saying reasonably, in a singsong voice. Garnet was sitting close by, holding a picture book and poring over each page. She looked up.

"Where you been, Lara? You're awful dirty."

"You gotta wash that clay off outside," Garnet said.

Gladwyn and Pearl, intent on chopping a pile of vegetables on a huge wooden board on the table, hardly looked up as she came inside.

"I'll come out with you and do the lamp," Garnet volunteered,

" 'cause the 'lectric light doesn't work out there in the bath-house anymore."

"She can light a lamp," Gladwyn said sharply, "and if she can't it's about time she learned. Take the matches, Lara."

Lara took the matches and went outside and around the house. She did not bother to go into the pitch-black bathroom and wrestle with the lamp. She knew as well as Gladwyn had known that she would not be able to light it easily. Lara washed instead at the old tank stand, her feet brushing against the ferns and bushes that clustered so eagerly close to the con-stant source of water and where she could dimly see what she was doing. She dried herself on the rough fragment of towel that was left there permanently for dirty hands and feet. And then she came back to the verandah and sank exhausted onto her bed. All was quiet within the house and she felt she did not have the energy to break in upon the unusual peace of it.

She reached under the bed and felt for the little trinket box she had hidden so carefully from the prying eyes and inquisitive fingers of the small children. She shook out her few treasures onto the bed. Mom's gold earrings — genuine fourteen-carat ones — that she'd got on her twenty-first. Mom's silver locket on a chain, that she'd received on her seventeenth birthday from her Mom and Dad. It was a pretty oval-shaped piece with delicate scrolling all over it. Mom wouldn't part with it even though she'd had to pawn her diamond engagement ring, the one that Larry had given her. She'd bought a little ruby fake in its place a few years later and said that only a trained eye could tell the difference really. And there were her own earrings and the matching opal ring that Mom had given her when the miracle of reading had happened. Mom had said to wear them only for best. Funny to think of "best" out here in the forest. And the coins. Mom had made an attempt, in an initial rush of enthusiasm that did not continue, to collect foreign coins. Lara touched the silver dollar gently, apprehensive again at the rush of memories associated with the gleaming coin. She thought of Mom seated at their kitchen table in the trailer, poking at the few coins she'd managed to collect, her eyes lighting up when she seized on the American dollar. "I'm going on the stage. Broadway, Lara. Chorus line. And you too, love, if you want. I'll teach you all I know. We can do it, I know it." Mom had only recently taken up tap-dancing and she and Bonnie had brought the house down at the Idle Hours Trailer Park Annual Concert with their brilliant tap routine to the strains of Jason Wenderoth's dazzling piano accompaniment.

"Hollywood or bust, girls," Stephen Pease had yelled out at them from the audience.

"After the house in Newcastle," Mom had said, "it's Hollywood for us, girl. Stick it on the list. And this silver dollar's going to be sort of an inspiration for us, Lara, okay? Proof there's this place across the other side of the world to be happy in. Of course we can be happy here too, baby. But you gotta have dreams. You'd better believe it!" And she'd jumped to her feet and tapped expertly to the other end of the trailer, finishing with high kicks that Lara had applauded loudly.

A grubby hand reached over the crochet cover and grabbed the silver dollar.

"Tar." Jasper's clenched fist moved to his mouth.

"No, Jasper. No. Dirty old thing," she said, prising the silver coin from his unwilling fist and distracting him with the other trinkets spread before him.

"What's that?" It was the brown-eyed Opal sliding round the bed now.

"Well, there's some pretty earrings," Lara began, her closed fist concealing the precious coin, "and a bracelet with a bird and . . ."

"No, that," Opal insisted, pointing to her clenched fist, so that Lara was forced to show her.

"Just an American dollar. A coin, that's all," Lara said.

"Mine. Mine," the baby whined, sensing his sister's interest in the glittering thing in Lara's hand.

She began gathering the things on the bed, tossing them nervously into the small box. Jasper set up a wail for the silver dollar which brought Garnet running.

"She's got jewels and things," Opal said, and Garnet had to be told the whole story of her mother's coin collection, particularly about the silver dollar.

"Let me look at it again," Garnet said, but Gladwyn's voice could be heard calling them inside and they took themselves unwillingly from Lara's bedside. Lara shoved the trinket box under her pillow, resolving to find a new and better hiding place when she went to bed that night.

"Lara's got a secret treasure," Opal announced importantly at the table when they were about to eat. Lara saw Pearl's eyes flash as she looked down at her plate and then up again at her mother's set face.

"With a silver dollar," Opal insisted.

"It was her Mom's," Garnet explained.

"Mom's!" Jasper put in.

"I wanna silver coin too," Opal pleaded.

"Eat up and be quiet," Gladwyn said.

"But I do, Mom."

"Me. Me!" Jasper added.

"Lara gave Jasper a coin from Bali," Garnet told them.

"Well, he doesn't want it," Pearl said, angrily. "He should give it back to her, Mom, shouldn't he?"

But Gladwyn had stiffened suddenly and turned in her seat, listening to something.

"Shh," she cautioned them and they all heard the sound of a motor, not far off on the forest road, but somewhere close at hand. A car coming up the driveway.

"Dad?" Pearl began eagerly but Gladwyn frowned and said "no" with such authority that no one argued. She left the table to look out the window. Lara was amazed that the children sat so quietly as the approaching car lights flung their long and ghostly shapes eerily around the walls. The engine stopped and they could hear the sound of footsteps approaching the unused front door. Now Jasper slid from his chair and found comfort in clinging to his mother's skirt but he didn't speak at all.

"Mrs. Ritchie," a man's voice called, causing Lara to start at the sound of her own mother's name.

"It's Bill Gadrey," Gladwyn said softly and opened the door. Lara sat numbly, thinking of Gowd Gadrey's pale moon face. Must be his Dad.

"News from Larry," the tall man at the front door explained,

"I thought you'd like to hear it now. He rang the post office and left the message for the general store. But he rang us as well so that you'd know real soon. He's contacted Cooper and it's going to be all right about your land. He's moving on from Cooper's place."

Mr. Gadrey's voice sounded so warm and so pleased that when Lara looked up into his smiling eyes, she could not believe the bearer of good news for Gladwyn was the father of today's unpleasant boy.

"Thank you," Gladwyn said, taking the paper with the message scribbled on it and smoothing it in her hands. "Thank you very much, Bill. I really appreciate getting the message."

"Well, I'd better be getting along then." He leaned a smiling face around the door. "Hello, good-bye kids. You'll be seeing your Dad real soon now."

They murmured some sort of response to him and then, after his good-bye to her, Gladwyn closed the door.

How stiff and formal she was, Lara thought, resuming her meal now as they all did, with Jasper chanting "Dad, Dad" and Garnet and Opal agreeing with him. "Yes, Jazzy. Dad, Dad."

Mom would have chatted to Mr. Gadrey, given him a cup of tea, thanked him profusely for the trouble he'd taken in bringing the message to her. But Gladwyn did none of these, only smiled politely and closed the door.

When Bill Gadrey's car lights had swept in a full arc and the sound of the motor retreated up the road, Pearl said: "The Gadrey boy's picking on Lara, Mom." Lara was so shocked by this unexpected remark that she felt her cheeks burn. But she said nothing.

"I don't like that Gadrey neither. He makes faces at me," Garnet said.

"And shoots little baby animals and things," Opal added. "He shoots them dead."

"Dead. Shoots dead," Jasper chanted.

"His Mom's dead, too," Garnet offered, looking sympathetically at Lara.

"We're not talking about that," Pearl flashed. "We're talking about him picking on Lara."

"Picking on Lara?" Gladwyn said absently, a far-away look on her face.

"He hates Lara too, Mom," Pearl insisted, "just like he hates me."

"I'm sure Lara can look after herself," Gladwyn said. Lara detected a change in the tone of her voice. It wasn't accusing. And there was a lightness in her step as she lifted the huge pot from the table. The children, too, sensed something different after Bill Gadrey's message. "C'mon, let's play slidings on the mattress," Opal suggested. "Will you help us, Pearly?" But Pearl remained at the table.

"He's horrible, that Gadrey boy," Pearl insisted.

"If it's a big problem, well, tell the teachers. Not me," Gladwyn said, closing the conversation. She let the kids play wild games for a time and hummed to herself over the dishes. But Lara felt sick. It might be good news that Dad was coming home soon. But when was soon? And in the meantime there was the Gadrey boy to face every day. It was clear that Gladwyn simply did not want to know anything about her problem with Gowd Gadrey.

"Look after herself!" Lara lay on her bed on the back verandah wide-eyed again until late that night. After the noise of the children in the confined house, she felt she needed time to herself to think. Funny how she'd never felt confined in the trailer with Mom, and yet it had been so much smaller than here.

Oscar had come down the tree, stared at her, head to one side, and then, when there was no response from Lara, begun busily feeding on the scraps. The night bird that cried its jarring notes all around the fields had come and gone. She lay listening to the silence.

She tried once again to talk to her mother but realized she could not even conjure up a picture of her beloved face any more. She clenched her hands tight. "You lied, Mom," she whispered. "You said you'd always be near. Well, where in the hell are you?"

There was only the sky through the trees, huge and black and pierced with hundreds and thousands of tiny lights that shed no warmth on her. She stared up into it for a long time.

When she closed her eyes at last it wasn't Mom she saw at all. It was Thunderwith leaping across the grassy hill at the top field and into her arms; Thunderwith running close beside her; Thunderwith sitting quietly by her, the big handsome head resting on her arm, the wise eyes knowing and understanding everything. Thunderwith.

And yet through the sweet dream of the dog came an unwelcome and persistent presence. The face of the Gadrey boy edged in and rose up pale and round and cruel. It was getting closer and closer. Something was happening, something she could not quite understand, and yet it was unbearable. She was falling, falling into an abyss of blackness and pain. She woke with a start, gasping for breath, but the terrible dream persisted. There was a black choking feeling of fear. It was Mom's great black bird hovering. It had spread its great dank-smelling wings over her face so that she was pushed down and down. She would suffocate if she lay a moment longer . . .

Lara jumped up from the bed, panting heavily, wanting to run to safety. But there was nowhere to run. She made for the door. She would have to wake Gladwyn. She would have to. Some pretext or other; the wind coming up and the need to roll down the canvas blind. She reached out her hand for the door handle and was about to open it when she heard the faint sound of music. Music that made the dream recede at once. Who was listening to music at this hour inside the iron homestead? It could only be Gladwyn.

She pulled the old crochet blanket off the bed and put it around her shoulders, glad that her panting breaths of fear had subsided. She knelt on the bed and looked through the small window. Gladwyn must have lit one of the small kerosene lamps so that its feeble glow would not waken the children They were all fast asleep up at the far end of the large room. She could just make out their inert forms. But Gladwyn in her nightdress was at the kitchen end of the house. Her eyes were closed and she was swaying to the music — well, dancing, really — in graceful movements, on the small free space of the carpet square by the dining table. The sight of Gladwyn's face stripped away all Lara's fear. Her expression at this moment was one that Lara would never have thought possible.

Gladwyn had let down her dark lustrous hair and it swept around her shoulders as she moved to the rhythm of the music. Her arms were clasped across her breast, hands gripping her own thin shoulders. Her lips were parted, not in a smile but in an exclamation of joy. The movements of her dance became quick and even fierce as the music rose and fell in its own strange syncopations. But there was a smoothness in her movements, like watching a fine piece of silk fluttering in a wind: streaming, floating, shivering. The fluid dance movements were beautiful to watch. She was beautiful to watch. Yes, Lara recognized with a start that Gladwyn was a beautiful woman. Her face had taken on an altogether different expression. It had come alive as she explored some rapturous place that the music had taken her. Oh, she wanted to be part of it too! To rush into the dimly lit room to say yes, she could hear the wonderful sadness, the strange satisfying beauty of the music too! If only she could.

When the music stopped, as it did at last, Lara ducked her head, afraid that Gladwyn would see her. She knew she was intruding into a part of the private world of Gladwyn Ritchie that maybe nobody else knew about. She wished she could speak to her right now for Lara had never heard such music. But she dreaded the hard cold expression Gladwyn seemed to reserve for her. She did not dare.

There was silence within now. When she peered through the window once more, Lara could see the lamp was extinguished. She climbed under the covers of her own verandah bed, feeling quite exhausted but not frightened any more. She had never heard sweet strange music like that before. It continued faintly in her head even now. She wished she could listen to more of it, even talk to Gladwyn about it. Gladwyn's music was like a doorway to some other place — a glorious place, a place maybe not even Mom had known about. She fell asleep with images of Gladwyn's wild and graceful dance on her mind.

Then next day, Lara saw Gladwyn at play with her children for the first time since she'd been there. Early evening in the sticky heat, Pearl had suggested a swim in the dam and to Lara's surprise Gladwyn had agreed. Pearl had stared at Lara's swimsuit and matching towel with hard eyes, but said nothing. They had walked across the rough ground with an assortment of towels and tires and plastic floats.

"Our dam's the best damn dam," Garnet chanted, "bar none." Then, coming close to Lara, she whispered, "And so is your swimsuit." Lara would have liked to have taken Garnet's hand, but instead she smiled at her.

"Dam, dam, dam," they all sang as they approached the white edge.

The water, somewhat replenished by the recent storm, was still low enough to reveal the harsh clay sides furrowed by rivulets of rainwater. In the dying light there was the strange white glow of the walls as they came up over the hump of the dam. Here and there patches of green hung tenaciously. "We're planting lots of grass here soon," Garnet explained.

The little ones, secure in their inflated arm-floats, surged into the grayish water at once. "Mom, Mom," Jasper cried, clinging to Gladwyn's leg, but finally allowing himself to be carried down the steep caked wall like a small baby in his mother's arms. She deposited him safely on top of one of the foam surfboards afloat on the water. "There, Jazzy. Lovely cool water," she told him, and pushed off easily from the edge, taking him towards the little island.

"Pearl!" she called over the noise of her kicking feet that drove the surfboard forward. "Look after the others." And she was gone.

Pearl dived into the water, splashing at Opal and Garnet, who shrieked in delight. She floated on her back to watch scornfully as Lara made her way in gingerly, recoiling in distaste at the feel of the sludgy wet clay underfoot.

"Don't you like the mud?" Garnet demanded, dog-paddling towards the older girl.

"I don't like the feel of it," Lara began, screwing up her nose. "It's all . . ."

"We love it," Pearl said, swimming towards the edge, quite close to where Lara was struggling. She came up the bank and stood there scooping up handfuls of the sloppy stuff, which she applied to her shoulders and arms.

"Erk ahh oooh," the others called from afar as Pearl applied final grimy streaks to her face. She stared defiantly at Lara, who was still poised at the edge.

The muddy spectacle of their sister brought the others in a flurry, screaming to be mud-painted as well. Pearl warmed to her task, applying handful after handful in startling patterns, until they all looked like gray water creatures, flailing arms and legs and gray moon faces.

"I am the Mud Queen of Willy Nilly," Garnet chanted, bowing to the line of trees across the dam.

"Me, too," Opal copied.

"And I am the Mud Queen of the World," Pearl said, raising her pale streaked arms to the sky.

When Gladwyn arrived, pushing Jasper in front of her on the foam float from the other side of the dam, she laughed at the sight of them. Lara stared in surprise at her. She thought she had probably never seen Gladwyn laugh. Then Gladwyn put Jasper in the shallows at the bank and returned to duck each muddy head in the water, playful in a way that Lara had not thought possible.

In a way, she thought after her brief swim and as she edged up the oozy banks to the hard baked clay, it was worse when Gladwyn was being so nice. Playing and laughing with her kids the way she was. There was the choking loneliness again for Mom's arms to be around *her*, Mom's love to make *her* feel alive again.

Lara sat, towel around her shoulders, huddled on the bank, watching with hungry eyes as Gladwyn played in the water with her children.

5

Lara was startled by a low humming sound as she came out into the huge expanse of playground at Palm Grove High. She could see a mob of boys gathered together in the far end of the grounds, jostling, pushing, jeering. The cry that had began as a sort of hum changed into words and rose to a crescendo, filling her ears.

"Get him. Get Reg. Get him," they chanted over and over again, and the slow accompanying clap became faster. "Get him. Get Reg," until it broke into a wild applause. The sound continued but now there was the thud of feet beating in the background as well. Then the mob, getting bigger each moment, swooped up the grounds. Like a herd of wild things, Lara thought, moving back towards the safety of the doorway. Like a herd of wild things intent on prey.

A small figure darted ahead of the crowd and up the playground right towards her. She could see it was Reg Breen, one of the friendlier boys in her class, fleeing in front of them. His face seemed frozen, his eyes wide with fright. His mouth was open in a huge O, denoting fear and superhuman effort as he ran faster than he knew he could, away from the vengeful wave of kids who lunged after him. Lara had no time to do anything but flatten herself against the wall as a wave of bodies seemed to break her and surge on. Pounding figures in a terrible pursuit.

They were gone in a few moments, Reg and all his pursuers, but Reg's face stayed clearly in her mind. It was the face of real terror.

She looked around to see if there was a teacher nearby. The yard was almost empty and from the other end of the school, behind the gym, she could already hear another harsh chant. It didn't take much imagination to work out what was about to happen to Reg down there.

"Punch-him, punch-him, punch-him," the group chanted. Lara turned away, not wanting to see anything of the struggling figures who'd attracted the eager crowd.

She darted across the asphalt towards the building that housed the large library where she was sure to find a teacher. But two girls appeared out of nowhere as she reached the top of the stairs. Suddenly there was a girl on either side of her and she felt herself being propelled down the stairs to the heat of the playground once again.

"We've been sent to get you," one of them said menacingly. She was the dark-haired girl that Lara had seen talking to Gowd Gadrey.

"Gowdie thinks you should come down to the back."

"Now," the other girl said, tightening her grip on Lara's arm.

"A bit of excitement going on down there, you know."

"I'm not going anywhere," Lara said, wrenching herself free of them and heading back up the stairs.

"Oh, dear, Gowdie will be disappointed. He wanted you to see him put an end to that dreadful fight going on down there. You should see Reggie's nose!" They both laughed at the look of fear on her face. "We'll tell him you won't come, then," the dark-haired girl spoke in mock-friendly tones.

"He'll just have to put you on lunchtime detention, I guess," the other one sniggered.

"For what?" Lara flashed.

"I'm sure he'll think of something."

"He said you were a city slicker and a snob." The dark-haired girl sounded annoyed now. "And you are."

Lara was confused by their attack. Why should Gowd Gadrey send for her? His daily taunting on the long walk home from the bus stop was obviously not enough. She was afraid. He'd guessed she was an utter coward. Or maybe he knew that she and Reg Breen got along really well in Mrs. Gilbert's history class. She stared down at the unpleasant laughing girls.

"See ya Bitchie — oops — Ritchie," they called as they ran off in the direction of the fight.

In the distance she could see two teachers who were obviously heading for the mob. She sighed with relief as the noise subsided in the lower grounds and then disappeared altogether. She could hear the raised voice of the teacher Mr. Croker, haranguing the kids, who were suddenly quiet. She was glad of the voice's loudness and firmness and anger.

Lara had only been at Palm Grove High a few weeks and yet she hated this school — with its bullies like Gowd Gadrey, and its mobs that went after kids as small and helpless as Reg. Hated it! Despite the teachers who'd been so nice to her. In her second week she had felt she might have liked it for that was when Mrs. Gilbert had said Lara's essay on the Aborigines of Lake Macquarie had been excellent. "A fine piece of work. Well researched," Mrs. Gilbert had written, making her glow with pride. And it was wonderful praise for a girl who, two years before, could hardly read. Lara wished Mom had been able to see the generous comments Mrs. Gilbert had made all the way down the margin and the A+ grading.

But history was only a small part of her day here. No, she didn't like big confusing Palm Grove High except maybe for one place. In the library it was always cool and quiet and peaceful. Lara found her way there every day. She'd checked for favorite authors, relieved that so many of the books Mrs. Robinson had insisted she read were to be found on the shelves right here. They were like old and trusted friends to her and she fingered the spine of each remembered book lovingly. And opening one or two she was grateful to see there were the same people and the same familiar places still there.

She sat down at one of the tables trying to re-read a favorite part of a story. But somehow, today, with the thought of Reg's fight and Gowd's request on her mind, she couldn't settle down to reading. Across the room, she saw a huge display all along the library wall. It was the one Mrs. Gilbert had told them to look at. Some of the senior students had worked on it last week with an Aboriginal storyteller who was visiting the school. It was all about Aborigines and the Dreamtime. She stared at the striped and checkered picture of the fat crocodile surrounded by so many tiny hunting figures. And all the others along-side it.

She went across to look closely at some of the bark paintings. And that was when she noticed the familiar cover of one of the books on display. It was the story she'd read to Garnet the other night, *Giant Devil Dingo*. The very one that had surprised her because she had only just found her own dingo dog.

Lara picked up the book with the fierce dingo face on the cover and read the whole story through again. Then she looked at the note at the back by the author that she hadn't noticed the other night: "*The dingo was very important in hunting and I have seen many sacred paintings of dingoes in secret caves in Cape York,*" the note said. "*. . . They make useful pets and are very loyal and a true friend of man . . .*" Thunderwith, her true friend. Yes, her *only* friend.

"It's a good display, don't you think?" A young woman with a pile of books in her arms was standing beside her. "My uncle — he's the storyteller — well, he helped put it up. Some of those are his paintings, too. Pretty good crocodile, don't you think?"

Lara nodded shyly, putting the book back on its stand.

"You interested in Koori stories?"

"I read this story to my . . . to a little kid I know. I was just looking at it. I like the pictures."

"You're a new kid here, aren't you?" the woman asked.

Lara nodded. "I'm Lara Ritchie."

"Well, I'm Joslyn Symon. I work in the library for a few days a week. Helping Mrs. Magill. With the books and the office and things. I've seen you here a few times." Lara smiled at her.

There was something about Joslyn Symon you liked immediately.

"If you like coming in here," Joslyn went on, "and I guess you do from what I see, well, a few of the kids help out sometimes. Would you like to talk to Mrs. Magill about it?" Lara nodded. "And if you're around on Fridays you can come and hear my uncle telling some Koori stories. He's just about the best storyteller you ever heard. Mrs. Magill's arranged for him to come once a week for a few months. And then if that works out — well, he's going to go all around New South Wales telling our stories," Joslyn said proudly.

Lara nodded at the friendly woman. She remembered a book of Dreamtime stories that she and Mom had once read, with magic titles like *Quork Quork the Frog*.

"Does he know any stories about dogs?" she asked.

"Better come and ask him. Friday lunchtime."

Lara came to the library on Friday with a handful of other kids to hear the storyteller, Neil Symon, the old man who was Joslyn's uncle. He began with stories of the times long, long ago at the beginning "that our people call the Dreaming." And later he talked of his own boyhood "a long, long time ago, too." And the group of kids in the library got larger and larger as his quiet voice went on.

Lara didn't notice any of the others, not even Stan Redmond, who stared over at her where she sat close to Neil.

The storyteller's deep, quiet voice rose and fell as he told the old stories. A voice that made you feel shivery and yet good at the same time, Lara thought. Like Mom's voice when she was reading her poetry.

The kids laughed, loving the quick, clever drawings Neil also made on a big white sheet of the animals and people he spoke about. And they laughed even more when he got some of the kids to come up front to act out the stories. Lara forgot everything under the spell of the old man's voice.

"A long, long time ago, back in the Dreamtime, there was no sunlight at all on the big dark earth. Do you know the tribespeople had to search for their food by the light of the moon? Oh it was

dark! And it could've stayed that way except for a fight. It was a good fight because it was the end of the darkness.

"The Emu and the Brolga had this fight about their babies. That old brolga got so mad she took one of the emu's eggs and hurled it up into the air. That egg flew up and up until it shattered against a pile of sticks that the Sky People had gathered high up there in the sky. Whoosh! it went, right against those sticks and they burst into yellow dancing flames.

"That huge fire lit up the whole world. And when the people down on earth saw how beautiful their world was — oh well, then they decided that they should have day and night. Oh yes!

"The Sky People agreed to gather a pile of dry sticks every day to be set alight when the morning star appeared. But if the day was cloudy, they couldn't see that old morning star. And so the Sky People asked the Kookaburra, who had a good big strong happy voice, to call them every morning. And this is what the Kookaburra does. And that's how we have the beautiful fire that lights up our world. That's how we have night and day."

And then when he'd finished the last story, he sang. He strummed a guitar and sang songs about his people, and the whole library came to life with clapping and stamping until Mrs. Magill had to quiet everyone down again.

Then Neil told them about when he was a kid like them. About how he had lots and lots of aunts and every one of them like a mother:

"I had one Dad. But I had so many mothers, you kids couldn't count them on both hands. And did they know all the old stories! Of course, most of them didn't want to tell me then. They thought it might be trouble for me to know them. They'd go all quiet when I asked. Call me Dirigeree. Willy Wagtail. Trouble.

"See, in those times some of my people were trying to forget the old ways. Learn all the white stories. Forget the Koori ones. And the Koori language. But one of my aunts, Urana's her Koori name, well, she told me. And my old grandfather, he told me, too. The very stories I'm telling you now."

Lara didn't want Neil to stop speaking. About his family.

About the old times. She liked being here with him. But then he sang his last song and it was over.

"Lara's a new kid round here. Lives in the Wallingat," Joslyn said at the end, thrusting Lara forward when most of the kids had finally drifted away from the old man's side.

"Well, we're both new then," Neil said, smiling at her. "I've lived around this area all my life, like I said. But this is my first time telling stories in a school. Going to new places and doing anything for the first time is hard going, I reckon." He seemed to be looking intently into Lara's eyes and she felt a little uncomfortable for a moment — as if he were looking inside her mind. But then he turned away, collecting his drawings.

"It'll get easier, you know. Things take time. Have a way of getting easier if you set your mind to it."

Had Joslyn maybe told her uncle how very unhappy she was here? But Joslyn had no way of knowing that. Why would she be talking about her, a new kid at the school, to anybody? And yet the old man seemed to sense something straight away about her. Guessed at her feelings, somehow, she was sure.

"You know, I was a bit worried about whether the kids here would like my stories . . ." Neil told her.

"Like your stories? They were the best stories I've heard since my Mom . . . in a long time. Really they were," Lara told him.

"Here. This is for you." The old man held out his sketch of the kookaburra.

"Oh, no. I can't." She looked at it, but didn't take it. "It's lovely, but I couldn't."

"Go on, take it," Joslyn told her, "Neil wants you to have it, Lara."

"There's a kookaburra comes every morning to our back verandah," Lara told him, shyly accepting the gift of his drawing.

"To light up your world. Say hello from me to your kookaburra, won't you?" Neil said, as he left the library.

"Thought you'd like Neil," Joslyn said. "Everyone does."

On the bus going home that day, although she sat alone as usual, Lara somehow didn't feel quite so bad. She thought about what Neil had said about being new. Maybe things would get easier, as he said. She had Thunderwith, didn't she? Maybe she'd tell Neil about Thunderwith. It'd be nice to ask him whether he thought Thunderwith could be a magic dog. Funny how she'd liked Neil so much. Joslyn was nice, too, but there was something special about the old man. Something about his voice that made you think of poetry — like Mom's poetry, only different. Something about the way he talked and stopped and looked at you so thoughtfully. As if he knew you from a long way back.

The sound of laughter from the back of the bus jolted her back to reality. There was the ordeal of Gowd Gadrey to come. Some days Gowd didn't speak to Lara and Pearl at all. He would stride ahead, disappearing up the dappled road as they lingered and lingered, united in their fear, until the tall, thickish form was out of sight. But there were other days when he goaded and teased and threatened, enjoying their hurried retreat.

She glanced quickly over her shoulder, noting with relief that, this afternoon, Gowd was not among what was called "The Royal Family" of seniors who lounged on the specially reserved back seat. The two girls could walk home in silence at a comfortable pace. At the old tin mail box on the gate Pearl gave a cry of joy and ran off up the driveway waving a letter excitedly. "From Dad, I bet," Lara thought, trudging behind her.

Gladwyn positively beamed when she opened it. It was good news for the family, she said. Things were going well for Larry. There was even a contact telephone number. She could talk to him and find out just exactly when he'd be home. They would need to go to the post office so that she could call him.

" 'Call at 10:30 any morning,' it says. We'll go tomorrow morning," Gladwyn announced. "It's Saturday, so you can all come with me. And afterwards we'll go on to the beach. For the day."

"To Seal," the kids yelled, "let's go to Seal, Mom!"

*   *   *

"What's that?" Garnet asked later when she'd caught sight of Neil's drawing as Lara sat at the big table with her homework spread around her.

"It's a Koori — an Aboriginal — drawing. There's an Aboriginal storyteller coming to our school. He's called Neil Symon. And he's coming every week for a while to the library —"

"Abo stories are pretty boring," Pearl interrupted.

"Have you heard any?" Lara asked. "Have you heard Neil's?"

"Nope. Library's boring. I don't go there. And I bet Neil Whatsit is boring as hell."

"He does real nice drawings, though," Garnet said, hanging over Lara's shoulder.

But Pearl refused to look at Neil's kookaburra. Later, however, Lara saw her look at it all right. When she thought no one was about Pearl took it out into the light. She stood by the remains of the campfire, largely unused now that Dad wasn't here, and stared at Neil's drawing for a long time.

And later still Lara noticed when Pearl did some of her own drawings at the big table there was one that had bold strong lines. It was of Oscar the possum, and it looked remarkably like Neil's.

"It's been ages since we've been to Seal, hasn't it, Gar?" Pearl said, early on Saturday morning as she packed their lunch into a neat array of containers. She said it loudly so that Lara could hear her plainly, but she didn't look Lara's way at all.

"Seal Rocks is our beach. And we all call it Seal," Garnet explained to Lara.

"I really love Seal," Pearl went on, ignoring her small sister. "It's the best beach in the world bar none. You couldn't have a nicer beach anywhere," she challenged Lara, who remained silent.

"We can show Lara the secret places, maybe, Pearl?" Garnet asked, approaching her older sister at the table and helping pack the slabs of bread and the pieces of fruit.

"Shut your big mouth," was all the reply she got.

"Grab the letter on the kitchen shelf and put it in my bag, real carefully, Pearl," Gladwyn called. "It's got your Dad's phone number on it and I don't want to lose it."

She was pulling a bright blue swimsuit onto Jasper's sturdy little body. He stood quietly, but his eyes were on the orange plastic bucket that Opal was swinging around her head now and that was tantalizingly close to him. "My bucket. My shovel," Opal teased.

"Well, Garnet, don't just stand there," Gladwyn snapped at the child, who was watching her mother's deft movements; dressing the baby, gathering towels and T-shirts. "Do you want to go swimming or don't you?"

Garnet rushed to get ready.

Lara could feel Pearl's envious eyes as she pulled out another bathing suit. She chose a high-cut strappy one-piece, a dreamy swirl of greens and blues, that she and Mom had taken ages to decide on in a big shop not so many months ago in a shopping mall in Wyong. "Sarah Green says you swim better in Speedos. She's the school swimming champion," Pearl announced to nobody in particular. She stuffed her sensible navy suit into an old canvas bag and strolled out onto the verandah, with Opal trailing behind.

"But I like Lara's suit the best," Garnet said. Then, when Pearl pinched her little arm in a great generous squeeze, she added, "after your Speedos."

"What's a Seedo?" Opal asked.

In the truck Gladwyn allowed Lara to hold the baby for he had landed on her lap when Pearl bundled him in the door. His cool little arms entwined themselves around Lara's neck at once.

"Get in, for goodness sake," Gladwyn said impatiently as Pearl attempted to extricate the baby from Lara's grasp. "And leave Jasper be, can you?" Pearl frowned but made no reply as she shoved in beside Garnet, pulling Opal in defiance onto her own knee.

Lara turned away from Pearl's stony glance and watched Gladwyn's thin brown hand as she put the truck through its paces, wrenching on the gear stick expertly as they bumbled

along the dusty road. Jasper gave the same little cries of pleasure when they lurched from side to side that he had given
when she had been at the wheel herself, not so long ago.

It had been right here that Larry had taught her to drive.
She remembered careering over these very potholes and Larry's
calm voice rising above the hubbub and the laughter of all of
them but Pearl. She'd sat through the whole thing quietly,
intent on the road. "Now clutch, love — that's it — now second — listen for the revs — now third — and watch out for
this one," as the car dipped and rattled over the uneven surface.

"You're a real natural, Lara!" he'd exclaimed with pleasure
as they'd swung onto the wider paved road that led out of the
forest, and she'd accelerated confidently. "A real expert at the
wheel."

Lara realized with a shock of pain that she was missing Dad
with the same sort of numb longing that she had missed Mom
when she'd been in the hospital, becoming more and more
remote as the days wore on. More and more part of there and
of them, less and less of herself. Until there was no more . . .

"*I just called to say I love you,*" Garnet was singing lustily.

"That's a stupid song," Pearl complained, but Garnet continued. She could see the soft look around her mother's mouth.

Lara was happy too at the thought that Gladwyn would soon
be dialing that number on the crumpled bit of paper that Pearl
had shoved into her bag. She touched the bag tentatively with
her feet, just to make sure it was still there. That number would
bring her Dad to life again. That number would tell them how
many days, how many hours before he'd be coming back. She
couldn't call here, home, somehow. It was not really home to
Lara at all with the mostly glumfaced Gladwyn and the kids
who were, after all, not the loving brother and sisters she had
longed for. But maybe it would be much more of a home, she
thought, when Larry came in the door again.

She gave Jasper a little squeeze. She wanted to hug the warm
round baby body to pieces, the way her Mom used to hug that
darned noisy little kid of Bonnie's who always kept wandering
up to their trailer for cookies and Cheryl's enthusiastic em-
braces.

But mindful of Pearl, she didn't hug Jasper to pieces. Instead, she leaned forward and pressed a silent kiss on the round little shoulder in front of her and then glanced anxiously from Pearl to Gladwyn. But Pearl was looking out the window and Gladwyn was intent on the road. It was funny for Lara to realize that she and Gladwyn had the same kind of feeling right now. That they were united briefly in their longing for the Man.

They reached the paved road and the truck fairly flew past the wide-verandahed home of the Toymakers.

"Can we stop here?" Opal cried out, unheeded as usual. Then they were on the open road. There was almost a smile on Gladwyn's face, Lara thought, as they took the turn-off where the sign-post told them *To Seal Rocks*. Oh, there was no doubt there was no one and nothing on Gladwyn's mind but that phone call to Larry.

At the sight of the lone telephone booth that at last indicated the Binwell Post Office, Gladwyn brought the car to a halt. They were right outside an old wooden house. Its front room, sectioned off from the rest of the house, with its rusty notices and mailbox, linked the whole of the district to the outside world.

"Wanna say hello to the Hemmingways," Opal said, sliding from the seat, remembering the old couple who usually found her something nice to eat if she lingered on the verandah of the post office.

"You'll stay put, Opal, or there'll be no beach for you today," Gladwyn said, sternly.

Lara and the other children listened to the metallic drop of the coins and then the rise and fall of Gladwyn's voice as she talked to that someone far away. Someone they couldn't quite believe was real and yet hoped was their father.

Gladwyn did smile when she told them: "You father'll be back two weeks from Thursday." And there was a smile in her voice, too. When there was a whoop of joy from the kids, she didn't tell them to shut up as she most certainly would have under normal circumstances. Not even Opal, who chanted continuously for the next few kilometers: "Dadda Fadda banana farna's coming home, oh yes." And when Jasper joined in hopefully and a fight between Opal and Jasper ensued ("Dadda Fadda not dar dar, you idiot!"), Gladwyn didn't comment at all.

They seemed to burst onto the raised road that ran down beside the beach. Lara caught sight of the high humped rocks plunging far out into the water and recognized at once the place that Pearl had so triumphantly referred to. Seal Rocks. It was all sea and sky except for that slash of rocky blackness that gouged into the blueness. She was about to exclaim at the loveliness of the sight before her but Pearl's single self-satisfied word silenced her.

"Seal," Pearl said, as if all that lay before them was hers.

They slipped and scrambled down the embankment that led onto the beach. The younger ones, unencumbered, surged onto the sand, running wildly towards the big surf. Pearl and Gladwyn, more sedate, made camp, dropping the towels and lunch boxes in a heap and hoisting the antique umbrella.

"Coming for a swim, Mom? Now, Mom?" Pearl asked.

"Yes, Pearl." And Lara watched as Gladwyn threw her shirt and jeans in a heap.

They ran straight down onto the wet sand. "Pearl, Mom, take us out there," the kids yelled. "C'mon, Lara, you too."

Gladwyn, ignoring the children, already wet and sandy at the edge, walked ankle-deep into the foam. She seemed to sniff the wind, for all the world like a seal herself, deliberating about whether to plunge her black-clad body into the waves. One moment she was standing surveying the surf and the next she was gone. Gone like a sea thing, a seal, dipping through the water effortlessly, a toss of her hair above the waves sometimes the only sight of her.

Lara, sitting beside Opal in the racing shallows, could not help admiring the slender, resolute body that seemed to skim through the waves and reappear far out in deeper, calmer waters. But Jasper, alarmed at his mother being so far away, burst into noisy sobs. And nothing Pearl or any of them could do would calm him.

"Don't cry, Little," Garnet said, "Mom's a real good swimmer."

"There's no sharks or anything," Opal told him.

"There are so sharks," Pearl said.

"Liar," Opal said, her bottom lip trembling at the thought.

"They usually net the beaches in summer," Lara said quickly, "a shark won't get your Mom, Opal."

"Well, they bloody well don't net Seal," Pearl said. "And I should know." Jasper's sobs were not abating and Opal set up a sad little howl too.

"What's wrong with you?" Pearl asked, furious.

"There's a shark out there with Mom."

"There's no shark today, so shut up, will you?"

After five minutes had passed, Lara spoke to Pearl. "You'd better go and get your Mom," she said quietly, indicating the sobbing little heap in the sand as Jasper, still face down on the sand, cried inconsolably.

"Why don't you go out and get her, smartypants? Or can't you swim either?" Lara turned away, stung by Pearl's words, and sat beside the small boy stroking the unheeding, twitching back.

"Idiot!" Pearl's word drifted back as she heaved her lithe body into the surf. She met the water as her mother had done, lovingly and angrily. Lara knew there was no way she could brave the pounding waves and she watched with envy as Pearl struck out through the water to her mother.

Gladwyn returned, a champion, riding a single huge wave right into the shore. She gathered the little boy into her arms and once more Lara was startled to see the change in her face as she soothed him. But always unpredictable, when Opal clung onto her arm, Gladwyn brushed her away. "Go onto your own towel. You're making me too hot," she said, impatient again.

"No, I'm not helping," Pearl told the little kids who began tunnelling and building in the sand. "I'm resting with Mom."

Lara sat a little away from all of them. She wanted to share the umbrella but couldn't bring herself to sit too close. She was glad of her floppy hat, for the midday sun was at its warmest now. There was a huge inviting stretch of rock at the near end of the beach that was crowned with a few persistent trees. Lara thought she'd like to climb it. You could go sliding down the front of it to the rugged promontory of rocks where the waves raced over. It would be a lovely place for rock pools and sea creatures. For seals of course, she thought, wishing there were some there now. Maybe you'd even find a *selkie,* the strange creature that she had read about once in a folktale, that was a seal in water and yet human on land. But if she went off on her own to explore, then Gladwyn might get mad. She might pack up suddenly and drive off in a temper, leaving Lara to wend her long and difficult way back to the farm alone. No, she wouldn't explore this pretty place.

Instead, she stared at the blueness of the sea and the greenness of the tumbling nearby cliffs and wondered why beautiful places like this could make you feel sad. At this moment she wished she could cancel out the whole beach with its tumbling vigorous surf and all the surrounding panorama that seemed to fill her longing.

Later when a strong wind came up, Garnet said, "Let's drive on to the Lighthouse Beach, Mom. There'll be no wind. And we can show . . ." she hesitated, glancing at Pearl's frowning face. "We can walk up to the Lighthouse."

"Jasper'll get real burned if we stay longer," Pearl said to her mother.

"He's not burned at all," Opal said, peering under his floppy hat and inspecting his pink cheeks and white zinc-creamed nose.

"I don't feel like walking. Anyway, I think we should go home now, Mom," Pearl insisted.

"No no!" the other kids yelled, wanting to keep their mother in her lighthearted mood.

"We'll drive around there if you like," Mom agreed, beginning to gather up their things. "If you don't want to come for a walk to Lighthouse, Pearl, then don't. You can wait in the car." Pearl glared at her small sister but said nothing. She was silent in the car as Mom drove the kilometer or so to the neighboring beach.

"There's secret places on the cliff we can show you," Garnet confided to Lara as they trekked across sandhills to reach the new beach. "Me and Opal call one of them Ritchies' Secret Cave. You should see it."

Lara, who could see Pearl's disapproving shoulders up ahead, squeezed the little girl's hand. "Perhaps not today, Garnet. I don't think Pearl . . ."

"But it's *Ritchies'* Cave. You're a Ritchie." It was the first time that Garnet had flouted Pearl's authority like this and Lara didn't know whether to be pleased or not.

Jasper had to be carried the last part of the walk, but the others, at the sight of Lighthouse Beach, sped down the naked sandhill, drawn by the still water. Here, out of the wind, the surf was low and Lara could swim in the water at ease. Up above them the old lighthouse gleamed whitely on the edge of a ragged cliff.

They ate the last of the oranges under the umbrella and then Garnet pulled on her T-shirt and jumped to her feet.

"Mom, I wanna go to the lighthouse. Who's coming up to the lighthouse?"

"Take Opal," Gladwyn said, stretching out on the faded towel with Jasper asleep beside her. Lara was surprised that there were such brief words of warning for the two little girls about to climb the cliff. "Don't be too long and don't do anything silly up there," was all she said.

Pearl, sitting under the umbrella, stared far out to sea.

The path up the cliff was steep but not so steep that the three of them couldn't make their way right to the top in a few minutes. Up there they felt the wind again but stopped to look out over the huge blue expanse of sea and more dark outcrops of rock that bobbed up here and there. Several tracks criss-crossed the tough bracken that covered the rock. Garnet chose one that led them windingly past the lighthouse and round the cliff.

"There's big caves over that way," she boasted to Lara, "but they're easy ones." She pointed carelessly out into the ocean where, again, Lara saw the fingers of black, black rock stretching out into the blueness.

"But straight up here's our secret one." She had dropped her voice mysteriously.

"But we're not allowed . . ." Opal ventured.

"You can shut up or go back down again to Mom if you want," Garnet warned.

Lara had no wish to leave the brightness and freshness of the windy cliff-top to seek out a cave. She didn't like dark places as she didn't like steep and difficult climbs, but Garnet seemed so keen to show her that she felt obliged to follow behind Opal.

Half way along the track Garnet left the well-worn path quite suddenly. She hoisted herself up an outcrop of rock, disappearing for a moment and then reappearing a few seconds later on a ledge higher up. "C'mon up. It's easy-peasy," she called. Opal climbed up, sure-footed, in front of Lara. They were on a narrow ledge that led between the actual cliff face and the outcrop. It was an easy walk for there were little sharp handles of rock to grasp as they went.

The narrow path swung around sharply and suddenly they were in it: a huge amphitheater in the cliff face. It seemed to Lara as if something or someone had taken a large chunk out of the massive cliff to form the cave and tossed it down into the waters that sucked back and forth so noisily below them.

"My God!" Lara exclaimed, impressed by the size of the cave and the din of the water that echoed with unnerving thumps below them.

"It's got bats, too," Opal cried out above the wind and water, as she lowered herself into the cave. "Come and see. Only you're not to tell, Lara. Not anyone. Specially not our Mom."

"We've never been right to the back 'cause it gets spooky," Garnet yelled, her voice echoing strangely. "I think there could be treasure around here," she went on, as she helped the smaller child over the threshold. "Coming, Lara?"

Lara followed them unwillingly. It was not so much the height, although that, too, sickened her, but the overpowering feeling of the great gulping hole of the cave. Its clutches of salty plants clung to the walls and roof. And there was a sweetly disgusting smell of what she figured must be bat droppings, years and years — millennia, the word they had used in biology the other day — millennia of bat droppings, exuding a pungent odor. She felt as if some ancient mouth would easily swallow them if they ventured any further than the lip of the place. There was something altogether unpleasant here, she thought, trying to dismiss the word *evil* from her mind. It persisted and she shivered.

Garnet's face beside her was filled with pleasure as she stood regarding the great arch of the cave and the clustered bodies of the bats above them. Lara knew she was required to say something about Ritchies' Cave before they could leave it.

"It's very big," she said, unconvincingly, her raised voice echoing above the pounding noise of the sea.

" 'Normous," screamed Garnet proudly.

When Opal slipped by them making her way over the rock-strewn floor of the cave, Lara leapt forward and grabbed the surprised child.

"No, Opal. Don't go in there. You mustn't!" The small child screwed up her face as if to object, but catching sight of Lara's face with its Gladwyn-like disapproval, she allowed herself to be led back to the entrance.

"Let's go, Garnet," Lara said, suddenly stretching a long leg across the track that would lead them back to the sunny cliff-top.

"Don't you like Ritchies' Cave, Lara?" Garnet asked outside as they filed around the rock ledge once more.

"No, I don't."

"Why don't you like our cave, Lara?" Opal asked.

"I didn't like it first time, either," Garnet said cheerfully. "But you get used to it."

"Well, I like it," Opal said. "I always like it except for the dark. And the smell. Pearl thinks something bad once happened there. She goes mental if Gar says she wants to come here. Someone died in there, she says, and it spooks her. Just like it spooks you, Lara. She always goes, 'You kids keep away from there or else,' she does."

"Shut up Opal, you talk too much," Garnet said crossly.

"It's true!" Opal was indignant now.

Leaping down from the black outcrop of rock onto the springy foliage of the cliff-top again they all felt lighthearted.

"Catch me, Lara," Garnet said, suddenly sprinting up the winding track.

Lara, seized by the fresh blueness and greenness of this wide-open place, ran so fast she tore past Garnet in moments. With the salt wind in her face she felt she wanted to fly. Oh, she felt so glad! She leapt and whooped and the two little girls, follow-my-leader style, pursued her as she ran in wild circles through the bracken, feeling a bit like a kangaroo bouncing across one of the back fields. When she tripped on one of the tough little branches underfoot she didn't seem to mind the scratches at all as she went down, arms outspread. She hugged Opal to her the way Gladwyn had hugged little Jasper this morning, while Garnet clung to her back.

"Love you, Lara," Opal said, suddenly.

"Me too," shouted Garnet. "Me too. Me too. Me toooo."

When they returned to the beach, Lara could see from quite a distance that Gladwyn's mood and expression had changed.

"You've fooled around long enough," she said disapprovingly. She wrenched her towel from the sand. "We've got lots to do at home."

That was all she said, but the briefly joyous spell of the cliff-top was broken. The girls left Lara's side at once and scrambled to help their mother and sister pack up. "You didn't go to the big cave, did you?" Gladwyn asked Garnet as she handed her some bags, in a voice that made the young child drop her gaze.

"We took Lara to an easy cave," she said.

"You know very well about those caves, Garnet. And one of them's very high and very dangerous."

"Someone fell out of that cave and died," Pearl said. "You know you shouldn't go there."

"It wasn't that one, Mom," Garnet said. "Oh, no, not that one," but Lara knew that she was lying.

Pearl did not speak again despite the fact that Garnet hung about her anxiously and Opal fetched and carried to her silent gestured commands. The way back up the sand dunes seemed long and hot for Lara with Gladwyn far ahead, carrying the sleepy Jasper, and Pearl behind her stoutly ignoring her little sisters' attempts to make peace. No one spoke to Lara all the long drive home. In fact there was a strange silence in the car which seemed demanded of them not through words but because of Gladwyn's changed, heavy manner.

When the lurching potholes jostled them against one another, Opal cried out fretfully. "Stop touching me, Gar. You're doing it on purpose."

"Towels on the line," snapped Gladwyn when they'd reached home, as if it were a punishment. She jumped down from the truck. And then over her shoulder she snapped out curt orders. "Pearl, you'd better feed the horses. The fowls, too. Garnet, come and wash up. Opal, you and Jasper in the bath."

After she'd placed her bright blue towel as far away as possible from the shabby faded ones, Lara thought briefly of the dog. But she knew work was expected of her before she could disappear. Pearl was heaving a huge bale of alfalfa hay from the store shed and she grudgingly allowed Lara to help. Not a word was spoken as together they hauled it to the gate, through the palm field and down to the horse pasture, where Pearl used the wire clippers expertly. The pale green stuff of the bale fell in halves, revealing a dark moistness and a smell that drew the horses from all parts of the large pasture.

Pearl had endearments for each one as she fondled them but Lara stood back, still unsure of the large animals. As she watched the girl caressing each of the horses in turn, Lara felt an anger towards her. It was as if she were being demonstrated the possibility of love. "Clever Mr. Ed. Darling Fifi. Darling beast Clive. Come to mother."

Lara withdrew. She crossed the creek and walked up the hill in slow steps. Her shoulders had "caught the sun," as Mom used to say, and she felt that summertime languor that happens after surf and sun. She felt like sprawling under a tree or on a bed and reading or just talking sporadically with someone who wanted to talk to her. She did not feel like trudging through a hot field but she knew she had to find Thunderwith before nightfall. Up on the hill there was no sign of the dog and, though she traversed the whole length of the field calling and calling for it, there was only stillness and silence.

"Don't you leave me, Thunderwith," she called out angrily to the trees and the hill and the trail of barbed wire that marked off the Ritchie land. The ring of the ax below meant Pearl was probably cutting a pile of wood for the stove. She should help stack the stuff. She began the descent but halfway down there was the sharp sound of barking and, looking back, she saw Thunderwith burst out of the bushes and bound towards her, just as it had done that day of the storm.

"Thunderwith, you darling beast." And she hugged it hungrily. "Don't ever let me down, my lovely old dog. Oh, don't ever let me down!"

The evening meal was tolerable. Gladwyn, with yet another inexplicable swing of mood, was full of plans for what would be done before Larry came home. "I want the second field started so we can get more things in straight away. I could ask Bill Gadrey to come and plow or maybe Henk Rangers."

"Oh, get Henk," Pearl implored, looking over at Lara.

"We don't like that Gadrey kid. He's mean," Garnet added.

"I might get Henk," Gladwyn agreed. "He was going to give me some more of his seeds for the veggie garden. And maybe we could enlarge that, too."

"Let's play King Jasper of the Wallingat," Opal suggested, hearing her mother's enthusiastic voice. "C'mon, Lara!"

But the mention of the Gadrey boy threw a shadow over any pleasure Lara may have shared with the little ones. She didn't hear the rest of Gladwyn's plans. Only snatches here and there as they cleared the dinner table ". . . and we'll do a big tidy-up outside here so the truck can get in more easily. Those logs are lying right down on the road. They're hard wood but they should be chopped and stacked. And the horse pasture needs . . ."

As Lara helped Pearl dry the dishes, one of the chipped plates slipped from her grasp. It fell heavily onto the concrete floor and smashed into a hundred pieces.

"Give me that!" Gladwyn blazed, snatching the towel from her. "Can't you do anything right?" Lara picked up the pieces carefully, aware of the woman's angry stare. Then she stumbled out the back door to her bed on the verandah, shamed once again by Gladwyn's scorn.

Out there with the moon up and bright-eyed Oscar at the vegetable peelings, Lara lay unseeing on her bed.

"Mom, for God's sake, speak to me," she whispered, reaching under the mattress to her secret hiding place for the silver dollar. She held it for a moment tightly, then placed the coolness of its round form on her hot forehead.

"You said you would and you're just ignoring me. Tell me what to do. Even with Dad here she hates me so much. She'll make me go away, I know she will."

The specter of the home loomed up again and a great wave of panic broke over her. Not the home. Maybe it'd be better to just run away. But run where? And she couldn't leave Thunderwith. The thought of the dog up there safe on the hill waiting for her return calmed her for a moment. But then there was a surge of anger at her mother. She snatched the silver dollar from her brow and plunged it deep out of sight under her pillow. "I can't keep on waiting for you, Mom. I can't keep on trying to remember you when you won't even answer me."

6

"Close all the windows," Gladwyn called, coming in from the bathhouse with Jasper wrapped in a towel in her arms. "Storm's on its way!" She brushed by the colored strips of the back door, rapping out orders, mainly to Pearl, who had been sharing the kitchen table with Lara for a short time.

They'd both been attempting to grapple with homework while the smaller children played noisily outside. Pearl had actually allowed Lara to help her with some geometry. Lara had seen the younger girl's pencil poised, her protractor deep frown. "You could do it like this," Lara had suggested gently and Pearl had watched her quick, sure calculations. "I get it," Pearl said, and almost smiled.

"Stack the tools in the shed. Help pull down the shutters. The washing!" Gladwyn called out. Though not addressed directly, Lara understood the orders were for her, too. She snapped her math book closed. She had been enjoying the power she felt over the figures on the white pages as problems fell out in an orderly manner under her pen. But she swept her books into her open bag. She went straight to the line where the clothes, stiff with unrinsed soap powder, assumed almost human form in her arms, and had to be forced down unwillingly into the old cane basket.

The smaller kids had been set in constant motion by the

gusty wind and the eerie green light that heralded the storm. But a sudden flash of lightning sent Garnet indoors and Opal under Lara's bed on the verandah. "Come out, silly," said Lara, pausing and allowing arms and legs to spring up out of the washing basket as if ready to escape. "It's okay. Only a storm."

"I don't like storms," Opal called from somewhere underneath the bed, but she raised the blanket a little to see if Lara was still there. Lara put down her load and began unrolling the canvas blind at the end of her bed. Then she spread a large piece of plastic full-length over the crochet rug to protect her sleeping place from the rain that could sometimes sweep across the verandah.

"Better come in, Opal," Gladwyn said from the door as gusts of wind sent a trail of toys on the back verandah swirling and skidding, "but gather up those toys first."

Opal came out reluctantly from under the bed, throwing the bits and pieces into the large cane box at the foot of Lara's bed. But at the first crack of thunder, she scuttled inside.

"I'm scared," she screamed, hugging Jasper who looked pink and pretty from the vigorous towelling he had received from his mother. He squealed too.

"Don't be silly," Gladwyn said, helping Pearl with the last heavy wooden shutter that closed out the light and the threat of rain at one end of the house at least.

"But I *am* scared of storms, Mom," Opal insisted.

"We need the rain."

"I'm still scared, though."

"Scared," Jasper squealed as Garnet grabbed him and carried him triumphantly around the big room. "The King of Willy Nilly, Jasper the King," she yelled. Opal, forgetting her fears for the moment, joined the parade until a resoundingly loud clap of thunder finally hushed all of them.

By now out at the shed with the ax in her hand, Lara had jumped, too, at the first boom of thunder, but not so much in fear. It was more surprise of the great heavy sound that seemed to roll round and round the forest. She liked the storms here now. They made her think of the dog. "One of Thunderwith's storms," she said to herself, retrieving a spade from where one of the kids had flung it during a game. And it was true. Thunderwith had come out of a storm. Funny about storms. You can't avoid them. Funny about Mom liking them so much. And yet Mom had said her own mother would take to her bed during storms. Cover her face in fear. "It's moody weather, love," Mom would say of the storm clouds. "And moods always pass."

As she stacked the ax and spade neatly against the corrugated iron wall, Lara remembered a story her teacher had read at school about a storm and a storm boy. Well, she had a storm dog, didn't she? Up on the hill, safe and sheltered somehow, she was sure.

Inside, Gladwyn had turned off all the electric lights in deference to the storm. She lit one of the lamps that Lara loved so much for their smoky gentle light. Opal had come and snuggled up against her when she had come inside. "Scared, Lara," the small child whispered.

"Don't be scared, silly. Let's look at it together, Opal," Lara said, kneeling on a bed by one of the shutterless windows, staring at the wildness outside. "It's lovely in a way. With everything waiting."

"To blow up," Garnet put in helpfully.

The outside they knew so well looked changed under the spell of the storm. Trees that had seemed solid suddenly slashed about like ribbons, whole branches snapping and crashing to the ground. And the gray swathes of clouds seemed to pulsate, pressing down on the landscape, obliterating parts of the forest. The intermittent flashes made Opal, thumb in mouth, press closer to Lara, despite the older girl's words of comfort.

"It's okay," Lara soothed. "It's angry for a while. But we're all safe and sound here."

"Jeez, listen to that one!" Pearl said admiringly. "That's close!"

"How do you know?" Garnet asked.

"You can tell 'cause the thunder follows fast. Hear that one. Two seconds after the lightning. It's just over the hill, I'll bet!"

There was another stunning flash that seemed to light up the whole hillside. The little ones had covered their ears, but too late. The next resounding boom was just seconds after. Even Gladwyn exclaimed at the reverberation in the iron homestead which seemed to shake the very ground. But Lara felt safe inside the house just as she had on the night of her first storm here. Just as she used to in the trailer where they had watched the storms active for miles across the nearby lake.

"We're safe and sound," she murmured to Opal again. The storm had made her feel united with the family and part of the squat strong little house. For a little while at least, it felt like home.

But then, Gladwyn, who was standing by the kitchen window, suddenly exclaimed sharply: "My God!" She sucked in her breath in alarm. And they were all upset again.

"What, Ma? What?"

She didn't answer, but pulled open the back door in a great sweeping movement, letting the wind tear inside in wild gusts. She disappeared into the rain that tore in under the verandah awning.

"Mom, where you going?" Pearl threw herself across the room and the rest of them followed her outside. Gladwyn at the edge of the verandah was pointing up the hill where a huge tree, still smoking, had been sliced in half by the lightning strike she had witnessed from the kitchen window.

"Just like that!" she was saying above the wind, and then, "It's the second tree that's gone that way in a year."

"I told you!" Pearl yelled triumphantly. "I told you the lightning was real close, didn't I?"

But Opal, impressed by the strength and fury of the strike, burst into tears. "Will we be bombed too?" she asked.

"No, not us," Pearl said, airing her knowledge, "lightning never strikes twice in the same spot."

"It's always the highest thing," Gladwyn explained to the little girl as she shooed them all back inside again. "That's it for our part of the forest. No more. All over now." But Lara knew Gladwyn had been shaken at what she'd seen: a magnificent sturdy forest tree reduced to a mere matchstick under the lightning blow.

The thunderstorm blew itself out all too quickly, leaving

them quiet and unusually indolent indoors. "Not much rain fell," Pearl told them, after she'd checked the rain gauge out by the water tank.

"All noise and no action," Lara said.

"Yeah. Worse luck."

Lara was surprised that Pearl had, for once, agreed with her.

Later Gladwyn and the children walked up the hill to look at the fallen tree. The earth, cooled by the brief fall of rain, gave forth its rich eucalypt-laden smells. Lara couldn't help taking deep pleasing breaths of it as they strode through the quivering wet bush.

Garnet and Jasper and Opal, who had recovered their good spirits once the last thunderclap had faded away, enjoyed scampering over the broken tree. They poked small fingers into the charred and blistered sections of the mighty trunk. And they demanded that their mother come and look and feel the burn mark. Gladwyn wouldn't touch it. She looked on silently, seemingly awed by the sight of it.

The broken thing was sad, Lara thought. What had been so grandly beautiful a short time ago was shattered now, seared black in parts, its life over.

Lara longed to take the path at the back of the house, over the creek and up the hill to Thunderwith country. But there was no question of that now. There were the outdoor chores to be finished and the tea to prepare, and it was already dusk. Out at the chicken coop, she stared upwards to her hill, sure that her dog was waiting.

"Tomorrow, Thunderwith," she promised silently. "Stay, Thunderdog, and I'll be with you tomorrow."

"You always think things a lot, don't you, Lara?"

She had been unaware that young Garnet had been standing by the chicken coop watching her, feed in hand, staring away into the distance. But before she could answer, Garnet said: "I do too, Lara. Oh, I think lots and lots of things. Sometimes sad things too."

It seemed to Lara as the last hot days of summer went by that Larry would never come back. Gladwyn seemed to have an astounding energy and drove them all into a frenzy of work to finish the daunting tasks she'd set herself for the next few weeks. Weekends were a drudgery for all of them and despite the endless pleading of Garnet, there were no more visits to the beach.

"Cool off in the creek," was all Gladwyn ever said when she was asked about Seal and Lighthouse, "and take Jasper with you."

"But there's only real muddy water in the creek," Garnet complained. "And the dam's nearly dry too."

"Well, you can help me if you can't find anything else to do."

Gladwyn attacked the two great logs out by the side road at daybreak each morning. The whole household would awake to the thwack of her ax as she gouged and chopped, throwing her slight strong figure into a perfect rhythm, up and back and down with the silver ax-head, reducing the hard timber little by little each day. From her bed on the verandah Lara had a daily view of this furious activity. She was only glad that the expert ax-woman was turned away from her. She could imagine the look of furious concentration on Gladwyn's face as she worked.

Sometimes Pearl would come out in her heavy boots and take over from her mother. But she could hardly make leeway, despite her energy, in the hard wood of the trunks. Once Lara tried, too, but the ax glanced along the surface and Pearl grabbed it from her in disgust. Lara wondered why they didn't ask Henk to bring his power saw. She had seen him working with it the day they'd gone over to his farm in the truck to ask about the plowing. But she didn't dare suggest it. It seemed to her that Gladwyn somehow liked punishing herself with this hard work. The little ones had to collect and stack the chopped pieces and there was quite a pile growing beside the store shed now. More than enough for the next few months, Lara thought.

The second field near the dam had been turned over by Henk's plow. Instead of being content with this, Gladwyn merely seemed eager to do more.

"We can surprise your father," she told Pearl, "and start putting some of the bigger palms in. Where Larry's going to build his shade house." It was not a suggestion. Pearl didn't make any comment but worked stolidly with Lara and her mother in the afternoons after school, digging up the half-grown trees in the far field where they had been stunted by the tough earth and lack of water, loading them on the old trailer, transporting and then replanting them where her mother had indicated.

The labor involved in digging out these small palm trees was surprisingly heavy. Lara began to hate the trees and pulled at the fronds angrily when they slapped into her face as she dug the neat square around the base of the palm the way Gladwyn had shown her. Why didn't she wait till Larry came back to help with the backbreaking work of it all? Why was she so insistent on working so hard? On making them all work so hard? Lara began counting the hours until her father's return.

Often, she was so tired by the evening that she had to drag herself up the hill to find Thunderwith. But under the trees high on the hill with the dog at her side, she found peace. She didn't think about Mom anymore when she was with the dog. She seemed so far away, so remote now. But Lara thought about the return of her father a lot. She imagined the homecoming, the hugs and kisses, how much nicer it would all be with his kindly face around the place again.

She wondered if she could tell Dad about the secret dog, and maybe bring him up here to . . . "No! Thunderwith, no one!" she said out loud, suddenly frightened. "Not even Dad should know about you, my beauty!" Something terrible might happen if she revealed the dog's existence, she thought, stroking its smooth coat. Even to Dad. "But when Dad comes back it'll be better. You'll see. I'll come here every day, Thunderwith. I promise I will!"

"I'm taking Pearl and Jasper shopping this time," Gladwyn announced, collecting her keys and best black handbag from the kitchen shelf. The others didn't complain at being left behind with Lara even though they were clearly disappointed. They loved the giant supermarket just outside Forster, with its treats paraded up and down the aisles so temptingly within their reach. "Two bags of chips, pleeease, Mom," Opal kept saying anxiously as her mother climbed onto the truck with Pearl and a smiling Jasper. Gladwyn was still giving orders from the car window as the truck pulled away slowly.

"The palms'll have to be handwatered. Garnet, you help with filling the buckets. But don't waste a drop, now. The water tank's down to half-way. And Opal, you pick some veggies for tonight's meal. And I don't want to see a thing on the back verandah when I get back. All in the toy box."

"Bye-bye," Jasper kept calling from the truck, feeling excited to be sitting on Pearl's knee so high up with the other kids left behind with Lara.

"Yes, Mom."

"Yes, Mom."

"Mom, mom," they could hear Jasper calling and see his little clenched fist out the window as the truck bumped its way up the driveway, slipping out of sight in the usual cloud of dust.

"Betcha she brings me salt and vinegar," Opal said. "I always say chicken though. Chicken flavor's my favorite. What's yours, Lara?"

But Lara was already on her way around to the water tank to line up the green plastic buckets that were stacked there. They had to be filled one by one from the tank tap, which would take ages. And then they had to be carried across the field to the thirsty palms.

Everywhere else, Larry had run his own bush watering system, a series of old pipes and plastic hosing which was fed by the pump from the dam. But the new palms they had so painstakingly replanted during those long hot afternoons stood splendidly alone in the freshly turned field where the black soil, unwatered, was already beginning to bake hard in the sun.

Opal turned to her scatter of toys on the verandah and Garnet followed Lara round the side to the tankstand. Lara and Garnet worked well together. Garnet began singing at the old tank as she filled bucket after bucket: "There's a hole in the bucket, dear Lara, dear Lara," and then straining with all her small strength to help Lara lift each heavy container into the old wheelbarrow. Lara trundled the precious water over rough ground, steadying the bucket if it looked like spilling, and then heaving it out of the barrow close to the tree to be watered. She poured each one slowly and carefully, pleased to watch the thirsty soil soak up the liquid so readily.

"I'm wading now, Lara. Okay?" Garnet called, already bored with the whole process. She dunked her grubby feet in each bucket. It was then she found the fat frog inside a half-empty tin, on the ledge where the soap and towel were kept. It was such a fat oily fellow she called out to her little sister eagerly: "Hey, Opie, look what I got here. The Frog Prince." But there was no answer from the back verandah. Garnet picked up the tin gently, climbed out of the buckets carefully, not wasting a drop of water, and went looking for Opal with her frog prize.

Lara heard her scream of alarm just as she was about to pour. She dropped the bucket, careless of its spill, into the parched furrow. She sped across the paddock to the back of the house. It was no ordinary scream. She knew that, familiar as she now was with the cries of excitement that accompanied the children's play. There was something about Garnet's voice that spelled danger. When she rounded the house she smelled fire and saw Opal running round and round in terrified circles. Her dress was in flames! And Garnet was chasing her small sister, screaming in alarm: "Stop Opal! Stop! Stop! Stooop!" But the panicking child could not hear, and did not stop as the smoldering flames climbed up from the hem of her skimpy dress. Fanned by her mad pace, the material burst into flames. Lara could see them licking upwards, towards the child's long unruly hair.

"Water! Get water!" Lara yelled to Garnet as she leaped at Opal, grabbing her by the arm and pushing her down onto the ground. She rolled her over and over in the dirt, trying to smother the leaping flames. But they were not easily extinguished. As Garnet sped around the corner with the heavy burden of the bucket, Lara had already plunged her own hands over the flames that had sprung to life again, crushing out the cruel tongues with her bare hands. The water Garnet threw drenched the charred material and finally extinguished the fire. It drenched Opal too. She stopped screaming and sat up at once, pushing back her hair. "You needn't have thrown it in my face, Gar," she said, crossly.

They inspected her legs and her stomach. Miraculously, there were only a few pink burn spots here and there, though the dress was seared and gaping. "It doesn't hurt hardly at all," Opal said proudly.

Garnet hugged her fiercely. "Mom'll be real annoyed 'bout your dress. Now let me get Mom's burn cream."

"I was helping," Opal said stolidly. "I got Mom's little wood chips from around the log. To cook us some potatoes in the fire for lunch. And then my dress caught on fire. And it wouldn't go out."

"You should have run to the water, silly. Not around and around in circles," Lara said, hugging her in turn.

"Where did you light Mom's little wood chips?" Garnet asked. But they could already see. Beyond the store shed there was already quite a grass fire. Some of the drooping leaves of the low branches of the nearby gums were alight, too.

"Quick, Garnet, before it gets away," Lara said, and they both fled back to the water tank. Lara snatched up the last bucket and made for the fire, but Garnet darted to the front.

"The hose. It's on the front tap," she called over her shoulder. "I'll bring the hose around here." But it was a job to disengage it with trembling fingers, then drag the heavy coils of it to the back, where she had to fumble at the rusty unused tap, trying to attach it. "Lara!" she screamed. "You gotta help me."

Lara threw down the bucket and together they somehow managed to screw the stubborn metal into place. But the hose only yielded a weak trickle of water when it was turned full on. "The bloody dam's empty," Garnet moaned.

It was a fierce blaze that had moved across the clearing. One or two saplings were burning vigorously, and smoke and ash filled the air. They were powerless and if a wind blew up Lara knew the house would be in danger, at least the wooden verandah part. "Tank tap," Lara said suddenly and again she worked furiously on the metal hose attachment. "We could put the hose onto the tank tap. There's water in there all right."

The hose wouldn't fit the old brass tap on the tank but Garnet and Opal could hold it in place and a steady stream of water issued forth. Lara doused the trees and flooded the grass near the house with water. As the smoke cleared she could see the fire was all but burned out. Then Lara and Garnet, telling Opal to stand well clear, took some old sacks from the shed and beat the charred grass. It was only when the last spark was extinguished that Lara felt the pain in her hands. She glanced down, surprised to see them swollen and bleeding.

"You burned them bad," said Opal sympathetically, leaning forward to gently kiss one of Lara's blackened hands.

"Mom says put burns in water. We always do and it works." Garnet brought one of the plastic buckets and Lara plunged both hands in, but an awful pain seared through the coolness of the water. She felt quite faint and was grateful when Garnet brought a cloth and washed her brow. "You've gone all white," Opal said. "You gonna throw up?"

When Gladwyn pulled up the truck back from the shopping trip, they were still on the step, Lara bent forward, her hands immersed. "What's going on? What's happened?" Gladwyn ran towards them with anxious eyes, Pearl and Jasper following. Lara shrank from those eyes. "I made this fire, Mom, and — and it burned me. But not bad, Mom. Not bad at all. And — and then it burned the grass. And Lara put it out, Mom. Lara put it out on my dress and — and she and Garnet put it out over there," Opal babbled anxiously, hopping about on one foot.

"It's okay, Mom, we're all okay," Garnet said, as Gladwyn's eyes swept over the three fire-blackened figures and the seared patch out in front, still smoking. "Opal didn't get badly burned or anything."

"It's all right now, Mom," Opal echoed, but Gladwyn had already caught hold of the little girl. When she saw there were no serious burns to the child, she began shaking her fiercely. "How many times have I told you, you naughty girl, not to play with fire? How many times?"

"But I didn't mean —" the small girl cried out.

"Didn't mean, I'll give you didn't mean!" And she struck the child on her bare arm. "Oh, get away from me! Go away! Into the bathhouse and don't come out. I don't want to set eyes on you, you silly little fool," she cried out. And Opal, released from Gladwyn's strong grasp, fled to the bathhouse, from where her weeping could be clearly heard. Jasper, a bag of chips in hand, followed his sister to offer what comfort he could.

Lara gazed up into the face of the hard-eyed Gladwyn, but she had already turned on Garnet. "Why did you let her have the matches? What were you doing?"

"We were watering the palms, Mom," Garnet said miserably, "like you asked. Me and Lara. And then Opal starts yelling. And then there's Opal's dress on fire and Lara had to catch her and put it out. She put it out with her hands. And she hurt her hands bad, too. And then there's this fire, and we had to get it out somehow — so we got the hose . . ."

"You're a silly little fool," Gladwyn flared. "Fooling around, all of you, I bet." And she smacked the child's upturned frightened face with a resounding slap. Garnet's hand flew up to her cheek, and she began sobbing noisily.

"I'd cry, too," Gladwyn said angrily, tiredly. "Oh, I'd cry too! Look at this mess!" Catching sight of the hose winding its way round the bathhouse she turned to Lara. "And I suppose you used all our tank water?"

"There was no dam water coming through," Lara said, rising to her feet to face Gladwyn's fury. "We had to use the tank water," she said, feeling sick to the stomach.

"You didn't need to use tank water at all. Don't you know it's a *clearing*? There's nothing much but grass to burn. It would've burnt itself out in any case. You didn't need to use our water at all." Her voice had risen. "It would've burnt out in a few minutes."

There was no point in arguing. No point in telling Gladwyn of the frightening spectacle of the shrivelling leaves as the flames jumped from branch to branch through the saplings.

"You're a fool. No common sense whatsoever," she spat out at Lara, pushing her to inspect the tank. "Don't just stand there, Pearl. Get the groceries in and get that lazy little sister of yours to help," she called over her shoulder. The older girl moved off slowly with Garnet, still sniffing noisily, dragging behind her.

Lara sank back down on the step. She didn't have the strength to help with the bags. Her painful hands couldn't have held them, anyway. She wanted to burst into noisy sobs just like Opal or Garnet had done but she was too tired even to do that. She wished she could just faint away, the way she'd felt she might just a little while earlier. Faint away in a heap and frighten the life out of Gladwyn. But she didn't faint. She felt annoyingly clear-headed. Only her hands burned and burned with the reminder of Opal's terrified face as the flames leapt all around her. She put her head down on her knees. Oh, the unfairness of it all! Gladwyn was a bitch, a beast.

"Show me your hands." Gladwyn was standing in front of her, all the fury gone from her eyes, but with her mouth still severe.

Lara slowly raised them. Gladwyn made an indistinguishable sound and left her. But she returned a few moments later with a pale blue tin in her hands. She placed it on the step and opened it. Inside were neatly placed rows of bottles, disinfectants, bandages, scissors — treasures that drew Jasper to watch. Gladwyn knelt in front of Lara, taking first one hand then the other, and tenderly laying squares of gauze with a cool jelly substance on them, until each hand was quite covered. Then she took up a roll of bandage and swatched first one and then the other hand in the thick white material. Her hands were cool and gentle and she made little noises in her throat as she caressed each new burn with the gauze. She snipped the gauze expertly and put the scissors back in the tin.

"Don't use your hands," Gladwyn then said wearily, gathering up the contents of the tin. "It's just as well you thought to put them in water. They'll still be painful tonight. But by morning, they'll feel much better." And then she left her.

Then Lara did cry. She put her head on her knees and cried freely, overcome by the unexpected kindness. She couldn't stop. Each time she thought of Gladwyn's attention and tenderness as she addressed herself to the problem of the poor burned hands, tears would flow anew.

"Wanna chip?" It was Opal who'd stolen from the bathhouse with Jasper's crushed gift of salt and vinegar chips in her hand. Lara allowed Opal's grubby little hands to feed her with some scraps of the salty chips. It was only then that she realized how hungry and thirsty she was.

"Mom's gone to finish the watering," Pearl called, "and she's left us all some sandwiches." She stood in the doorway. "Mom said, what you did with Opal was quick thinking. Very quick thinking." High praise from Gladwyn and from Pearl, daughter-of-Gladwyn. But Lara felt too tired to care. Opal came out and took her tenderly by the arm. "You can have all the chips, Lara," she said, "all that's left."

Lara sat heavily at the table where Gladwyn had left the sandwiches. They all watched as Lara managed her food with her large bandaged hands.

"You look funny like that," Pearl said.

"Lara's the bravest person in the world," Garnet said, bringing her a drink and glaring at her big sister. "Bar nobody!"

7

On her way to the school library a week later, Lara came face to face with Gowd Gadrey. He hadn't spoken to her for days, but that morning as they left the bus, he'd taken Pearl aside. She'd hated to see Pearl's terrified expression as he cut Lara out in that smooth and smiling voice.

"It's actually a private conversation, so excuse us!"

He'd done this a few times before and though she'd asked her, Pearl would not say what these brief conversations entailed. Lara knew he was up to something and she dreaded it, whatever it might be.

"Look what we have here," he said now, gesturing to the knot of kids around him. "The new Ritchie girl. Our stuck-up city kid. And it's carrying its library books. Sucks up to the librarian, I hear, the new girl." They all smiled approval at Gowd's taunts.

"I hear from the *old* Ritchie girl," he turned to his companions, "that *Pearl* of a girl, that this one brought a coin collection with her from wherever it was she came from. Nothing much else, but she does have a coin collection. Quite a coin collection. And a silver dollar. All the way from America. What do you think of that?" Her eyes flashed when Gowd said this, but she could not speak.

He put his finger lightly on her arm and punctuated his

words with short sharp jabs that seemed like blows to the terrified Lara. "We think you should share your coin collection, Ritchie. Donate it to the school. That's be nice now, wouldn't it? New kids should give something. Don't you think?"

She didn't trust herself to speak but the others assented for her as his finger pressed harder into her forearm. "You'd better bring it in."

She stared at him and then shook her head slowly. No, she wouldn't. "No, you won't? Well, that's not nice, Lara Ritchie, to refuse a reasonable request like that. But you're new. And we like to be fair to new kids, don't we? Until they get the hang of things. I'll tell you what: we'll give you some time to think about it. Until the end of the term. Okay?" His voice was sweet and reasonable again. "You'll consider it, won't you? I know you will. Of course we would never *force* you to do anything you didn't want to, but it would be a very nice thing to do something, however small, for your new school . . ."

He withdrew his hand, smiled pleasantly and, as he passed on, said over his shoulder: "You got the message?"

She stared after him, unspeaking.

"Doesn't say much," she heard him laughing as they all passed out of sight. "You can see she's quite dumb."

Lara's thoughts were in a whirl as she went on her way. Pearl must have told him about the coin collection! But why would she do a thing like that? She knew Pearl had been softening towards her since the fire: she would sometimes talk to her while they were doing their homework, in an unguarded manner — almost as if she'd forgotten she had to dislike Lara. And she knew Pearl hated and feared Gowd Gadrey as much as she did. Oh Pearl, why do something like that? Perhaps he'd twisted Pearl's arm, she thought, the way he'd done it to her once. Got her in the playground behind the sheds and twisted her arm till she cried out in pain. Yes, that was it. Demanding something of Pearl about Lara so he could get at her. But Mom's coin collection!

Oh Pearl, why did you mention the silver dollar? My only good luck charm. My *mother's* good luck charm. Pearl, you shouldn't have done that!

She trudged on down the corridor. She'd bring the coin collection for Gowd. She'd have to. But the silver dollar — no! She couldn't part with that. She'd say she'd lost it. That Jasper had taken it. And she'd bury it under a rock on the hill at the back. Thunderwith's hill. In Thunderwith country. She couldn't give her mother's precious silver dollar to Gowd Gadrey. Never! Thunderwith would have to take care of it. But a shiver of fear passed over her as she thought of facing the Gadrey boy without it.

Lara was so lost in thought, she didn't notice Stan in the corridor or respond to Joslyn's friendly greeting or see Reg and Dieuwer waving at her. In the library, Neil was just about to begin a story to the largish group gathered around him. "You look like you've seen a ghost, Lara," Joslyn said as she passed by. "You've gone all white. You okay?"

Lara nodded and sat down to listen to the calm of Neil's deep voice. It was like magic, that voice, a balm that soothed and soothed her. The storm inside her subsided as Neil spoke about another storm. She was safe here, inside one of Neil's stories, where she could forget everything else, even Gowd and his nasty laughing friends.

"There was this terrible storm," Neil was saying. *"Oh, it was a bad one. The wind blew like mad and there was thunder and lightning. It blew so hard, that wind, the leaves and sticks and sand swirled around in it, even small animals. Yes: goannas and baby possums and little birds and snakes and frogs flew round in it too. And everyone in the tribe took shelter. They were pretty scared, that lot."*

As he spoke he drew big swirling lines in soft crayons that showed the storm, the path of the wind and then slashes of lightning. On top of this he made bold sketches of the swirling tumbling animals. The kids watched spellbound.

Lara thought of the Willy Nilly storms and the broken tree . . . and then of Thunderwith.

"No one had been in a storm quite like this one. The tribe huddled together in a gully watching it pass over. And there in that big storm, in all the debris flying around so madly, they saw some strange creatures. They pointed in wonder, they were so strange.

*Some of the people even laughed. Those creatures with tiny heads
and small arms had such great long hind legs, and their back legs
seemed to be getting longer and longer every minute as they tried
to reach down on to the earth for a foothold.*

"*Suddenly, that storm passed over. The wind dropped and all the
creatures fell to earth. They stood up on their big strong hind legs.
Can you guess what they were? Yes, you're right: those Kangaroos
stared around. And then they hopped off in giant bounds, away,
away and the people followed them. But they were too fast. In no
time, the first Kangaroos were out of sight. It took a long, long time
before the Aboriginal people learned to catch a Kangaroo, I can tell
you. But that was how the first Kangaroos came to earth, long ago
in Dreamtime.*"

The kids applauded Neil's story as he drew a handsome kangaroo for them with his fast sure strokes. They clapped more
noisily when he sang his great gray kangaroo song. And then
they listened, quiet once more, as he spoke of the old ways and
how, when he was a little kid, "My old Grandpa could build a
bark shelter that quick. A good one, too. Kept us good and
dry in the rain. Looked like this." Again, the big bold strokes
with his crayons.

Lara waited behind after the bell when all the other kids left.
She wanted to stay, safe in the library all afternoon. She went
up close to see Neil's sketches of the animals whirling around
in the storm.

"Something very good came out of that storm," Neil said.
Lara stared at him. He stared back. His eyes seemed so deep
and dark. What did he know about her? she wondered. About
Thunderwith? She had the strangest feeling that he knew a lot.

"Do you think someone could find a sort of magic dog?" she
asked him at last, looking back at the swirls of Neil's drawing.
"Like, not in a story but you know — now. In real life? A dog
that, say — came out of a storm?"

"Depends on the person." He smiled at her. "Where did you
find your magic dog, Lara?"

So he did know something. And she wanted to tell him
everything about Thunderwith. "Here. I found him here," she

said eagerly, "not long after I came to live in the Wallingat . . . See, when I first came to Willy Nilly Farm, I felt — well — I felt I didn't belong." Lara had never been able to say things like this to anyone but now they came tumbling out.

"After my Mom died, I just didn't seem to belong anywhere anymore. Then I found this dog. Or maybe he found me, I don't know." Neil nodded but didn't speak, and so she went on: "He came out of a storm, Neil. Honest to God he did. Up on the hill right at the back of our farm. The part where it's not cleared and there's big trees and things. Right out of the storm. He came down the hill and straight to me as if — I don't know — well, as if maybe he knew me already." Neil nodded, as if what she was saying was making good sense.

"I kind of felt we were meant to meet like that. He's there every day now. He always seems to know when I'm coming. He knows lots of things, I think. And I — well — I kind of talk to that dog, lots. He's a beautiful dog. A bit like a dingo to look at."

"A dingo, you say." Neil spoke for the first time, his eyes widening with curiosity. "You say he looks like a dingo?"

She nodded. "I thought he was a dingo at first but he's bigger and he's darker. Beautiful like a dingo, though. I call him Thunderwith, but maybe that's not the right name for him. He came out of the storm and there was thunder so I . . ."

"Thunderwith," Neil said, lingering over the name so that it sounded like the beginning of a song. "Thunderwith and he came out of a storm. A good name for a dog that came out of a storm. A very good name," he approved. "I might call him Purnung but you've called him Thunderwith. Yes, I like that. You spend a lot of time with Thunderwith?"

She nodded.

"I'm glad the magic dog came when you needed it, Lara. And I think you're right. You were meant to find that dog. He was meant to find you. It's good to have something to hang on to. And now you've got a friend. Your magic dingo dog out of that storm."

"I just worry he'll go away one day, just like he came."

"Maybe. Maybe not," the old man said thoughtfully. "But I suppose if that dingo dog leaves you, well — it's for a purpose," Neil said. The bell rang.

"What do you mean, for a purpose?" she asked, afraid of the words, afraid of the idea of Thunderwith not there anymore. But Mrs. Pickard put her head around the library door. "Come on, Lara. Bell's rung, you know," she said in her kindly way. "You're wanted in the gym. There's a special sports meeting right now."

As Lara made for the gym she realized that for the first time since being with Mrs. Robinson, she had talked easily with someone. It was good talking to Dad, of course, when he was there. But it was almost impossible to be alone with Dad at Willy Nilly. And there were so many things she just couldn't say. She didn't want to hurt him. With Neil it was different. He seemed to understand that she was sad.

She'd told Neil her precious secret expecting and knowing the man of stories would understand. She had the feeling Neil would understand a lot about all the other confusing feelings she had, too. The way he told those stories with a softness and sometimes a sadness in his voice and yet always a singing strength in it — well, it made her think that maybe one day she could tell him all about Idle Hours. All about Mom.

She sat at the back of the gym, behind a post. She could see someone she didn't want to see out the front with the sports teacher. And it all came flooding back to her. The coin collection and the awful Gowd Gadrey and his friends who wanted it. She didn't dare tell anyone that worry. Not even Neil.

She knew Gowd could outsmart her with his fast persuasive manner. She'd watched him talk to teachers, so respectfully and pleasantly, on dozens of occasions in the playground, and at special assemblies where he sometimes took part. She knew he was well liked by the teachers and by many of the junior students as well. Why, with her own ears she'd heard him ask so convincingly on several occasions for any new member of the school to seek help from him or any of the other class officers sitting so tall and serious in that half-circle at the front of the stage. And he'd sounded so reasonable, she knew they'd believed him. She'd almost believed him herself.

But then there was the memory of Gowd Gadrey on the dappled bush road, his eyes hard and his hands cruel, so that she'd had to stare down at her feet and bite her lip, not wanting to look up at his face. Why would they believe any complaint she made? The new kid who had no friends and whose own sister — half-sister — didn't talk to her? Why would they believe that Gowd Gadrey, the respected class officer, was nothing but a bully!

On the bus home that afternoon, Pearl glanced at Lara guiltily as she passed by with her friends. She must know that Gowd Gadrey had asked about the coin collection, Lara thought, and was sorry she had blurted out Lara's secret in her fear of him. Sorry, yet somehow relieved to get rid of some of her own fear of the ever-present threat of Gowd. Lara saw him get on too, but he didn't look her way at all. He made for the very back of the bus and just occasionally she could hear the distinct sound of his deep voice as he talked with the Royal Family. Lara thought that some of the shouts of laughter might be directed at her but she didn't turn around. Not once. Oh, she'd like to be somewhere quiet and peaceful where she didn't feel frightened and lonely. Somewhere away from all these kids and their noise.

She stared out the window at the glimpses of the shining expanse of water they were passing. Yes, here. Right here. She'd love to jump off the bus and go and find the lovely secret place Dad had showed her weeks and weeks ago on one of their trips to town. A cathedral of ferns and palms that led down to the water's edge.

The bus was already leaving the lake and the Green Cathedral behind, and thoughts of Dad. The prospect of Gowd Gadrey and the lonely walk home chased out all her pleasant memories. She saw the trees flash by in a blur. The open fields announcing their arrival at the turn-off filled her with anxiety.

When the three of them leapt off at the familiar corner, Gowd pressed close to the girls at once. They quickened their pace, both dreading the voice, and the inevitable taunts. But as he came level with them, a horn was blasted directly behind. Lara and Pearl turned to see Henk's battered truck almost enveloped in a cloud of dust. He called out to all three of them. "Give you kids a lift? Long walk on a hot day." He pulled up beside them. The girls climbed in, silently grateful. Gowd heaved himself up last of all, sitting next to Lara on the broken seat. She held herself stiff and straight, trying to maintain the space between them even when the truck lurched and swayed as they reached the rougher road.

Neither girl spoke, but Gowd took up a conversation with Henk all the way. Farm talk of crops and clearings and cattle. It was only when he hopped down from the truck at the turn-off to the Gadrey farm that he acknowledged the girls at all. Looking up at Lara, he smiled and said, "Oh, Lara, don't forget that coin collection you told me about, will you? All the kids want to see it." She stared at his smooth round face but did not reply. "Well, see ya, then," Henk called out to him as the truck roared on its way.

Towards the Willy Nilly turn-off, Henk said, "Talks too much, that boy, doesn't he?" as if he sensed their intense dislike. When Henk had deposited them near the driveway, Pearl ran ahead. But Lara called out to the younger girl: "Why'd you have to go and tell him about my coins, Pearl? You shouldn't have done it." Pearl made no reply.

Gladwyn seemed in a strange mood when they reached home. The children scuttled around her trying to please but she pushed them away, even Jasper, who took refuge on Pearl's knee.

"You two'll have to help out in the back field," she said. "There's been a big delivery today — a thousand plants."

Lara could have exclaimed in weariness at the thought of the back-breaking work that lay ahead of them, but she merely acknowledged with a nod of the head that she'd heard. They ate their afternoon meal in silence and then changed into work clothes and followed Gladwyn down to the field at the back of the house. "Your father's been delayed," Gladwyn said grimly as they began moving the seedlings into the shade by the creek.

"But why, Mom?" Pearl asked.

"I don't know. Just got the message from Bill Gadrey that he's moved on again. And that he won't be back next week after all. Something's come up."

That was all she said, before throwing herself into a frenzy of work. Between the three of them the load of pots was moved out of the cruel sun in less than an hour.

A wind had sprung up and clouds scudded across the sky as they headed back to the house.

"Don't tell me it'll rain now that we've put them all under the trees," Gladwyn grumbled. "You can't win." Her voice sounded raspy as if she were close to tears. But when Lara looked up at her she was regarding the heavens with perfectly dry eyes.

"You wash up, Pearl, and get the dinner on," she said, and headed for the two logs she'd been working on. There was the sound of vigorous chopping outside the house.

"I didn't want to tell him," Pearl said, looking at Lara nervously as they cut up the vegetables, "only he made me do it." Then she turned away. Lara knew Pearl was trying to apologize in her own way about the coins, but she still couldn't understand the girl's cruelty.

"Why's Mom always chopping?" Garnet asked Pearl.

"She's angry," Pearl told her sister.

"She's *always* angry now," Garnet observed, and Pearl did not correct her.

Lara went out to the verandah to find the coin collection that now, because of Pearl, would have to be given to the Gadrey boy. Opal came to sit beside her, fingering each coin lovingly. "These are real nice things, Lara," she said appreciatively.

When her mother's lucky silver dollar fell onto the bedspread, Lara took it up at once. She wrapped it carefully in a tissue and stuffed it in her pocket.

"What you doin', Lara? With that one?"

"I'm showing my coins at school sometime soon," the big girl explained.

"But what're you doing with that one?" And she pointed to Lara's pocket.

Lara, groping for an explanation for the inquisitive child, never actually answered. There was a long blood-curdling scream that brought them both to their feet. It was such a chilling cry of alarm or pain. And what made it even worse was the realization that it must have come from Gladwyn. Lara darted across the verandah and jumped down the step to reach her. Lara knelt beside the giant log she'd been attacking with the ax only moments before. The ax had fallen out of her hand and she was bent double, cradling her foot. Her old split boot lay on the ground, dark with blood. Awful sobbing gasps were coming from her as she rocked backwards and forwards.

"Pearl!" Lara screamed as she reached the stricken woman, frightened at being alone to face whatever it was. She could see the blood dark on the ax which had been flung in the dirt.

"What's happened?" she shrieked when she saw Gladwyn's eyes dilated and black with pain.

"Towel, get a towel," Gladwyn grunted at her from between clenched teeth. There was blood gushing from between the fingers of both hands which were gripping her cut foot.

Pearl was half-way across the yard to her mother.

"She's cut her foot off," Opal was screaming at her sister in distress. "Mom's cut her foot off."

"No, she hasn't. She's *cut* her foot," Lara corrected, but her heart was thudding at the thought of the great deep gash under the clenched hands. It was giving forth such a volume of blood.

Pearl rushed to her mother's side. "Keep back," Lara heard her scream at the others, and then: "It'll be all right, Jasper," as the little boy burst into frightened sobs.

Lara's hands were trembling as she rummaged in the big old wooden box that served as linen closet for their sheets and towels. She grabbed her own bright blue towel, the thickest by far, and sped out the door with it.

Gladwyn had turned an awful pale color but she wrenched the towel from Lara's grasp and wound it round and round the awful wound the ax had made.

"She's going to faint," Pearl said, forcing her mother's head down.

"She's going to bleed to death," Lara thought, well aware of the stain of dark blood already appearing on the towel.

Gladwyn gasped. "Help me to the car."

"You can't drive, Mom, not like that," Pearl said.

"Have to . . . get to the hospital."

Together Lara and Pearl helped her hop to the car, the great bundle of her foot held tightly in front by the grave-faced Garnet. When she was seated shakily at the wheel, Lara sent Garnet and Opal back for more towels. She gathered Jasper into her arms and sat beside Gladwyn, who had started the motor with a little gasp of pain at the effort involved for her. Lara, turning to check they were all on board, felt a little stab of something, of pity or love or both for the anxious children, as they sat so silent and frightened, aware of their mother's awful plight.

Gladwyn managed to get the car up the driveway but there were beads of sweat standing out on her forehead and her breathing was loud and labored by the time they'd reached the first corner. No one spoke. Only the sound of that strange labored breathing could be heard in the car. Until the rain.

Long before the paved road, great gusts of it descended. Gladwyn, hanging on grimly to the wheel, began weaving all over the road. As her head began falling forward, Lara tried to grab the wheel, but it was too late. The car careered off the side and down into a hollow as Gladwyn slumped across the driver's wheel, unconscious.

"She's going to die. She'll die," Pearl sobbed. And the little ones set up such a crying and wailing that Lara screamed at them: "Shut up. Now shut up all of you. She won't die if you all help. I can drive this car. I can drive it. And I will! Help me move your Mom and I'll drive her to the hospital."

She was surprised at her own conviction and amazed to find herself giving orders. "Wind another towel around her foot, Pearl, and press on it. Don't let go — not for a moment. Sit down, you kids, and be real quiet. I've got to think my way out of this mess."

They dragged the unconscious Gladwyn across the seat and while Pearl attended to the great bandaged foot, Lara took Gladwyn's place, her hands trembling on the wheel.

She prayed silently that she'd remember reverse, the most difficult gear of all to find and the one that would lift them up out of this hollow and set them back on the road.

She turned on the ignition. "First, second, third, fourth, reverse," she mouthed as she worked her way through each gear, the way Larry had taught her, oh so long ago now. There was complete silence in the car as they all watched her.

"Reverse. That's it, I'm sure," she said out loud, and then she pressed hard on the accelerator and the car lurched backwards and bumped up onto the road again. She braked so violently they all shot forward. The children screamed but not with the fun of it as before. They screamed in horror. They screamed in real fear. Pearl, catching hold of her mother's inert form, gulped back her sobs but there were tears streaming down her face too.

"It all depends on me," Lara thought, as she tried to wrench the heavy gear stick out of reverse. "It's not fair. It all depends on me." And as she tried to peer through the sheets of rain she hated them all. All these Ritchie kids and their mother who would probably die out here on this Godforsaken road. And it would be all her fault. All her fault if she didn't get this stupid car going.

"I can't do it." She covered her face with her hands, wanting to wail like the small children had.

"You gotta do it, Lara," Pearl said quietly, beside her. "I saw you do it with Dad lots of times. You can do it. You're a better driver than me and you know it. I don't even know reverse, so you gotta do it!"

There was no time to argue about it. It was true she'd driven this car a number of times as far as the paved road and she'd done it well. But that had been with Larry beside her, with Larry to guide and advise and encourage. It was different in the rain with the night falling all too quickly. Still, Pearl was right, she realized with dread in her heart. She had to do it and that was all there was to it.

But first she'd have to see, to be able to drive the truck anywhere. It seemed strange that the rain they had longed for, during all those long, hot, dry weeks and through all the short-lived storms, fell with such a vengeance now. She twisted every knob on the dashboard and on the steering column, feverishly looking for the windshield wipers. Colored lights winked and blinked, the headlights shot on, then blessedly — the wipers jumped to life.

"Now concentrate," she said aloud. "Out of reverse, like this. Out and find first. And then go, go!" The car hopped and bounded through first gear and then settled into second, third and fourth, and they were bumping their way cautiously along the rain-wet road towards the paved one and then the turn-off that would lead to Forster and the hospital.

"Good going, Lara," Garnet said softly.

"Go, Lara. Go!" little Opal said, leaning over to kiss the back of her neck.

Lara steered the car in the middle of the road, afraid of the edges that sometimes fell away into gullies, but aware, on that lonely road, that they'd probably meet no other car.

"Can you go faster?" Pearl asked miserably. Gladwyn's body slumped against her seemed so heavy and so still.

Lara's foot pressed down again on the accelerator but when the car leapt forward with speed it rocked from side to side and she was forced to slow down again. In this manner they rolled onwards towards the main turn-off. It wasn't until this was in sight that she thought of the Gadrey farm and the possibility of help there. But it was too late now. They were too far past any other farm on this road. What an idiot she was! Oh, what an idiot! For despite her fear of the boy, Lara knew Mr. Gadrey would have done all he could for them. But now there was no going back. On the main road she'd have to get help. There'd be other cars. She could stop and flag one down and they'd help for sure. But then when she glanced at Gladwyn's face cradled in Pearl's arm and its funny grayish color she thought she might not stop. Any delay would be bad.

She turned the car off the small paved road onto the highway as the rain pelted down with a heightened fury. She took the car slowly and carefully as far as she could but in the gathering darkness and the fury of the storm and the force of the rain, despite the flicking wipers, she could hardly see. Finally, unsure of the direction, she was forced to bring the car to a halt.

"It's no good, Pearl," she cried out. "I'll kill us all. I can't see. I can't see a thing."

"Don't turn it off," Pearl warned, screaming over the thundering noise of the rain. "It'll never start again. For God's sake, don't turn it off!"

Pearl put her head out the window. "I think I know where we are, Lara. It's not far to the village. You gotta keep going. If we can get there, there's houses. There's the post office and a phone. You gotta keep going. I can tell you where the road is. Go on, Lara. You gotta."

"Go, Lara," Opal said again, imploring.

And so the car limped towards the village, all of them in it soaked to the skin by the driving rain that poured in over Pearl's head. Her body was half out the window as she guided Lara down the dark empty road. Then, when she saw the light of the small village, Pearl turned to the little ones. "She's done it! Lara's done it! We're there!"

They jumped up and down on the seat, clapped their hands and leaned forward to hug Pearl and kiss Lara. But she said, wearily now, "Sit down please, kids. We're not quite there yet."

"Maybe I can run faster," Pearl said. "Maybe I could get out and run."

"No, Pearl, you mustn't. Don't let go of your mother." And don't leave me, she thought, please don't leave me.

Lara stopped at the sickly yellow light that indicated the lone gray telephone booth, peering up through the deluge of rain. She could see beyond it the brighter lights of a house and a tiny post office. They were here and someone else could take over. Only now could she lean forward over the wheel and forget the wet black windscreen and the dark shapes of the road that had so frightened and confused her on their terrible journey. Now adult help was at hand. Pearl leapt from the car and bounded up the wooden stairs at the front of the house, sure-footed even in the wet and dark.

"Mrs. Hemmingway!" she screamed, not bothering to knock. "Mr. Hemmingway! Marcey! It's my Mom. Come quick! We gotta get her to the hospital."

Mr. Hemmingway lifted Gladwyn into his car, and left, taking his daughter, Marcia, who was in training to be a nurse's aide at the local hospital. She had checked Gladwyn and bound the foot with extra towelling that Mrs. Hemmingway had brought to the car through the pouring rain.

"Your Mom's in real good hands now, kids," the old woman told them as the Hemmingway Ford Falcon roared off powerfully into the night.

Then she had taken them all into her kitchen, the whole frightened sodden group. "It'll be all right," she said, bustling to get them something to eat and to find towels and dry clothes. "George'll have her there in minutes. Marcey has bound her foot real good. It's never as bad as you think. Don't look so sad. It'll be all right."

But they were silent and afraid until the phone finally rang.

Mrs. Hemmingway relayed the good news at the top of her voice, sentence by sentence, as Marcia spoke to her. "They've stitched the cut real nice, Marcey says, her ankle — you don't say! A broken ankle. And put a cast on her ankle, kids. A bit weak from the loss of blood, and she's resting now. But she's had a nice hot cup of tea, too. I told them she'd be okay. She's tough, that Gladwyn Ritchie. And they said she should stay put in the hospital a couple of days. Good, Marcey. Now you tell your Dad to just watch that road. Take it easy on the way back. Yes, they're all here, Marcey, and they're so happy you phoned!"

They did smile then, and ate more toast and jam. "Your Dad's away still, isn't he?" she asked Pearl. "Never mind. You kids'll just have to stay here for the duration."

"And you say you drove all the way by yourself?" Mr. Hemmingway was saying admiringly as Lara and Pearl had told their story for the third or fourth time. "You're a bit of a smartie, isn't she, Dulcie? All that way in that storm and on that dark road. And only had half-a-dozen lessons with her Dad."

They were sitting in the large sofa with scratchy material that prickled the back of their bare legs while they drank mugs of tea with the Hemmingways. The little ones, "all fed and watered" as Mr. Hemmingway described it, had been bundled together into a three-quarter bed in one of the big old pleasant rooms of the house, and had finally fallen asleep.

"It was a pretty bad cut all right," Marcia told them, "and just as well you acted so fast. She was so glad when she woke in a hospital bed, your Mom. So glad to know the lot of you were okay, too. Said she thought she might have killed you when she ran off the road in the storm."

"Why they won't get a telephone hooked up, I don't know. In emergencies like these, well . . ." Mr. Hemmingway began, but Mrs. Hemmingway cut in quickly: "Your eyes are half closed. You kids better hit the sack now, too."

Lara and Pearl climbed into the high old-fashioned twin beds in another large slab-walled room, both of them dressed in the large Mrs. Hemmingway's floral nightdresses. Lara, feeling utterly weary now, was glad to let her thoughts go, to drift towards much-needed sleep. But she was dragged back from the lulling feeling of first sleep by the sound of a muffled sob from Pearl's bed. She listened and a few minutes later there was another tiny choking sound as if Pearl had her face pressed into the pillow to hide her distress.

"It's okay, Pearl," Lara said to her across the dark space between them. "Your Mom's going to be okay."

Then the young girl burst into tears and Lara left her own bed and knelt by Pearl. She threw her arm around her quivering shoulders. "It's all right now, Pearl. Honest."

When the sobbing finally ceased, Pearl turned to Lara in the dark. "I'm sorry, Lara. About the coin collection. Honest to God, I'm sorry. But he frightens me. And last year I had a really bad fight with him. After the rabbits episode, Dad told him to keep off our farm. But he didn't. And I told Dad I'd seen him up at the back with his gun putting holes into our old shed. Mr. Gadrey took Gowd's rifle away from him then. And Gowd said he'd get even with me some way for that, and if I dared to tell my Dad . . . And then you came. He kept pestering me about you. And I got frightened. So I told him about your coins just so's he'd leave me alone. But I'm sorry I did it."

"I know that. And if it makes you feel any better, I don't care about those coins. Well — except for one of them. And I'm not giving that to him. No way."

"The silver dollar."

"Yeah, the silver dollar." A shiver went through her at the mention of it, but Lara spoke calmly and slowly to the younger girl. "So don't worry about him. Your Mom's okay, Pearl. That's the main thing, isn't it? You okay to go to sleep now? Pearl?" Before Pearl turned her face to the wall she crushed Lara's hands in hers gratefully.

Lara, back in her own bed, lay awake a while then, sensing from Pearl's deep breathing that the younger girl had at last fallen asleep. It seemed Pearl had finally accepted her. Her tears had indicated she wanted Lara's friendship and Lara's forgiveness. A kind of weary gratefulness came over her. She knew she loved these kids who were now her family. If only Gladwyn would accept her, then maybe this ache of loneliness inside her . . . She didn't dare let herself think about her own mother tonight, she wanted her so badly. Instead she concentrated on her father, the Man. "Please come home, Larry. I need you to come home now. We all need you badly." With the thought of his cheerful face on her mind she eventually drifted off to sleep.

But Lara's sleep was interrupted at midnight by Jasper who had slipped from his bed and was wandering up the hall crying "Mama, Mama." She took him into bed with her as she knew Gladwyn or the kids did on the nights he found it hard to sleep. He snuggled up to Lara and soon fell asleep in her arms. Then Garnet came softly, also crying for her Mom, followed by Opal a few moments later.

"Get in Pearl's bed," Lara whispered to the two little shivering girls as they clung to her arm.

"No." Garnet spoke for both of them. "We want to come in your bed, Lara, with you."

"Get down in the bottom, then, and go straight to sleep." After a few whispered giggles they soon did.

With first light at the curtainless window Lara wakened, feeling the heat of a tumble of legs against her own. The two little girls were sound asleep, as was Pearl, all alone in her bed. Lara lifted Jasper carefully from her bed and carried him across the room, where she placed him, still sleeping, in Pearl's arms.

8

They were traveling fast down the forest road. It was cool here, out of the full sun. But the dust rose up behind in a thick brownish swirl reminding them all that the weeks of rain they'd had were long gone.

The kids cried out, as they did every time they passed the small clearing at the side of the road. "Here's where Mom conked out," they said. "And here's where Lara drove from."

They knew when they'd identified this now familiar piece of bushland that the dust would be left behind pretty soon, and they would soon reach the smooth paved road.

When they did, Gladwyn, her ankle out of its cast, put her foot down and the car shot forward at unaccustomed speed.

"Why we going so fast, Ma?" Pearl asked.

"Because," Gladwyn answered tersely. And Pearl knew there'd be nothing more said because her mother's lips were held tightly together the way she did when she didn't want to answer. But Pearl was wrong. "Because the office closes at four o'clock, that's why," Gladwyn said, glancing down at her daughter, "and we gotta get there before it does, that's all."

"Why, Mom?" asked Pearl, surprised.

"So we can eat, that's why," her mother snapped. And there was such indignation in her voice that Pearl didn't dare ask another question but lapsed into silence, as her mother did for most of the trip.

Lara had wondered at the sudden burst of energy mid-afternoon at the farm. The feeding of the horses and the ducks and the hens was usually left until late in the evening. But Lara had complied with Gladwyn's requests and hurried to do what was asked, helping Pearl first heave the food down to the horse pasture and then working with Garnet to make the mash for the hens.

She had glanced up to the hills several times. She had hoped to take Thunderwith for a walk late this afternoon. Now this sudden announcement of the town trip for all of them meant they would probably not be home till nightfall.

It had been harder of late to get away. Ever since the accident. Ever since Pearl had stopped hating her and had at last accepted Lara as part of the family. Lara didn't know why Mom had receded so far now. Only Thunderwith seemed to be some kind of link to her. She longed to spend more time with him up there. Early in the morning was no good, for the little kids rose with the sun. Sometimes lying awake at night on her verandah bed she wanted to see the dog so much she considered making the trip up the hill by moonlight. But she hadn't the nerve to face the creek with its clinging leeches and cutting reeds. And she knew the ghostliness of the trees and bushes clothed in darkness would terrify her. So she'd lie and think of the dog safe and sound on the hill. And she'd plan for how she'd get up there the next day, and go walking with the dog into the forest. It had been days since she'd spent time with him. And now this afternoon, since Gladwyn had bundled them into the car on her mysterious errand, once again it was going to be impossible.

"Both you girls wash up and get into clean shorts. We're going to town," Gladwyn had told them in the early afternoon after they'd done the chores. Then Lara had heard Jasper's cries of indignation at being washed thoroughly long before nightfall and Garnet's complaints at having to get Opal ready.

"Our best clothes, Mom?" Garnet had asked, not wanting to leave her game of marbles.

116

"No," Gladwyn had answered sharply, "just clean clothes, you silly child. You didn't listen. And get Opal's too."

"Okay, Mom," Garnet answered cheerfully, but then with lowered voice she complained to her sister as she threw down the marbles in disgust. "You should be able to find your own things, silly child."

"I don't want to," Opal announced capriciously.

"Well, neither do I."

"But Mom said you had to help."

She pushed at Opal as they went through the door together. Then there were muffled cries as Garnet flung the clothes she had found in the huge chest of drawers across the room and into Opal's face.

"Be quiet," Garnet said, alarmed at the howl Opal set up. She ran across the room to comfort her sister. "Don't cry, Opal. If you shut up right now I'll help you and then I'll give you something nice this afternoon."

"Can I eat it?" asked Opal, recovering.

"Yes," Garnet said. "Now here are your sandals, Opal. Put 'em on and I'll do 'em up."

Lara had pulled on a fresh pair of shorts, once bright blue but now faded and stained like the rest of the clothes that had seen hard work on the farm. She brushed her hair in quick strong movements, not even bothering to look in the cracked mirror in the bathhouse, the only one there was. And then she took Jasper's hand. Cleanly dressed and with his best sandals on, Jasper clearly expected a treat of some kind.

"Coming for a drive, Jasper?"

Every time Lara climbed into the Land Rover these days she silently remembered that awful night and the drive into the village through the storm. And the children remembered out loud, repeating bits of the drama as if it were a well-loved fairy story. "And then the storm bursts. And then the car goes all over the place. And then . . ." until Gladwyn or sometimes Lara herself silenced them.

Gladwyn had seemed more remote than ever after she'd come home from the hospital. She couldn't look Lara in the eyes now and made only fleeting references to the long

117

dangerous drive the girl had made on her account. She'd never really thanked her for her effort either. Gladwyn limped about the farm on crutches for the few weeks it took her ankle to heal, demanding that Pearl and Lara do this and do that.

Gladwyn now seemed so weary and so crabby that not even Jasper was able to make her smile much any more. The children, sensing their mother's unhappiness, had stopped asking when Larry was coming home again. Dad simply wasn't mentioned.

Despite the awkwardness of the stiff leg, Gladwyn insisted on still doing the cooking, balancing at the sink with a crutch under one arm. She prepared meals that to Lara, hungry from a full day's labor, seemed to be getting sparser and sparser.

And though it was rough going over the uneven ground with her painful leg, every morning, without fail, Gladwyn would hobble down to the small palm plantation and inspect it before she gave her daily orders. The little kids, once they'd tended the vegetable garden, which they did together — even Jasper could tell when the lettuce was ready to pull — kept well and truly out of her way after that.

Up at the house she'd organized pots and seedlings and soil that the girls carried up from the dam. And there, on a hastily contrived table made of two large drums and an old door, she began the huge task of transplanting hundreds of plants that would go into the greenhouse Larry would one day build over by the dam.

She labored at the back of the house, with her foot up on a stool when it became too painful, for hours on end. The children took to playing at the front, away from the commands of their mother, although Garnet was called more and more to be on hand. "I don't see why you shouldn't help more, Garnet," her mother said one day when she complained that she wanted to play ball with the two younger ones. "You're getting to be a big girl now. Pearl and Lara work very hard, you know. And they can't do it all." That was the only time Lara ever heard her admit to their unrelenting work.

But Lara never saw Gladwyn rest. The only thing she didn't attempt was to resume her attack on the old log. There was enough firewood stacked by the old shed for a whole season, anyway.

Henk had come over a few times when they'd got back to the farm, with fresh fruit and vegetables, which were eagerly accepted. Arlie had sent a couple of cooked meals the first days after the hospital, which had been devoured to the last morsel. And Bill Gadrey, calling by, had asked if there was anything he could do to help.

"Any shopping in town?" he asked in his kindly way. "I'd be only too happy to do it for you while you're finding it hard to drive."

"We're fine for shopping," Gladwyn said quickly, frowning at Pearl who'd been about to say the cupboard was almost bare. "Fine for a long time yet. We bought up big last time."

They'd not eaten any meat since the accident for they'd not bought any. And no bread, either. Gladwyn had started baking a kind of rolls out of flour and, though no one really missed the grainy sliced bread, Lara had wondered why. They'd worked through the packets of pasta and all the big jars of rice from the shelves and over the last week, with only vegetables on their plates, the younger kids had begun complaining. "Can't we have a stew, Mom?"

"Or spaghetti and tomatoes?"

"Be thankful you have anything," Gladwyn retorted. But later that evening Lara saw her inspecting the vegetable garden, and several times after that she asked how many eggs had been collected that day.

Fresh milk from Henk's farm was dropped at the gate every day. Apart from that, nothing else came to the table other than what was produced in their small garden.

Lara hadn't liked seeing the friendly Hemmingways driving off up the driveway waving goodbye so cheerily when they'd brought Gladwyn home early from the hospital on her insistence. Gladwyn was the only adult here and Gladwyn was still in pain. It was obvious with every step she took as she went about her daily tasks with her usual determination. It was clear she was suffering in some other way as well. She was more distracted than ever, more worried. Lara wished she could say

119

something, sensing a loss and loneliness that was akin to her own. But Gladwyn had that closed-in look, so she didn't dare.

And now this unexpected drive into town this afternoon. Lara thought it must be something to do with Gladwyn's worries.

They were approaching Forster. They passed the enormous shopping complex on the outskirts of town. Both Opal and Jasper cried out, at first in excitement, but then in disappointment as Gladwyn pressed firmly on the accelerator, indicating there would be no stopping. When they finally pulled up in front of an official-looking building like a post office, Gladwyn ushered them hurriedly out of the car.

"Can't we wait for you, Mom?" Pearl asked, somehow sensing an ordeal before her.

"They've got to see you, you stupid girl. Otherwise why would I have gone to the bother of bringing you? Don't hang about, Opal. Come on. And Garnet, get your fingers out of your mouth."

It was a strange building to the young children who were not even used to a school house, and an oppressive one to Lara and Pearl. Pearl was reminded of a court or a hospital, and for some unaccountable reason thoughts of an orphange for kids like her welled up in Lara's mind. She shrank back behind the group, trying to memorize the name she'd seen on the glass in large black official letters outside. The Department of Social something or other: she couldn't quite remember. It sounded official and scary, anyway, she thought.

Inside, there were long lines of people at counters, like in a bank, Lara thought. Gladwyn made them all sit down on the low spongy chairs that stood in a neat row against the wall. The plastic on the chairs was an awful dull blue color, Lara thought, sinking down onto one of them with a funny feeling, just as if she were starting at a new school. She watched Gladwyn waiting her turn in one of the lines to reach the fresh-faced young woman behind the counter. The one with the loud voice and the black pen in her hand, that she waved in the air from time to time as she talked.

Lara noted the best leather bag held so tightly in Gladwyn's brown hand that her knuckles looked white.

Opal and Jasper didn't last long sitting still, but slid off the chairs furtively. "Let's play hide and seek," they whispered, finding the tunnel the chair legs made down the room. Eventually Garnet peered down under the chairs to see what the others were doing, and very soon she'd disappeared too.

Pearl and Lara sat stiffly, waiting, knowing that Gladwyn was doing something she didn't like doing and that somehow they were part of it or even the cause of it.

When Gladwyn glanced back at them for a moment, they felt the cool stare of the dark-haired woman with the waving pens as well. Pearl then fished the three kids out from under the chairs and made them sit up on the wedges of blue foam again. But Jasper, annoyed, slid down again.

"Play," he said hopefully to Opal, taking her hand. But Opal had seen her mother's expression. "Sit down, you naughty boy," she said. He yelled indignantly when Pearl lifted him up and placed him on her knee, where she locked her arms around him. "Mom, Mom," he shrieked, fighting to get down. She glanced worriedly at her mother's back.

"You've got a Lifesaver, Garnet. I know you have. I saw you put it in your pocket. Give it to Jasper to shut him up. Or there'll be trouble."

"It was for Opal," Garnet protested, "for being good and getting dressed. I promised I'd give her half. On the way home."

"Well, that's too bad. You give it to me, now," Pearl said, sternly, sounding like her mother, "or I'll smack you one."

Garnet scowled but she gave the precious thing unwillingly. "There you are, pig!" she blazed as it was stuffed into Jasper's mouth. Opal had come forward to watch the operation, her mouth longingly half-open too.

"It's mine though, Pearl. Gar said so."

"Sit back there and shut up, both of you," Pearl said angrily.

They did sit back, but Lara saw Opal's fist wiping her eyes and knew that silent tears were falling at the thought of the

Lifesaver she'd earned being gulped down by her greedy brother.

Gladwyn finally left the counter and came back to them with the piece of paper clutched in her hand. "I've got to see the man in the office. You're to come with me."

They went through a bubbly glass door at the end of the room and into a small partitioned space rather like a principal's office, the girls thought, but with less space. A large rather weary-looking man at a desk stood up as they entered. Gladwyn handed him the paper and then sat down, taking Jasper on her knee.

"Murchison's my name," he said in a friendly way, "and I'm here to be of service."

"I've explained my circumstances in no uncertain terms to the lady outside," Gladwyn told him, in a strange little strangled voice, "and it seems that's not good enough. I have to explain my case further. To you. So here I am. Here we are. Well, it's all there on the paper. I need money and I need it now. Simple as that. That's why I'm here."

He took up the piece of paper on his desk and stared at it in an unhurried manner.

"Gladwyn Ritchie," he said slowly and deliberately. "Your husband's whereabouts are unknown at present."

"He's been sending us money regularly but he had to go up north. The mail can't get through from where he is. It's only a temporary thing. We just need some to tide us over. When he comes back I'll . . ."

"Four children. Pearl, Garnet, Opal and Jasper — unusual names if I may say so. Very pleasant." He smiled at her again across the desk but she remained straight-faced. "All Ritchies, the four of them."

"All Ritchies," she replied, icily.

"But there are five children here at the moment?"

"There's Lara, too," Garnet piped up. "Lara Ritchie."

"Be quiet," Gladwyn rapped out at her.

"Is Lara your daughter?" he asked, "making five dependants in all?"

"No," Gladwyn spoke loudly now. "She's not. She's nothing to do with me."

"Mom," Pearl gasped, and then, seeing her mother's wild eyes, looked down at the carpet squares on the floor and said no more.

"I see," Mr. Murchison said smoothly, looking at Lara, whose cheeks flamed with embarrassment and hurt.

"I've explained about her, too," Gladwyn said.

"But she's a dependant at present," he insisted.

"She's staying with us, yes," Gladwyn agreed unwillingly.

"For a period of time?" he asked.

"Yes," Gladwyn agreed, "for a period of time."

"I'll make a note: five dependants. And if you'll just sign here, Mrs. Ritchie, there'll be no problem about the money you've requested. Fill in this pink form and take it to the cashier. The regular payments could take a few weeks. However, if there is any hardship, come in to the office again and I'm sure we can help."

Lara didn't remember much about leaving the glass cage of the office and the smiling Mr. Murchison, who patted Jasper's dark hair and was almost bitten for it. She didn't remember too much about the walk across the shiny floor past the counters and through the swing doors. Gladwyn's words were ringing in her ears: *"for a period of time."* The home loomed closer than ever before. There was a terrible feeling in the pit of her stomach.

"She doesn't mean it, really," said Pearl. She's just mad 'cause Dad's fooling around in Queensland. That's all. It'll all be okay, Lara, when Dad comes home. Honest to God it will!" But Pearl's kind words seemed meaningless.

"Yes, some chips and a whole packet of Lifesavers each." Pearl told them at the supermarket where they had stopped on the way back home. Gladwyn had gone off eagerly to plunder the shelves. "Take the kids and go and find the sweets, Garnet."

With her mother out of sight in another shopping aisle Pearl was anxious for a moment alone with Lara. She watched Lara pull down one, two, then three big jars of peanut butter. "She didn't really mean it, Lara," she said again, but the older girl, intent on searching the shelves, didn't answer.

The little ones had gone sliding over the floor, shoving aside shopping carts in their eagerness to find their favorite aisle and take the treasures down for themselves.

"Garnet already ate her whole packet!" Opal told Pearl when they'd finished their shopping marathon. With three packed carts and Gladwyn at the helm, they were waiting in the check-out line. "So she better not think I'm giving her any of mine. 'Cos I'm not."

On the way home Lara sat lost in thought. *"For a period of time. For a period of time."* It went over and over in her head like a recording. Gladwyn had said that Lara was only with the family *for a period of time.* She would like to have asked Gladwyn, who was suddenly more cheerful and relaxed with Pearl and the others, for *what* period of time. But words stuck in her throat every time she attempted to speak and tears welled up in her eyes. There was a strong smell of chicken-flavored chips, and when Opal held out a sticky Lifesaver for her, Lara felt quite sick.

At the house she didn't pretend to help unload the great mound of white plastic shopping bags that bulged with good things to eat. She darted off across the field.

"Where you going, Lara?" Pearl called. "Mom said we're all to help. It's getting dark. Don't go off by yourself, Lara."

But Lara couldn't trust herself to reply and darted away, entering the thick grove of trees by the creek with enormous relief. She leapt across the old log with a sure-footedness that was in large part anger. Deserting the track she'd worn through the grass and mindless of warnings of snakes, she sped up the hill by the steeper, shorter way, arriving breathless and hot, whipped by thick grasses and bushes on her way to the top.

"Thunderwith!" she called. "Thunderwith!" And her voice was a strong cry that seemed to echo in the opposite hills. She demanded that the dog come to her and it did, within seconds.

Leaping and bounding, flying across the hilltop, it was at her side. It licked her hand and she looked into its sad, wise eyes. "Oh, Thunderwith," she said, sinking down beside it.

"They won't take me away. I won't go. She can't make me. We're going to be together forever and ever. You and me. And nothing and nobody's going to stop that."

They sat motionless on the hillside until darkness had almost settled. Then she could hear activity and calls down below: Garnet and Opal and Pearl all searching for her in the lower fields. "Lara, where are you? Lara, come home. It's dinner, Lara."

She left the dog, who seemed for a moment as if it might follow her down the hill. "Stay, Thunderwith. You must stay." It stood stock still and then, as always, faded off into the darkness to that secret place where she never attempted to follow. She made her way down the hill, carefully this time on what she could see of the track, calling to them when she reached the bridge, for she could see they were carrying lanterns that bloomed in the dark for her.

"I'm here. I'm coming."

Pearl lit the way for her across the old log bridge and the other two escorted her back to the homestead.

"It's spaghetti bolognaise, Lara. You could've missed it," Garnet told her, clutching her hand.

But she couldn't eat much anyway. The strands of it seemed to stick in her throat. Garnet and Opal fought about what was left on her plate and ate it between them with an eagerness that made her turn away.

It was a mild night outside on the verandah. Lara lay dully on her bed, aware of the murmur of voices within, as Pearl talked to her mother. The night ahead loomed long and dark. Mom's big black bird was around, she was sure, although there was still no sign of Mom. She concentrated on the dog. Even with the thought of Thunderwith up there on the hill for her, she felt powerless, lost and afraid.

"Thunderwith," she whispered, seeking some kind of help in the looming blackness. "She hates me. Oh, she hates me more than I knew. What can I do?" But there was a strange silence all around her.

9

Lara dreamed she was running very fast and that Thunder-with was at her side. Running and running through the forest and up into the hills, effortlessly, gliding over rocks and bushes. Almost flying. But all at once she stumbled and fell and the forest floor opened up into a black abyss. She fell down and down into blackness and then she stopped. She was trapped in a dark, suffocating place. There were invisible wet strands enveloping her with a clammy obstinacy. She could hardly move. But she could see the brilliant light of day at the top of that dark hole. And there was the dog's face. Oh, yes, she could see it quite clearly. She tried to reach up to him for the dog seemed poised ready to leap. But invisible bonds held her arms fast to her sides. Thunderwith! Oh, Thunderwith! Then, as the dog tensed, ready to jump down into the blackness, to free her, its face melted in a blaze of light. She saw the dear familiar eyes break into fragments and burn away until there was nothing there any more. She struggled and broke out. She reached upwards to the empty air. She tried to call his name but the cry froze in her throat. Thunderwith! Oh, Thunderwith!

Lara sat up, alarmed. Where was she? What had happened to her dog? When she realized she was safe in her bed at the end of the verandah, she breathed easily again. It had been a dream. An awful dream. She knew Thunderwith was waiting at the top of the hill, as always. Always there for her.

126

She lay back again, glad to be awake, and watched the dawn break from her open-air bedroom. There was the usual clatter of bird cries. Yes, a kookaburra, she thought, concentrating on the hubbub both near and far. Yes: Neil's fire-people had faithfully lit the fire up there so that the earth was being slowly illuminated once more. The birds seemed extra loud this morning, she thought, watching them come and go in the great tall gums. But there were other sounds too. A kind of bass accompaniment of rustlings and scurryings and whisperings, only to be noticed if you listened really hard. Lara did listen. What had Neil said about the heartbeat of the old earth last week? Something about listening to it as if it was the beat of your own heart, too. *"I am the earth,"* he had said in the middle of one of his stories about his mother-aunts, in that special serious voice of his. It had made everyone go quiet and feel a bit shivery, just the way he said it. So sure and so strong. She loved the singing words Neil used. *"And the earth goes on and on."* Then those other less kind words came back to her. Gladwyn's harsh words of yesterday. The dawn seemed suddenly sickly pale. A hot and lifeless day was dawning with no sheen at all. Lara turned her face to the wall.

She knew she must get away from Gladwyn's disapproving stare somehow today. She was hungry again for the company of the dog after the sharpness of her dream, and she knew she must go up the hill and find it as soon as possible. Gladwyn, much happier now the cupboards were stacked full again, told the little ones last night that they'd go and see Henk today about shoeing one of the horses. And then they'd go down to the river for a swim. Lara would invent some reason not to go with them. She'd go instead to her beloved dog.

As the light grew she could hear the kids stirring inside the house. Opal's indignant voice: "He got more cereal than me. Jasper's a greedy guts!" And Garnet's game: "Arise, King Jasper — aw go on, Jazzy, let me put Mom's flower hat on you." Then Gladwyn's voice, cutting across all of them: "C'mon now, all of you. Get dressed or no breakfast."

They scampered outside to the bathroom, Opal shooing Jasper ahead of her, hoisting her own shorts on as she came, calling out to Lara. "Mom's making pancakes for breakfast, with honey or maple syrup or jam!" There was still the strange feeling in Lara's stomach at the mention of food. And at the thought of Gladwyn at the stove, preparing that food for her. But she went inside to see if she could help. Gladwyn and Pearl were busy.

Lara found the plates they'd need, wiped down the table and set jam jars and sugar and honey and syrup in the center. And then she tried to distract the little ones from the pervading smell of the cooking batter which was making them hop about in anticipation. They waited hungrily, eyeing the growing stack of pancakes keeping hot on the stove. Licking his lips, Jasper began whimpering for them.

"Shut up, Jazzy or you won't even get one," Opal advised.

"There's four each," Garnet announced. "I counted."

"None for you, guts. None for anyone if you don't sit down," Pearl told them. They sat.

"I'm not coming to Henk's or to the river," Lara told them when Gladwyn had left the table. Pearl shrugged her shoulders, a sign she was disappointed. But she didn't question Lara. Opal was eyeing the last pancake, untouched on Lara's plate.

"I'll eat that pancake now for you," she said hopefully.

"You already had more'n me," Garnet said, quickly. It was cut into three, for Jasper cried for a piece as well.

Garnet screwed up her face. "I bet I know where you're going, Lara," she said between mouthfuls, "and I'm coming too."

"No, you're not," Pearl said sternly. "We're watching Fifi get new shoes. And then we're going swimming."

"Well *I'm* not," Garnet said again. Pearl had begun clearing the table and didn't bother answering.

The morning passed slowly for Lara but eventually Gladwyn came in from where she'd been working and told the kids to get ready to go to Henk's. "Please yourself," she'd said shortly when Lara told her she wasn't coming with them.

Pearl had given her brief instructions about Lara's plan to walk towards the Bulahdelah Mountains. "There's hardly any paths. But there's plenty of landmarks. I've been there a few times with Dad. Take a stick in case of snakes, Lara. And if you get lost, cut down to the river and that'll lead you back this way in the end. You can take my backpack if you want."

Lara crossed the log bridge with ease. She burst through the stiff reeds wanting to break into a joyous gallop at the thought of the dog up there waiting for her and the whole day ahead for them. Then she did something she'd never done before. She called for the dog before she made the ascent. "Thunderwith, Thunderwith!" Her voice echoed round the hills, making her feel strong and glad. "Thunderwith!" she called again. Then something flung out of the bushes behind her and clung on to her legs, pulling her down. She turned back in fear and fury as another body hurtled through the air on top of her.

"Oh, Garnet!" she exploded. "Opal! What do you think you're doing?" She sat up. "You scared me silly."

"We want to come too. We don't want to go to the muddy old river. We want to go with you."

It took five minutes to extricate herself from them. "Pearl said she might take you rowing too," she assured them. "And your mother'll be real mad if she has to come looking for you both." Reluctantly, they turned back.

"Bye, Lara," they called mournfully, at least ten times. She waited until they'd crossed the log bridge and were heading for the house again before she made her own way up the hill.

She didn't call out and she didn't run, sobered by being discovered by the little girls with the dog's name on her lips. She walked swiftly, her eyes searching bushes, tree trunks, hollows and rocks. Right at the top she found Thunderwith, waiting. The dog seemed very flesh and blood, she thought, sitting and panting as it was in the shade, its long pink tongue hanging out. She hugged it to her eagerly.

"We're taking a long walk today, Thunderwith. Just you and me. A long, long walk way over there. Through the forest. To the top of a mountain. Come on, boy."

Despite the heat in the air, their walk across the hilltop turned into a run. They bounded through the grass and across the paddock, happy to be together. To run like this made Lara feel that she wanted to go on forever. She felt as if she could outstrip her longing, go faster than the sadness that seemed to be lodged permanently inside her. Forget it all, with the dog like this at her side.

It was an easy path down the smooth-sided hill where the vast area of cultivated land that was probably the Gadreys' lay suddenly exposed. Exhilarating as their run was, Lara was glad when they reached the shelter of forested land again. The dog seemed to hesitate here. Several times Thunderwith turned as if to head back the way they'd come. But Lara called it to her side each time, reassuring: "C'mon, boy, it's all right. We'll come back home later."

As Pearl had said, there were no paths and though they made good progress at first, it seemed to take a long time to reach the foot of the mountains. The nature of the countryside seemed to change altogether once the ground swung sharply upwards. There was no easy weaving through palm fronds and bushes. The going was tough. "Let's rest," she suggested long before they'd reached the top. The dog, who seemed willing enough to stretch out on a smooth outcrop of rock, watched as she unpacked some of her food from Pearl's backpack. She offered it a wedge of dark bread and cheese. But though it sniffed the food, it refused as usual. "You are a magic old thing, aren't you, Thunderwith. You don't live by bread, that's for sure."

It was peaceful here within reach of the mountain top. Lara felt elated to be alone and free, even if only for a short while. There was nobody to pull you down, nobody to fill you with fear, she thought, glancing up the cliff face. And there was the great effort ahead of fighting to the top. That supreme effort she knew would obliterate all unpleasant thoughts. As she sat here in the little glade where patches of sunshine made everything glow so greenly, she wished she might stay forever. She and Thunderwith, like some sort of bush spirits from one of Neil's stories.

She lay back on the rock when she'd eaten, breathing deeply. It was smooth and warm under her as she gazed up into a tangle of branches and vines. You didn't have to concentrate on the heartbeat of the old earth here: you could feel it right

130

inside your bones. But in a few moments she sat up suddenly, just as if something had bitten into her. Gladwyn's words *were* there after all, hanging in the air, burning into her brain. They had flashed through her head like one of the slides Mrs. Gilbert had shown on Ancient Egypt, sharp and clear, only there was no pleasure in them, no pleasant voice explaining them. "*For a period of time*" was what Gladwyn had said. And that was what she had meant, no matter what Pearl or anyone else said about it.

"*For a period of time,*" she said out loud. The dog pricked up its ears and its alert gaze met her own. "That's what she said." It was too awful to contemplate. She stood up, gathering her things together. "C'mon boy, let's get to the top," she said.

The last part of the climb was over exposed rock and the dog went ahead, climbing easily. "Good boy," she said, heaving herself up a rough boulder which took her to the very top at last.

"See, it was worth all the effort, Thunderwith." There were sweeping views of forest all around and somewhere far off to the east the pale smoky blue of the sea. "Top of the world, Thunderwith. Must be." Lara could see storm clouds rolling home again. The prospect of the leeches on the flat near the water made her decide not to stay too long.

They slipped and slid down the rock, beating their way down a fresh path that seemed easier going than the way up had been. But the storm rolled in faster than she'd expected, and when it broke the thunder and lightning seemed directly overhead.

"You're not worried, old fella, are you?" she asked the dog. "We met in a storm, remember." But an extra loud rumble of thunder that accompanied a brilliant flash of lightning worried her. She remembered Gladwyn's felled tree all too clearly, and her words about high places and lightning. Trees began to shake in the force of the wind and the earth seemed to reverberate with each rumble of thunder. When the dog darted into an opening, a kind of slim fold of rock at the base of the wall that they'd reached, she galloped straight after him.

"It's a cave," she said, and her voice, echoing in the blackness, confirmed the high vaulting space up above and beyond. And it's okay, she thought slowly, remembering the feeling of the frightening beach cave Garnet and Opal had shown her. Here, it wasn't like that at all. She caught a glimmer of the back wall shining in the half-light but didn't venture any further inside. Just sat in the entrance, watching the storm.

After the first cascade of heavy rain, the quivering lightning began again in thrilling non-stop flashes. That was when Lara looked back over her shoulder more intently, to see what she could of the interior of the grand space.

"It isn't a bit like the sea cave at Lighthouse, Thunderwith," she said, recalling its threat again and enjoying the contrasting sense of safety here. "But we're not going too far inside it, Thunderwith. Not without a flashlight."

They left the cave in a light drizzle of rain to find their way back down again. Once more the dog seemed unwilling, turning back to the cave entrance once or twice. "Silly old dog," she said, urging it down the hill. "We'll come back here, too, Thunderwith," she promised.

At the foot of the hill the forest was awash. Lara's boots, an old pair of Gladwyn's that she now wore around the farm, disappeared into the sludgy mud at each step. It was slow going. She lost her sense of direction, panicking when no cultivated fields came into view after what seemed like hours of walking.

She had picked up a stick to flick off leeches that climbed her boots or fell out of the trees in the denser wetter parts. She smiled to herself at the ease with which she was now able to remove the fine black cotton threads with their little sucking mouths, recalling all too well her horror of the slimy creatures in the first few days at Willy Nilly Farm. As they trudged on and the forest appeared to roll on endlessly, she began to think they were walking in circles. That they were lost.

Lara didn't want to spend a night here. She was cold and tired and longed to reach familiar ground.

"You know which way to get home, Thunderwith, don't you?" she asked the dog as she hesitated in the trackless forest. "Let's go home, Thunderwith. Home, boy!" The dog moved off confidently then and within minutes she glimpsed water. "The river! Good dog, I can follow it now. Well done, Thunderwith!" And follow it she did as it curled and twisted and finally led them to places that were familiar. She saw the small landing where Henk stored the row-boat that the kids might have used if Gladwyn had brought them to the river before the rain today. She realized they had made a huge half-circle through the forest but that they were now quite close to home.

It was already dusk and there was no sign of the storm any more as she took Thunderwith to the top of the hill. "Stay," she said, patting its head. "Stay right here, my brave dog." Then she turned for home.

Lara could see that there was another vehicle parked at the side of the house as she broke out of the trees near the creek and came through the front yard. Garnet sped out of the house and ran half-way across towards the rain-wet girl. Her face was flushed and her eyes bright and Lara's heart did a strange little dance of fear at the sight of her.

"Oh, Lara, quick, oh, come quick, quick, quick, Lara!" she called and Lara could tell by her voice that there was no disaster to report. "Dad's come home. Truly. Really. Dad's home, right now. It's him. It's really him. He's been up where there's crocodiles and everything — honest to God! He sent Mom a letter and money and everything from way up north. But it got lost. And Mom's so happy to see him!" And she did a wild little kick and a turn and raced back inside, announcing loudly: "Here's Laaaaara!"

Lara couldn't help bursting into a flood of tears when the suntanned Larry threw his arms around her, lifting her for a moment clear off the floor.

"Lara's blubbering," Opal said, trying to inspect her face up close. But it was buried in her father's shoulder. And Jasper caught at her trouser leg. "Lara. Lara!" he called, anxiously.

"She's not sad," Garnet explained to her brother. "She's crying 'cause she's so happy to see our Dad."

"He's her Dad, too," Pearl said quietly.

"She'd better get off those wet shoes. Trudging mud in all

over the place," Gladwyn said. But there was no bite in her voice. When Lara relinquished her father for the other little ones to cling onto him again, she saw Gladwyn's expression. Her eyes were on Larry's face and they were soft and curiously light. It was quite evident that for the moment at least, Gladwyn, too, felt genuinely happy.

10

"Thunderwith took me to this cave. A few weeks back, in a storm. I swear he led me to it. It wasn't by accident or anything. We sat there for ages. The two of us." Lara spoke softly so that no one else in the room would hear what she had to say to Neil.

"I meant to go back there the next week, with a flashlight, so I could explore. But it's a long walk from our place. Back through the forest towards the Bulahdelah Mountains. You know where I mean?"

"Yes, I know."

"Well, my Dad came back home the day I found the cave. He'd been right up north into crocodile country. Away from phones and everything. And we didn't know where he was for ages. And then he came back, out of the blue. And he's found all these lovely palms that are going to be sent down for us to grow on the farm. And to sell in Sydney."

"That's good, Lara. About your Dad."

"Then after he came back, I couldn't get away by myself again. Not until yesterday. I took a flashlight to the cave. And Neil, I just couldn't believe what we found. I couldn't wait to tell you . . ."

She leaned forward on her chair, her eyes bright. "There was something in the cave meant for me, Neil. It kind of spooked me when I saw it, in a nice kind of way. But it spooked me all the same. I think it was . . . " She groped for words ". . . a — sign. A sign meant for me and Thunderwith."

"What was there?" the old man asked.

"It was just inside the entrance, but hidden. I don't know how I missed it the first time in the storm, except that it was so dark that day. Right there, bang in the middle of the wall. This giant painting. It was of him! I just couldn't believe it!"

"A painting of the dingo dog, you mean?"

She nodded eagerly. "Yes! It was him all right. All patterned and beautiful. I knew it must've been there a long, long time because you'd told us how old those cave paintings are. But I knew it was Thunderwith, too. The way it was so big, and its head held up, just like him. I stood looking at it for ages and ages. It glowed wherever the flashlight beam hit it. I just couldn't move. And then when Thunderwith barked it echoed really loud in there. I nearly jumped out of my skin!"

"You were frightened, then?"

"That's just it, Neil. I was jumpy when he barked. Just for a moment. But I wasn't frightened in there. Not one bit. It didn't feel like other caves I've been in that are spooky. This one's such a beautiful place. Peaceful. And the painting. You'd like it a lot. It's a bit like some of the ones you do, Neil."

"Maybe a bit like mine," he said. "But I'm sure the one you saw was very, *very* old. In that cave."

"Do you know that cave? Have you seen the dog I'm talking about?"

"No, I haven't. But I reckon I know exactly what you're talking about, Lara."

She smiled at him. She'd known Neil would understand.

"Just a little way inside the cave, you say?"

"A little way inside. But you wouldn't see it easily without a flashlight."

"And there was a boulder, kind of blocking the entrance?"

"Yes," she nodded. "A big rock blocked most of the entrance. I'd have missed it if it hadn't been for Thunderwith. It's quite secret, really, that cave."

"Must've fallen there, that big rock, years ago," he mused,

looking away into the distance. "Perhaps thousands of years ago. More. You're probably the first person to see it in a long, long time, Lara." He had that dreamy far-away look for a moment. But then he looked back at her inquiringly. And she knew that he was aware she hadn't quite finished her story. She looked down at her hands and then back at the kind face of the old man. And then she went on: "I looked at the picture of the dingo dog for ages and I had this funny kind of feeling, Neil. It's hard to explain, really. It was weird but it made me feel like — well — as if I'd come home. Crazy, isn't it — to feel like that inside a cave? But I felt comfortable, you know. As if I belonged: I don't know why. I've never really felt that way before." She looked down, embarrassed for a moment, feeling close to tears.

"I would like to see that place one day, Lara. Maybe you could take me to see it."

She nodded eagerly as he went on. "You're lucky, you know," he said, slowly and thoughtfully, "to be able to see what you see."

"What do you mean, Neil? Lucky to see what I see?"

"It was meant for you to find the cave and your dingo dog picture, Lara, that's for sure," he smiled at her. "Someone else might not have had the eyes to see it."

"I haven't told anyone else, Neil. You're the only person. I think it's meant to be a secret, like the dog's a secret, don't you?"

He nodded. "Be careful who you tell about that cave, Lara. Maybe it was meant only for your eyes."

Lara didn't know why the large painting of the big dingo dog on the wall had affected her so much. There was a rightness about it that she had recognized at once. Something familiar, yet almost forgotten. She had the distinct feeling that she'd known all the time it would be there. And yet she was overwhelmed by the surprise of it, as well. It was like finding part of yourself, she'd thought, with a start. A wave of feeling had broken over her. It was very much like the feelings she'd had when she heard Gladwyn's music playing late at night.

She had gazed up at the painting and felt somehow, as Neil

understood, that it was for her. For her and Thunderwith. And she knew then that she, Lara Meredith Ritchie, was meant to be here in the Bulahdelah Mountains, right now, at this exact spot. And she knew suddenly what it meant. As Mom had said, over and over again, it was meant for her to find the Man and her new family, to find the dog and now this cave with its glowing painting. "Oh, Mom, I'm here," she'd whispered. "I'm here. I'm right here."

At the same time Lara had known the only person she could tell about her wonderful discovery was the storyteller. And of course Neil had understood. But he'd warned her as well: "Be careful who you tell." Well, she'd tell no one else. Not even Dad. But she'd think about it, the place and the good strong feeling. She'd think about it all the time.

With the end of the school term fast approaching, Lara found herself thinking more and more about other matters. For a while she'd been able to forget Gowd Gadrey's demand for her coins. But she knew he hadn't forgotten. She'd been forced to give them to him very soon. All but one, anyway.

He had reminded her one day in the school corridor as she was on her way to the library. "Don't forget the coin collection, now, will you, Lara?" Mrs. Gilbert had been passing and had smiled at them both. "You know, the one you're always talking about. We're all really interested to see it." Gadrey's voice was friendly.

Lara nodded wearily at his smiling eager face. "I'll bring it," she whispered.

"What's that, Lara? Did I catch that right? You said you'll — oh great. How about next week? A fitting gesture, Lara, before your vacation, don't you think? I'll tell the others. Say Monday. Good!" he'd said in that pleasant voice she hated so much.

The evening before she arranged to give Gowd the coins, she found the bundle she had prepared and almost taken to school weeks earlier — the evening of Gladwyn's awful accident. They had been wrapped carefully in some tissue paper she'd found in the back of a drawer that had been left around some scarves and ribbons from the gentle days of Mrs. Robin-

138

son's house. Lara put them in a brown paper bag from the kitchen. The silver dollar, which had been wedged under the window sill near Lara's bed for some time now, had been extricated and taken across the yard to be buried under one of the tallest trees, the one with the fat pinkish branches that Dad liked so much, not far over the creek.

Lara had meant to take it up to the top of the hill to be hidden in Thunderwith country. But she'd never got there. Garnet and Opal had seen her setting off across the paddock with a spade. They'd followed her so she'd had to explain to them that she was burying treasure and the two little girls were so excited at the idea that she decided to let them help her. They helped choose the big tree just over the log bridge and took turns digging the hole.

"Where's the treasure, then?" Garnet asked, when the hole was big and deep and Lara produced a small glass jar. They peered inside and saw the lone silver dollar.

"Is that it?" they asked, disappointed at the sight of just one coin, silver or not.

"Yes," Lara answered, "and it's very precious. Very precious. You must swear never never to tell a single living soul that it's here, okay?"

"I promise," Opal said at once, but Garnet asked, "Was it your Mom's?" And when Lara nodded, she hugged her and said, "I'll never tell nobody, Lara. Cross my heart and hope to die!"

"Can we tell Pearl?" Opal asked.

"Not even Pearl," Lara said, "because there's a nasty boy at school who could make her tell where it is, maybe —"

"I know who," Garnet said, "that creep of a boy G . . ."

"Shhh, Garnet. You mustn't talk about it. We've got to make sure it stays with the right people, okay?"

"The Ritchies?" Opal asked.

"Course, silly," Garnet answered, "and it'll stay here till our dying day."

When they'd covered the jam jar with soil again, and scattered leaves and twigs over the top, Lara said that no one could tell the ground had ever been disturbed.

"Not even Dad?" Opal asked, as they took the spade back to the tool shed.

"No, silly," Garnet told her, but when they met him at the back of the house she said at once, "Hi, Dad. We have a secret and we're not allowed to tell, so don't ask."

"Okay, I won't ask," he said and went on his way, leaving Opal standing there rather crestfallen.

"Let's play tips," Garnet said, lifting Jasper down from the verandah where he'd been playing with a scatter of plastic pegs. "C'mon Lara," and they went careering round to the rough lawn at the front of the house.

But Lara sat thoughtfully for a while alone on the back step. She couldn't put the silver dollar in the jam jar under the tree out of her mind. Or the prospect of tomorrow and the coin collection and Gowd Gadrey.

He hadn't spoken to her for a while on the bus into school. Nor did he this morning. He ignored her all the long morning at school while the brown paper package of wrapped coins weighed so heavily in her school bag. But he just happened to be waiting with some friends in the long passageway between two buildings when Lara came by at lunchtime. He knew full well she cut down here on her way to the library every day.

"Here's Lara, the bookworm of a girl," he said, stepping out of the shadows with two boys and a girl at his heels. She was the dark-haired girl who had been sent to fetch Lara the day of the Reg Breen fight, and she was grinning with curiosity.

"Bookworm I said and bookworm I meant. Not hookworm or anything as unpleasant as that particular parasite. I said worm of the book variety. She loves the library, our Lara Ritchie. And our school, it seems. Lara wants to make a contribution to it. You've got the coin collection, I take it?"

Lara didn't speak but tremblingly reached inside her schoolbag for the brown paper parcel of coins.

"Good girl," he said, when he saw it. But when she tried to brush by him he said, "Hey now, just hold on there! What's the big hurry?" He stepped in front of her, blocking her way, his pasty moon face unbearably close to hers. "As class officer

I would want to make a personal vote of thanks to you, wouldn't I, for this wonderful gift you're contributing to senior members of the school. So just stand by while we have a little look. I mean, how would I know it really is the coin collection, worm, until I see it is?"

She hated the thick back of his neck as he squatted with the others in front of her, shaking the wrapped coins one by one on to the asphalt. She wondered how a boy who lived on a farm could be so pinky-white as she watched the pale short-fingered hands unwrap each coin eagerly. "A Japanese yen, ah so — and this lovely old Roman coin. Quite a beauty! And a few old pennies. Junk really. 1904, 1918 and all that. And some little coins of the Republic of Indonesia. Then *Victoria Dei Gratia 1879!* Veery nice! A gold sovereign, no less. Am I right? I thought so. And some German money, too. Sieg Heil and all that."

He pointed slowly to each one. "Now which one's the most valuable, worm? The gold sovereign?"

She pointed dumbly to the gold coin in its slim pouch of plastic, the special gift from the Robinsons to commemorate her reading success. He pocketed that one, leaving the others to divide the rest of the spoils.

She tried to leave them then, the avaricious grinning group, but once again Gadrey detained her. "What's all the rush, book-worm?" he asked and then, touching her arm lightly, "You mustn't leave just yet because there seems to be something missing. Where's the prize, bookworm? Come on."

"I don't understand."

"I think you understand very well. The coins. They're not all here. You've forgotten one, haven't you?"

"They're all here," she said, but he grabbed her on the upper arm, pressing his fingers into the muscle.

"The silver dollar's not here. It's no use denying it, little book creature. I know everything. The pearl of a girl told me about the prize. Where's that?"

"I don't know what you're . . ."

"What a shame!" he interrupted, pressing so hard on her arm that she cried out in pain, as he had wanted her to.

"It's not worth anywhere near the gold sovereign," she gasped. "It's not worth anything much at all."

"So you suddenly do know what I'm talking about. That's strange." And he turned to the others to take in their glances of admiration. "Remarkable how the memory can be jogged, isn't it?"

"I lost it," she cried out, near tears and in terror of his harsh hand. "I lost it, I tell you!"

"Well, you'd better find it then, hadn't you?" He leaned down to her, talking softly and pleasantly. "Or you might find yourself in a tight spot. You see, your coin collection's not really worth anything to us unless it's complete. And we need the silver dollar to make it complete. So you'd better take a real good look for it."

And then he was gone with the others and she was left alone in the cool passageway still fighting back tears.

She leaned against the cold brick wall for a few moments trying to compose herself before she went on to the library. But she straightened again when she saw someone coming. One of the seniors. It was Stan. He hadn't been part of the nasty little group with the coins. In fact, she remembered, Stan had been the one to apologize for Gowd's harsh words to her on her very first day at the school. But she was afraid of him right now. Stan seemed uncomfortable as he sensed her fear, but he came straight out with what he wanted to say.

"I've just talked to one of the others about what happened here, Lara. Listen, Gadrey can play a bit rough sometimes. Act the real dickhead. If he's giving you a hard time and it sounds like he is — well, maybe you should talk to someone about it. Maybe Mrs. Gilbert. He's not the type to leave things alone. Maybe I can help. Do you want me to . . ."

"No, it's okay." She turned away from Stan and his offer of friendship. She couldn't trust anyone at this school. Not really, she thought, as she stumbled on towards the library.

The thought of Gowd's moon face rose up in front of her like a creature she and Mom had read about in a book so long ago who was prepared to go to any lengths to get the prize he wanted. Only his prize was a ring, not a coin. What had he called the magic ring he wanted so badly? "My precious," that was it. And now another vile creature in human form wanted her precious gift. Well, he wouldn't have it!

But as she walked her knees were shaking so badly, she knew she was extraordinarily afraid of Gowd Gadrey and his lust for the silver dollar. If only Mom's silver dollar was as magic as the ring had been in the story. Then she would rid herself of Gowd Gadrey once and for all.

In the library she didn't talk to Mrs. Magill or even seek out Joslyn to have their usual chat. And when Reg and Dieuwer and Shelley came in to look at a project they were sharing she showed them her research automatically. Her gaze kept shifting out of the window to the threshing cabbage palms she could see in a row. The place where Gowd and his friends often gathered during the lunch hour.

"It's great stuff, Lara," Dieuwer said enthusiastically. "Maybe you and Reg and Shelley can come to my place one afternoon. We can do a recording and finish the typing there."

"Yes," she said absently, scarcely aware of the friendly faces. "Okay, that'd be good."

She dreaded the bus ride home all afternoon and hoped for a miracle. That Larry would be outside in the Land Rover when school was over, his lean smiling face a promise of safe passage: that Gowd would be detained at school for something, a student council meeting or a game of soccer, and not come home on the bus at all; that there would be a freak storm that would be so wild they wouldn't be able to go home at all but would have to find shelter in the town, or with the Hemmingways.

But at 3:30 they were on the bus together. She and Pearl sat side by side these days, about halfway down the bus. Lara didn't look behind her but could see Gadrey from time to time in the mirror. He was sitting alone at the back, busily making notes today. Not looking up at the kids around him at all, looking down all the way.

When they got off, the three of them at the usual corner, he was right behind them. He didn't speak to the girls although he stayed fairly close behind them until he reached the place where he turned off. Then he called out as they strode down the road, glad to be free of his heavy presence.

"You won't forget your little promise? One silver dollar and by tomorrow." Pearl gasped, but Lara hissed: "Shut up. Don't answer."

They walked in silence for a few moments and then Pearl burst out anxiously when she was sure he was out of earshot.

"What are you going to do, Lara, about the silver dollar? Why didn't you give it to him along with the others? He'll break your arm. I know he will."

"I've buried it," she explained, "in a place he won't find. I'll never give it to him. Never." But even as she said this she wondered about it for the brave words seemed to stick in her throat.

"Oh, yes you will," Pearl said. "You'll give it to him all right because otherwise he'll make your life unbearable. And if you tell any of the teachers, he'll lie till he's blue in the face. He's a class officer and always doing things in the school for other people and all that. They won't believe a word you say. They'll believe him, Gowd Gadrey — because he's a real little goodie-goodie around the teachers. And you'll look an idiot and they'll think you're a little liar."

"Then I'll tell Larry," she said, grasping at straws, "and he can go over and see Mr. Gadrey and then," she faltered because she had visions of Gowd with Dad, all serious and intent as he would say, meekly, "Well, yes, she did give away a few coins, Mr. Ritchie, sir. I mean everyone knows Lara hasn't got too many friends at school. And she's kind of trying to buy them. I must admit when she gave me this beautiful gold coin I took it just to please her. I was going to give it back to her later. It was just a gesture of friendship. I'm awfully sorry if this caused any trouble, really I am. Coins mean absolutely nothing to me. And I can get the rest of them that she distributed. I was going to talk about Lara's situation at the student council meeting. See if there wasn't something we could do to help her."

It would be all so reasonable and he'd be bound to believe it, just as the teachers would. And then there'd be empty explanations to Larry and to Mr. Gadrey and Gladwyn's scorn to bear. And afterwards in a dark corner of the playground or on the bush road home, there'd be the taunting and Gowd's cruel hands.

"Dad'd try to help, Lara," Pearl said as if reading her thoughts. "But I think he'd make things worse for you, too. Please Lara, I know it was your Mom's and all. And I know it was my fault 'cause I told him about the silver dollar. But give it to him" — the younger girl's face was dark with fear — "and honest to God we'll work out a way together to get it back. We'll go over there and steal it back. We will."

"I can't give it to him," she said dully as they came through the home gate of Willy Nilly.

There were still the after-school chores for the girls to complete after their tea but the load had lightened considerably since Larry had been back. Lara would like to have fled to the top of the hill to Thunderwith but instead they both went over, after they'd changed, to the dam where Larry was working with Gladwyn.

"Take you for a swim in the river after," Larry said, and the little ones who had trailed behind squealed with pleasure. "And a row in the boat, Dad. Please, pretty please!"

It was dusk when they set off, towels in hand, for the river. Lara was glad that Gladwyn had stayed behind at the house, for now the party could be light-hearted.

In the brownish cold water of the wide river Lara swam out into the current, letting it tug at her and carry her along a little way. Then she swam strongly back, forgetting school and the silver dollar and Gowd's pasty face in the pleasure of her movements through the coolness and deepness of the water. She loved hearing the kids' sighs and squeaks — as their toes encountered the squelchy mud — mud that no longer worried her — in the shallows where they played.

"Let's go in Henk's boat," Garnet called. She had left the water and was exploring underneath the old wooden jetty where the boat was stored.

"Hey, there's another boat here. A real neat row boat."

"It's Gadrey's. Brand new. And Bill said we could use it any time," Larry called to her.

"Only you've got to get the oars from that old shed up the hill first." He swam towards Pearl and Lara. "Either of you girls like to go up to Gadrey's shed and get the oars?"

"No," they chorused, so quickly that Larry laughed. "You've still got something against the Gadrey boy, Pearly?"

"I hate him," Pearl exploded.

"Oh, he's not so bad, is he? Since he's gotten over that rifle incident he seems to have a bit more sense. His Dad says he's been really happy at school since he became class officer this year."

Pearl and Lara exchanged glances, but said nothing.

Larry persisted. "He's not giving you girls a bad time, is he?"

"I hate him," Pearl burst out again.

"Oh, he's not that bad," Lara cut in nervously. "He's okay," and she frowned at Pearl.

"Well, if he's giving you the slightest bit of trouble, Pearl, I'll speak to him." But Larry was interrupted by cries from the shallows. "We wanna row, Dad. Now, Dad!"

"Tomorrow," Larry promised as he heaved them out of the water one by one. "We'd better head home now."

"In Henk's boat," Pearl said quietly.

"Fine," Larry said. "In Henk's boat, if you'd rather."

Though Gladwyn smiled more frequently and spoke more kindly since Larry's return, Lara was still aware of the barrier between them. In his absence, Gladwyn had been forced to rely more on Lara. Now she could almost entirely exclude her. There were no orders issued as there had been in rapid-fire succession. Now Lara automatically attended to the chores she'd previously been assigned. There was not even grudging acknowledgment from Gladwyn of anything she did around the farm. And if there was comment from Larry when Gladwyn was in earshot, Lara always winced for she saw the shadow that fell over her face. It seemed worse, if anything, between them. Lara felt she was waiting, waiting as Gladwyn was waiting, for some awful sentence to be passed. She would be banished, she was sure of it.

That night Gladwyn seemed to be more accusing than usual. She spoke quite angrily, "You'll have to do something about those cases, Larry."

"Cases?"

"Hers." She inclined her head towards Lara who looked up, surprised at their mention, but said nothing. "That stupid school teacher sent the lot of them up here by rail. After I said we didn't want them. A note came while you were away. Whole heap of things at Taree Railway Station. Box of books, too, the station master said. What do we want with more books, I'd like to know?"

"I love books," Garnet said looking at Lara. "I really do."

"You just shut your mouth, miss," Gladwyn said, frowning in her direction for a moment but then directing her gaze at Larry. "So now we've got to get all this junk, I suppose. She's got more clothes than she needs already."

"Why didn't you tell me before, love? I've been into town a few times now."

"Well, I forgot, didn't I?" she flashed. "I've had a lot on my mind. And we've got no room, anyway, for more of her stuff. Bad enough as it is," she muttered.

"I'll run in and get it this week and then we'll sort out what to do with it. It'll be okay," he soothed.

"Waste of time," she sniffed, having the last word. She slapped the desert tray down so hard on the table that their plates danced.

"Do it again, Mom," Opal said, banging her own fist on the table so that Jasper gurgled with pleasure. "You made everything jump." But Larry said, "That'll be all now, Opal. We've had enough of your noise," and Lara left the table quietly.

On her bed she could gaze up at the sky and think about nothing if she tried hard. But not for long tonight. Gladwyn's cold indifference was a persistent ache and now there was the fresh terror of Gowd Gadrey to contend with.

Mom had said: "Face your fear." Well, they were fine words of Mom's. But she had gone off somewhere and left Lara all by herself in this mess, without telling her just exactly how you do face up to a flesh and blood fear who has big hands, who can bend your arm back and use cruel slimy words that make you feel so weak you want to die. Someone who knew your fear so well. She stank of fear, she was sure, whenever he was around.

Well, why not give him the silver dollar and be done with it? What was the use of Mom's dollar anyway stuck over the creek in a hole at the foot of a tree? Lara couldn't even look at it if she wanted to. And she didn't really need it, did she? Why not give it the loathsome boy so the nightmare would be over?

She could almost close out the memory of Mom's high kicks in the middle of the trailer kitchen and her singing "New York! New York!" at the top of her voice, her lovely freckled face all crinkled up in a showbiz smile. She could almost close out the enthusiasm of her words as she tossed the silver dollar on the kitchen table: "You gotta have dreams, Lara. You'd better believe it!"

Lara closed her eyes and clenched her fists. She would block it all out.

She concentrated on the little scuffling movements up in the tree that would be Oscar. She went to tempt him down and feed him an extra, a half-eaten apple that one of the kids had discarded on the verandah step. Then the door opened and Pearl came out as she often did now to sit and talk with Lara. Just the two of them.

"There are two new baby possums, Lara. Garnet saw them tonight when she went to the bathroom. They were on the roof peeking down and now she's trying to work out a name for . . ."

"Pearl, will you help me?" Lara asked suddenly. "I've changed my mind about the silver dollar. I'm going to give it to Gowd Gadrey after all. I've thought about it a lot and that's what I'm going to do." She spoke quickly, staring out into the blackness of the night beyond the outside toilet and the toolshed, the image of the baby possums far from her thoughts. "But I need your help to do it."

"I'll help, Lara. 'Course I will. But what d'you want me to do?"

"The silver dollar's buried over at the creek. I'll take a spade and if you hold the flashlight we can —"

"But can't we get it in the morning, Lara? Real early?"

"I want to get it now," she said, staring miserably at the younger girl, " 'cause I don't know whether I'll be able to go through with it in the morning."

11

"Okay, okay," Pearl said. "We'll get your dollar, Lara. But I've got to go inside and get the flashlight and then the kids'll want to know what's happening. It might take a few minutes. You get the shovel and wait by the tank. I'll come as soon as I can."

Pearl didn't take long at all. She returned with a flashlight concealed under her sweater. They set off quickly across the black yard, picking their way carefully through rows of young palms. But it took a long while to find the bridge of logs in among the thick foliage. It was a cloudy night and they were both glad of the bouncing flashlight beam which showed the way. On the bridge of logs they held hands and shuffled across, clinging together. On another such trip they might have giggled at the danger and excitement of such a nighttime expedition but there was no light-heartedness tonight. Only a grim determination to find what they'd come for and get back quickly before they were missed.

"How will you know where it is?" Pearl demanded, when they'd reached the other side.

"I know," Lara answered, falling to her knees at the foot of the huge familiar tree and clearing the leaves and debris. "It's right here. Hold the flashlight and I'll dig."

It didn't take long. She'd probably been digging for less than a minute when they heard the soft thud of glass on the spade edge. She flung her hands down the hole and retrieved the bottle, shaking it. The clink of the coin on glass reassured her the contents were untouched. They didn't bother filling in the hole but turned back to the dark creek, searching for the log bridge once again. It was when they were halfway across that they heard activity outside the house and Larry's anxious voice across the still night air.

"Pearl, Lara! Where are you, Pearl?" They froze for a moment.

"Don't tell him what we're doing," Lara whispered.

"We'll drop the spade at the side of the creek, then I'll get it first thing tomorrow," Pearl hissed back, and then called, "Here, Dad, we're here."

"What the hell are you doing?" he called angrily.

"Just going for a walk."

Lara left the jar by the tank stand and they both appeared empty-handed in the full light of the back verandah. Larry's face was angry. "What do you think you're doing?" he asked roughly. "Walking off like that without a word." The children's anxious faces peered around Gladwyn's skirt in the doorway.

"We went down by the creek," Pearl began guiltily, but Gladwyn, towel in hand, interrupted from the doorway. "It was her idea, wasn't it? You've never gone off to the creek at night in your life, Pearl. All her idea."

"Get inside and help with the dishes," Larry said to Pearl who ducked through the door but not before Gladwyn flicked at her angrily with the towel. "You're a silly girl," she said, "to go running down there in the dark when there's jobs to be done here."

Then Larry turned to Lara who stood helplessly by her bed. "Would've thought you'd have more sense than that. What'd you want to see over there in the dark, anyway?"

There was nothing to say, so she hung her head, grateful when he too walked off with an exasperated sigh.

"I bet I know why they went to the creek," Opal's shrill voice began from inside. "I know, Mom, it's about a secret."

"Get to your bed," their mother scolded. "I don't want to

hear anything more of secrets or creeks or anything else." And very soon there was quiet within from the kids and only the soft murmur of adult voices.

When she went inside the cool bathhouse to change into her night clothes and wash, Lara retrieved the jar from the tank stand. She brushed the dirt from it, inspecting it in the dim light to see that the silver dollar was unchanged. It was the same silver dollar, she thought but now it was no longer hers. It had become Gowd Gadrey's already and because of this she could not even allow it near her bed or her things on the verandah. She left the jar with the shiny dollar in it on the bathhouse floor beside the sink pedestal, with a towel flung over it. Tomorrow, before they left for school, she'd hide it in her school bag and then she'd get rid of the thing as soon as she could. Maybe on the bus. But she knew Gowd would want to make a big thing of receiving what he'd wanted so badly. He probably wouldn't allow it to be slipped into his hand unnoticed. He'd want his friends around him and to make his speech and mock her fear. No, she knew he wouldn't cheat himself of that opportunity.

Maybe she'd be able to tell Neil about it in the library afterwards. But she knew in her heart of hearts that she wouldn't. The words wouldn't come out about Gowd Gadrey, not to anyone, they were so choked on the fear she felt for him. And she was so ashamed of what she was doing. Ashamed she'd given in to him. Mom had slipped away somehow. Perhaps the silver dollar was the last part of her memory. The thought of it wrenched at Lara. She wanted to go back to her bed but there seemed no possibility of sleep now.

Then she thought of the boxes sitting on the station at Taree! Maybe there'd be something as good as the dollar she was giving up to remind her of Mom. Bet there would be! She felt a great surge of relief, at the thought of it. She couldn't remember much about what she and Mrs. Robinson had packed, though. She didn't know what Mom herself had packed. But how she longed to see the books! It would be wonderful to have them round her once again. Maybe to read some of her stories to the little kids.

But no, she thought, no, no! Not even her favorite book could replace the silver dollar, and she knew it.

"What's the use! What's the use!" she murmured as she tossed and turned in her bed. Nothing would ever replace Mom's special gift to her. Their gift of hope. She was giving away that hope. Yes, that's what she was doing. She was giving away hope to a creature like the book creature she and Mom had detested. The slimy pathetic creature who had wanted the gift he had called his Precious.

Then something even more unpleasant occurred to her. It wasn't Gowd Gadrey who was the pathetic creature at all, pasty and unpleasant and cruel as he was. She was the really detestable one. *She* was the creature. For a moment she thought of returning the bottle to the naked hole over the creek, but all her strength had deserted her. Maybe she'd just leave it out of sight beside the bright yellow pedestal in the bathhouse forever.

But in the morning, after she had packed their lunches, while Pearl ran across the yard to fetch the shovel, Lara slipped into the bathhouse with her school bag over her shoulder. She felt carefully for the jar. But where she thought she'd placed it, her hand groped nothingness. She dropped to the floor, searching wildly. It was gone! A terrible fear choked her. It had been twice lost now. What was she going to do? She couldn't go to school, that was for sure.

"Lara!" It was Garnet's voice from outside. "I got something."

She wrenched open the door and saw Garnet standing there in her pyjamas, the jar in her hand. She snatched it from the child's grasp. "You needn't grab like that, Lara. Opal brought it inside to bed real early this morning. She found it under a towel." She watched Lara stuff it carefully into her bag.

"What are you going to do with that silver dollar, Lara?"

"Nothing." She tried to walk by Garnet.

"You're going to give it to that creepy boy, aren't you?"

Lara gazed back at her. "Yes, Garnet," she said tiredly, "I'm going to give it to that creepy boy."

"But you said it was our secret," Garnet accused. "You said

it should stay here. With us, the Ritchies, forever, till our dying day, you said. You shouldn't do it, Lara."

And then Garnet ran away, leaving Lara standing at the door alone.

"Dad's ready to drive us." Pearl's voice summoned Lara from her unhappy reverie. Several times on the journey up the bumpy bush road to the bus stop, she felt she could almost tell her father the whole sorry story. She wanted so much to be saved. But he was still a bit annoyed with them about last night's escapade, she could tell, even though he joked about it. "You two runaway night owls," he'd said a few times. Anyway, the words would probably stick in her throat if she tried.

"Have a good day!" Larry called as he swung the car around, leaving them at the bus stop with Gowd who simply ignored them both. They waited in silence, Pearl afraid to open her mouth and Lara deliberating as to whether to give him the wretched jar now or wait until he asked. When the bus finally came he pushed past both of them to get to his seat at the back. "I'll see you later on," was all he said to Lara as he went by.

She waited all day, tense and unable to concentrate. At the first recess she searched the grounds for Gadrey but he was nowhere to be found. She wanted to get rid of the silver dollar as soon as she could, for it weighed heavily. She wouldn't allow herself to think of Mom, or what Mom might have done in the same situation. "It's a silly, stupid American coin and nothing much to get excited about anyway," she kept telling herself. "I'll be glad when it's gone. Glad!"

In the library at lunchtime, Neil told another story.

"You know I told you kids how my people have totems that sang them alive — way back there in the Dreamtime — platypus, snake, goanna, kangaroo, possum — all of them. Well, everyone has a totem, see. Mostly an animal but sometimes even a rock or a part of the land. The totem is them. And today I'm going to tell you about some people that belong to the dingo totem."

He looked across at Lara's pale face as he said this. "Do you know why?"

154

" 'Cause you're a dingo," a seventh-grade kid called out. The others laughed. But Neil said, "Yes, you're quite right. The dingo is my totem."

Lara felt a little shiver of something she couldn't quite describe pass over her. So Neil's totem was the dingo! Dingo! She didn't know why but she felt Neil was telling her this for a reason. He'd never said it before even though he'd already talked about totems. Maybe it was to do with . . . but no . . . it couldn't be . . .

"I wouldn't want to be a dingo," the same kid said.

"They can be a true friend," Neil said, "a lovely dingo dog. Believe me!"

Then the big man stood up and in a few easy strokes there was a dingo before them. A big proud creature that looked like . . . Lara looked down at her feet but Neil's voice, strong and insistent, made her look back at his face, like every other kid in the room did whenever he began his stories. His voice made her listen to every word:

"You see, there were these seven lovely emu sisters. Oh, they were beautiful, all right, with their big strong wings for flying. Yes, way back in the Dreamtime, these emu sisters flew around everywhere. But these dingo men wanted the emu sisters for their wives. The emu sisters had other ideas. And did they go! They disappeared so quickly and found a good hiding place in a big, big outcrop of rocks — you know, like over the back in Buledelah, those big rocky outcrops. They were clever women and they knew the good hiding places, all right!

"Then do you know what those dingo men did? They followed, all right. And then they lit a huge fire all around the rocks and smoked the emu sisters out. And the fire burnt their lovely wings so they couldn't fly any more. But they could run. Oh, yes, they could run! See the long legs." Neil slashed a few strokes up quickly on the white paper that became the emu sisters stretching their great long legs in flight. *"See the long legs — well, they grew longer and longer as they ran, but the Wanjin — that's the dingo men — they followed to the end of the earth, they were so made for those emu women. But the women leapt up into the sky to get away. And there they are today. You can see the Seven Sisters at night in the sky.*

"Those dingo men, they were so desperate, they threw themselves up into the sky after them. And they're a constellation of stars now, all of them. That constellation some call Orion today. But I call it the lovesick dingo men.

"Now who wants to come out here and be an emu woman? And who wants to be a dingo?" Neil asked.

Lara wouldn't stay for the play about the emus and dingoes. It was one chase that she didn't want to see.

"Are you okay, Lara?" Neil asked when he came down the back to watch the kids perform.

"I've got to go and find someone," she said sheepishly. "I'm sorry, Neil."

"No need to be sorry," he told her. But there was. Lara felt there was. She shouldn't go out there to find Gadrey. She should stay here and talk to Neil. But the awful feeling rose up again, the black awful fear that made it impossible to speak. She slipped away while the kids were laughing at the chase and she searched the grounds for him. But Gadrey and his friends were nowhere to be found.

Then at the school assembly, she saw him all right. Large as life, up on stage. Gowd Gadrey beside the principal. She felt sure he was looking right down at her when the principal announced a new student welfare program. There would, he said, be an opportunity to discuss any problems or to seek advice from older students in the school. It was being organized by the class officers.

Later, when they were divided into groups, Lara found herself, with about eight others, allocated, as she had known she would be, to Gadrey's group. They gathered at the back of the hall and he assigned them one by one to senior students. He read their names from a list he held, slowly and importantly.

"It's Lara Ritchie, isn't it?" he said, looking at the paper and saying her name as if for the first time. "Ah yes — you're assigned to Margot Hillier. She's in the library at present discussing settling-in problems with other new students. Now, Lara, if there are any problems at all for you with Margot, you've only to let me know and of course, I'll assign you elsewhere. Okay? The principal is very interested to know how this is going to work, from everyone's point of view."

She nodded dumbly, wondering what game he was trying now, as the other students looked on, apparently unaware. When she rose to her feet to seek the library and Margot Hillier, the unpleasant dark-haired girl who was part of Gowd's group, he added: "I'll be along to the library later to see how you're all getting along."

She found them in a small study room at the end of the library and Margot gave her a dazzling smile of welcome.

Gowd Gadrey came just as the buzzer rang for the next lesson. The others left at once, with trusting smiles for Margot, but Gowd detained her. "Oh, Lara, there is something Margot and I would like to ask you. Do you mind waiting just a moment?" His expression changed then, just as she'd seen it do on several other unpleasant occasions.

"The little bookworm has held out on us, you know, Margot. She promised to donate her coin collection to the school. Ages ago. Wants her name up on the honor board, I guess. As class officer, I had to accept her measly offer. But I said I would only do so as long as the collection was complete. Sad to say, she held back one particular item of interest. Now I told her very nicely that I thought the coin collection was incomplete without that particular item. And she made me look like a fool in front of my friends. Said she lost it."

He turned from Margot then and and leaned forward towards Lara. "You lied about it, didn't you? Worm. You had the coin all the time — the one I particularly wanted."

"I, I'd forgotten —"

"You lied about it," he insisted. She nodded.

"Well then, tell Margot you lied or otherwise she might get the mistaken idea I'm making this up." He smiled nastily. "And we wouldn't want that, would we? Speak up, Lara, please."

"I, I —" she faltered, looking down at her feet, her heart racing. She could get up and walk out now, couldn't she? They couldn't stop her. The librarian was at the other end of the library somewhere. And maybe Joslyn was about. Or Neil, still.

Maybe she could go to them. But to get to the door! Maybe it was locked, anyway . . .

"Look at Margot when you speak to her, Lara," Gowd insisted.

She looked up, her cheeks burning with shame. "I lied about the coin," she said, loudly and clearly.

He leaned back, satisfied. "That's better, that's much better. Well then?"

She undid the satchel with nervous, shaking hands and proffered the bottle holding the coin. But he did not take it.

"What do you think we should do with a student who lies to her class officer like that, Margot? It's not a very good beginning at Palm Grove High, now, is it?"

When Margot, who had been silent and impassive up to this moment, spoke, Lara's heart fell. She was playing his game and Lara knew she was victim to both of them.

"I think she should apologize. We don't want liars here, we really don't." She sighed loudly and looked with hard eyes back at Gowd.

"In what manner do you suggest she apologize?" he asked earnestly now. "We want it done sincerely, of course."

"On her knees perhaps," Margot suggested. "That would be impressive."

"Excellent idea," he said, and then there was a silence in the room. "Well, you heard, Lara, didn't you? Margot suggests you apologize sincerely on your knees."

"I am not —" she flashed at him but he jumped to his feet and stood over her.

"I'd do as you were asked, if I were you." There was no leering smile now. Just cold glittering eyes watching her.

Then there was a sudden rap on the door. Gowd went to answer it quickly. "Oh, Mrs. Magill, you need the room. We're just finishing. Sorry to hold things up," he said. Then, turning back to them both, he continued smoothly. "Thank you, Margot and thank you, Lara. It was a really interesting discussion. We'll have to take it up again later." And he was gone.

She would liked to have said something to Mrs. Magill but

a class had arrived at the door. "Do you feel all right, Lara?" the teacher asked, noting her pale face. Lara nodded and then returned unwillingly to her classroom. She sat dully through the rest of the afternoon's lesson, so distracted that even Mrs. Gilbert reprimanded her in her gentle manner, "I thought you were really interested in this, Lara." But Lara's mind was racing and the tombs of Ancient Egypt, no matter how fascinating, could not hold her attention this afternoon. Not for a second.

She still had the silver dollar, she reflected, and she still had to face Gowd Gadrey on the bus and afterwards. But since the library interview, she had had a frightening realization. She knew now that with or without the silver dollar, the Gadrey boy was intent on making her life a misery. Why give it to him then? Why give Mom's precious silver dollar to that miserable creature? She would keep it after all, she resolved. It would be lost again when he asked for it. Lost to him. He would never have it. Never! Even though she knew she was terribly afraid of what might happen this afternoon and other afternoons, there was a terrible gladness once she had decided this. She'd wanted to be saved from delivering the precious thing to her enemy. And now she had been. The joke was that it was Gowd himself who had saved her.

At finishing bell she dashed along to the library so fast that when she burst through the swinging glass doors she almost knocked Mrs. Magill flying, "Library's closed, Lara. You should know that," the teacher said, recovering herself.

"Is Neil still . . ." Lara began. And then she saw him still there at the end of the library, with Joslyn. "Please, Neil," she said urgently, "take this and keep it for me." And she thrust the jar at him. "It's my mother's silver dollar and someone wants to take it from me. And I don't want to give it to him. I want you to take it for me. Please hide it. Please!" The words tumbled out, almost incoherently. But Neil took the bottle at once and put it in his bag alongside the crayons and paper he always carried.

"I'll look after it for you, Lara," he told her in his calm unruffled voice. "Of course I will. It'll be safe with me."

"Got to catch a bus, sorry. 'Bye Neil, 'bye Joslyn." Lara flew past Mrs. Magill. "Sorry, Mrs. Magill. I'll come and shelve some books for you tomorrow morning," she apologized.

Lara was out of the library in a flash, running light-heartedly now, relieved of the awful weight of the dollar. She felt strangely, wildly glad to be facing the moon-faced boy again without the gift. She would take whatever he meted out, oh, she would, even though she dreaded it. But she'd be safe in the knowledge that her mother's gift was secure with Neil. Oh, she could cry with the relief of that thought. It was a miracle that Gowd hadn't taken it when she'd offered it to him. And now there was another miracle. Dad smiling at her and Pearl's loud cry of relief when she spotted Lara at the crowded bus stop.

"Where've you been, Lara? Dad's been here with the trailer for ages. And we're all going to Taree to get your things." Lara jumped in the back and hugged the ragged little urchins there as if she'd not seen them in weeks. "You're squashing," Opal complained, but Garnet showered the big girl with kisses. "Lovely, lovely Lara," she said, pleased at the ferocity of the hug she received. Then Garnet kissed Pearl too, and crooned "Pretty, pretty Pearl."

"Get off. You're filthy dirty, Garnet," Pearl told her, but she patted her arm affectionately.

They'd been helping their Dad plant more palms and obviously Gladwyn hadn't been there to order them to the tank stand to clean up. The grime of wet earth clung to their hands and legs. But to Lara they were as splendid as angels on high.

"Jasper, you little darling," Lara said, gathering the baby boy in her arms. As Dad's car swung out, she caught sight of the cold eyes she dreaded over the top of Jasper's head. But she didn't shrink back, merely stared at Gowd for a moment and then buried her face in the softness of Jasper's hair again. "You beautiful little boy," she said loudly.

She was safe and tomorrow seemed such a long time away. In the truck with her Dad and the kids, she could be happy all the way to Taree station and her Mom's things. She sang so loudly and so happily that the little ones stared.

12

That's mine, Dad!" Lara pointed out the large cardboard carton obvious to her among the conglomeration of boxes and packages. "Must be the books." She recognized Mom's inscription in bold felt pen: *Lara Ritchie,* large and untidy letters written several times. Then, as Dad pulled the box down from the shelf, more untidy scrawl: *Books — handle with care.* She turned away for the moment, realizing Mom must have packed these things long before she went to the hospital. Larry set the box down on the floor of the store room on Taree Railway Station and hugged her. "Don't be too upset, love. I bet we'll find you some lovely surprises here, Lara."

They heard Garnet's voice call through the lock. "Dad, Lara. We just saw a train go through the station. What've you got in there?" Then they all burst into the tiny room and the things belonging to Lara were pointed out. The box and two more large trunks.

"Presents," Garnet announced.

"For us," Opal agreed.

"Us," Jasper echoed hopefully, and their excitement lifted Lara's spirits. But Jasper lost interest quickly when he realized they were not going to be opened then and there. And when Opal started sneezing because of the dust, Pearl took them on to the station to look for a cart and to watch for another train.

"Dad, what are we going to do with all this?" Lara was worried by the size of the boxes and the memory of Gladwyn's contempt for her mother's things.

She wanted to see inside them so badly and yet the thought of taking all of them home worried her.

"It's okay, kiddo," he said. "I've worked it all out. There's the shed up on the back of the farm, right next to Gadrey's property. Top of the hill. Few tools and things in it. We can put 'em in there. Tomorrow after you've had a real good look you can decide what you want to bring down to the house. And the rest — well, it can just stay there." He looked at her worried face and said, softly and apologetically: "Now don't you go and worry about Gladwyn's grumbling."

"I'm kinda used to it," she murmured, but she remembered with a start Gladwyn's haunting words *for a period of time.* "Wouldn't it be easier just to leave it here until . . ." Her voice trailed off. Somehow she couldn't tell Dad what was nagging at her and he'd already started dragging the heavy things across the floor.

"It would not. I'd have to pay to store it any longer and there's no sense in that, now, is there?"

"Hey, guess what? Lara! Dad! It's Stan from school who's going to help us get these things to the car. He just told us he works here after school." Pearl announced as Stan arrived behind her, wheeling a large cart.

He smiled at Lara as he greeted her and for some unaccountable reason she felt her cheeks color. She was glad when Stan turned to work with Dad, loading the things and then wheeling them down a ramp at the back of the platform to Dad's battered trailer. But Garnet watched her intently.

"You love Stan, don't you?" Garnet asked, as the car moved out of the yard where Stan stood watching.

"No, I do not," Lara replied, blushing again.

"And he loves you," Garnet insisted.

"Shut up, Garnet, for goodness sake," Lara snapped at her.

"You're turning very red, Lara."

"Yes," Opal agreed, "you are."

162

"I'm not. And if you're not quiet there'll be no presents. So there!"

"Oh, all right, Lara, just because I said you were turning red . . ."

"Shut up, Garnet, okay?" She had never spoken sharply like this to Garnet before.

Garnet turned away from her, looking out at the swaying cargo with what appeared to be great interest. She began singing a monotonous little song and for a moment, just a fleeting moment, Lara thought she heard the word *Thunderwith* from the child's lips. Or something very like it. Lara was furious with Garnet. Why was she being so annoying? And was it *Thunderwith* she was saying or not? But when Opal asked, "How many presents for me?" Lara laughed in spite of herself.

"There'll be enough presents for everyone," she promised, and Garnet turned back hopefully then. "For me too, Lara?"

"Yes, of course you too, silly."

"You're nice, Lara." Garnet said, sighing and turning back to play with Opal. "You're always nice."

When they came up the driveway at last, Larry turned off at the rough overgrown track. It took them quickly to the top of the hill at the other end of Willy Nilly Farm. Lara felt a little nervous being here with all of them. To her this high place at the back of the farm was Thunderwith country. But there was no sign of any life — no stray kangaroo or inquisitive horse looking for food. And certainly no sign of the dog.

They found the small shed that was well hidden behind mimosa and saplings, and helped Larry slide the chests off the back of the trailer into the wheelbarrow that Pearl had fetched. Inside the shed the children did a wild dance around the precious new cargo and Garnet pleaded: "Please Lara, open up just one of them. Pretty please."

But Larry shook his head. "Not tonight, kids. These are Lara's things. I think she'd probably like to come back here, tomorrow maybe, and look at them first all by herself, wouldn't you, love?"

Lara smiled agreement at him. "The box of books still on

the truck's for all of us. So Lara says," Dad told them and they dived out the door eagerly at that piece of welcome news. Garnet and Opal again watched the box with solemn eyes all the way home.

"Stick 'em on the shelves, kids, once you've all had a look at them," Larry told them when he'd put the precious box inside the house. And then he was gone to join Gladwyn, who was still working far across the field by the dam.

It was strange that the very first book Lara saw, as the lid was lifted, was the one that had set her mother dancing across the caravan floor. The day she'd announced to all the world that Lara could read. She reached out for it but Pearl had already picked it up. *"The Dark is Rising.* Oh this! Mrs. Magill read us a bit and it was pretty boring stuff."

Lara stopped herself from exclaiming in disagreement about the book. She was too happy seeing the familiar covers to enter into any conversation about it. Maybe later she'd tell Pearl something about that particular book — how she'd loved it and how Mom had loved it, too, and how it had helped change her life. But not now. She was too busy searching through the tightly packed piles of books. Books from her childhood that now seemed so long ago. So completely left behind.

"What else?" the others demanded, jostling against each other so that she was forced to throw books this way and that all over the floor. She was so pleased to see them that she read out some of the old familiar names. One about a secret garden. "I'll read it to you, Garnet, and you'll just love it."

"A veggie garden, like ours?" Garnet asked hopefully and then frowned. "There aren't many pictures."

"And here's the one about the spider and a pig, Opal darling: just for you. Nope, I didn't say you were a pig, Opal. It's *about* a pig. Oh, and a magic wardrobe book for Pearl. You'd like it too, Garnet. You'd all like it."

"I'm not interested in wardrobes much either. But I liked that pig one when I was little. I'll read it to you, Opal," Pearl said, flicking through the books.

"Oh good, and some comics." Garnet seized them.

"Me, me," Jasper demanded, so that her hands delved deeper until she found it. "Look here, Jazza. Look here at this lovely story about a balloon."

Then Lara pulled out a thick blue-covered book with little gumnut creatures on the front cover. It was Pearl this time who gave a cry of pleasure. "Look, Jazza. I remember Dad reading this one to me when I was very, very little."

Lara glanced up at her with a strange look. She had been about to say "Me, too," for a sudden little shivery memory assailed her. Something long forgotten, buried deep, that had surfaced for a flickering instant. Dad and Mom sitting on her bed. Dad reading something about Snugglepot and Cuddlepie and Little Ragged Blossom and the Big Bad Banksia Men.

They emptied the chest and lay on the floor among the spillage of books, with Pearl and Lara reading snippets here and there to the younger ones until Opal, looking out the door, called to them. "Here comes Mom. Better tidy up, quick."

Pearl and Lara jumped to their feet at once, stacking the books quickly and neatly on Pearl's shelves and then dragging the box across the floor. Even Jasper sensed Gladwyn's potential disapproval for he dropped the book he'd been looking at and scattered Opal's box of dominoes over the floor.

Gladwyn made no comment about the books, although it was obvious they had been absorbed into the house. The kids hung about Pearl's bookcase, now crammed to capacity. Opal made frequent requests that evening for someone to read her a story please, a new story. And Jasper had taken the book with the picture of the boy flying across the sky held up by a large red balloon, proudly to show his mother. "My present," he told her.

Later that night, Lara took one of Mom's own books from the shelf. It was the old poetry book that Mom had kept with her always, because it had once belonged to her Dad. The one called simply *The Treasury of Verse*. It had a plain gray cover with a simple drawing of a candle aglow in its holder. She remembered Mom reading some of these poems aloud, so long ago now, with her stage voice ringing through the trailer. Oh, she remembered lots of the strange rich singing words:

> *In Xanadu did Kubla Khan*
> *A stately pleasure-dome decree;*
> *Where Alph, the sacred river, ran*
> *Through caverns measureless to man*
> *Down to a sunless sea.*

She could see Mom now, reciting this one by heart. Or reading the lovely one about the bell-birds or the sad one about poor Harry Dale, the drover. It all came flooding back as she glanced down the titles, flicked through the familiar yellowed pages. Then she closed the book and pressed her lips to it for a moment. She put it down gently on her pillow where she could reach out and touch it. Just having it there helped give her the courage she needed to think about tomorrow. Now that she had made her decision about Mom's silver dollar, and now that it was safely with Neil, her feelings seemed to have changed.

She was scared, there was no denying it. But she was secretly pleased with herself too. She hadn't given Mom's precious possession to the enemy. She hadn't gone down on her knees to him. Mom would be pleased about that, for sure. Victorious though she was at this small triumph, she didn't feel the flow of happiness she'd imagined, out here in her bed under the stars. Once again, she tried unsuccessfully to conjure up her mother's face. She concentrated instead on tomorrow and the day after. School she could manage. Stick to the library and Mrs. Magill and Joslyn in the breaks. But the bus rides to and from school, and the long afternoon walks up Old Creek Road, with only Pearl to help stand up to Gadrey's cruelty and mockery, were not a pleasant prospect.

When Larry took Lara back to the little shed where her mother's packing cases were, he left her alone with them. "Be working in the field. Back later, okay?" She was glad for this private time even though she knew the jostling noisy kids had helped her through the shock of seeing the books again last night. But these boxes were different. They were filled with the everyday things of the life she and her mother had enjoyed at Idle Hours together, from the toaster to the bedspread. It was the unexpectedness of what she might find under the three wooden lids that made her feel so tentative.

Nevertheless she lifted off the first lid and worked her way down through the contents, disappointed to find some of her own clothing and more towels and sheets for Gladwyn to scorn. It was in the second box that she found the letter. It was wrapped in one of Mom's Indian scarves and marked *For my darling daughter, Lara* which was unusual in itself. Mom rarely used words like darling. The writing was unusual, too. It was not as firm and sure as usual, though it was unmistakably hers. By the date at the top of the page Lara worked out it must have been written during those last days in the hospital, then given to Mrs. Robinson to put away with the stuff in the boxes that Mom believed, so fervently and so rightly, would eventually reach Larry and Lara's new life. It read:

Dearest Lara,

It makes me sad to see you so upset about what is to happen very very soon. I've tried to say things to you but I can see now is not the time to say them. So I thought I'd write this and later when you find it, it might be the right time — or a better time at least. I'm not going far from you, believe me. I know it just as I know by the time you get your letter you'll be with the Man. That thought makes me feel so happy.

Do you remember the painting of the rock pool that used to be over Mrs. Robinson's desk? Well, it's somewhere under this letter now, waiting for you to unwrap it, and it's a present for you. I thought a lot about that painting and Mrs. Robinson brought it in here to the hospital for me to look at because I feel a bit as if I'm in a rock pool now, almost submerged. The next wave or the next over the rock platform is going to be the one that takes me out of here and washes me away gently and easily to some other place,

Lara. That's all. And I'm not worried about that one bit and nor should you be. But whatever it is that ties us together — as we are tied together — can't be lost because the tide's flowed up and over, Lara. I'm for you and you're for me and okay, I suppose my big black bird might be around you sometimes, probably a lot in the first year of our being apart, Lara, but just think of this — I'm kind of in the same place as that big black bird inhabits, but among all the good things as well and I can help send it on its way if you want. Just reach out for me and I'll be there, I promise.

I'm looking at this lovely little rock pool and glad you are in it with all kinds of things still to discover. I'm sorry I'm leaving it, but I'm calm, very calm. My love for you Lara Meredith Ritchie is big as all the universe — you'd better believe it!

Mother.

P.S. Be brave and talk to the Man. He'll understand what you're feeling. And love me always, won't you?

Lara wiped impatiently at her eyes, where tears swelled ready to fall. "Mother." She'd signed it "Mother." It seemed so strange Mom calling herself *Mother*. She'd always just been Mom and yet because of the importance of the moment the word *mother* was so right. She dug down feverishly into the box and there was the little framed water-color of a beach not unlike the one at Seal Rocks. Mrs. Robinson had attached a little card: *Your mother wanted you to have this, Lara, and so did we — Marjorie and Albert.*

It was a wonderful little painting, pale blues and greens, and the rock pool Mom spoke of glowed like a jewel. It was a perfect oval of deepest green except at one edge where a wave had foamed over the rock, disturbing the perfect surface, and about to send ripples right across. Behind it again was a larger wave and Lara stared and stared at it, wanting to believe that Mom's final moment had been as easy as she'd said it would be.

She didn't really want to explore the rest of her things, but sat clutching the painting until Larry returned.

"Mom wanted me to have this, so I'd like to take it down to the house."

"It's a great painting, Lara, and if you want it then I'll put it up on the wall for you, right above your bed. It'll look real nice there. And when I finish that bedroom for you and Pearly, well, it can have pride of place in the middle of the wall."

She smiled at him and then held out the paper: "There's a letter here from Mom, too. Do you want to . . ."

He took it from her and she stood there silently while he read it. He didn't say anything for a long moment and she wondered if she should have given it to him. But then he looked at her. "She always had a way with words, Cheryl did," he said huskily. "And it was a nice thing to say about the rock pool. I believe that's how it would have been for her."

Lara knew that neither of them could say anything more about Mom for the moment. The look on Larry's face made her turn suddenly to the last box and search it thoroughly, pulling things this way and that.

"The three bears," she said at last, seizing the old battered things that were at the very bottom of the box. She smiled up at him with real pleasure. "Thank goodness they're here. They used to always sit on my bed — the koala minus a nose, the panda, looking a bit chewed now, and the baby bruin. One for Jasper and one for Opal and one for Garnet. And I'll give the scarves to Pearl. She'll like that."

"You're a beautiful little kid," Larry said, "always thinking of the others. They'll be real pleased."

"I don't want any of this other stuff, Dad. Just the painting. I'll come and look again some time. There's really no room down there for any of this." She knew he was relieved to secure the wooden lids again and leave the memories of Cheryl up on the hill behind the house. Out of sight, though not entirely out of mind, until another day.

She climbed into the Land Rover clutching her bears and her painting. Larry was silent almost halfway down the hill and then he said, "It must be hard on you, kiddo. I know it is. With no proper room and all the kids and missing your Mom and all . . ."

"I don't care about the room, Dad, honest I don't. And I love the kids." She wished with all her heart she could say something to Dad about Gladwyn and the *"period of time."* She knew she had to have it out sooner or later.

She would, she'd say it now. This was surely the moment. She'd tell him of her awful fear about the home and Gladwyn's cold words. "Dad, there's something I want to . . ." But the truck slewed sideways suddenly and there was a loud hissing sound. Larry jerked it to a stop and jumped out at once.

"Bloody puncture," he muttered. Lara had to run all the way down the hill clutching her gifts and into the house to get the flashlight for Larry because it was quite dark. She dumped the painting on her bed on the verandah and the gifts into Pearl's surprised hands.

"You find the kids and give them one bear each," she called, as she rushed inside to the shelf with the most powerful of Larry's flashlights on it. "The scarves are for you."

"What took you so long?" Gladwyn asked sourly. "I hope you're not bringing back a whole load of rubbish from up there, are you?"

Lara ignored the question. "The truck's got a flat," she explained.

"Here, I'll go," Gladwyn said, seizing the flashlight from her hands. "You can help Pearl do the potatoes."

Lara was glad she was there when the kids came in helter-skelter to Pearl's loud cry of "Who wants a prezzie? A present from Lara?" For they screamed with pleasure and then swarmed all over her, hugging her and kissing her.

"Mine's better than yours, Gar," Opal observed, hugging the worn koala with its pretty face to hers. "It's fatter, too."

"Is not," said Garnet, looking down at her curly-haired bear. But then glancing at the battered face of Jasper's panda with its bald patches and missing bead eyes, she said generously, "Jasper's is the best, don't you think, Opal?"

Pearl tied a bright purple floaty scarf at her throat. "It's beautiful, Lara. Don't you want it?"

"No, I've got this." And she went to get the painting of the bright rock pool and held it up for them to see. Again they clustered around.

"All those fishes and things," Garnet said, admiringly.

"It's lovely, Lara," Pearl said. "Did your Mom paint it?"

Lara shook her head. "No, but she liked it very much."

"So do I," Opal said, squeezing her bear hard.

"So do I," the other two echoed.

When they heard the motor, the two older girls left the bears and the small children and set about hurriedly scraping the large pile of forgotten potatoes.

Gladwyn was furious. "Get out of the way, both of you," she said, grabbing a knife herself when she saw that nothing had been done. Then, glancing at Pearl, "And get that silly thing off your neck."

Pearl's hand flew up to her throat as Larry came in the door. "I think it looks pretty on our Pearl, Gladwyn. Why don't you let her wear it?" It was the first time Lara had heard Larry oppose Gladwyn and she froze, waiting for Gladwyn's scornful reply. But she merely sighed heavily.

"If she wants to look ridiculous, she can do as she pleases, I suppose." Pearl left the scarf at her neck and stood resolutely by her mother, peeling and peeling down to the very last potato. But Lara didn't have the courage to move in beside them and help.

That night Opal wakened Lara by slipping into the bed beside her. "I wanna sleep here with you, Lara. On the verandah," she whispered, and Lara could see the battered teddy in her arms.

"Go to sleep now," she whispered, settling the small child down in the bed beside her and wondering what Gladwyn would have to say about this in the morning.

She yawned, closing her own eyes once she heard the heavy even breathing of the sleeping child. Tomorrow, maybe, she could talk to Dad about the period of time that might be coming to an end all too soon. Mom had said in her letter that she should talk to the Man. Well, she would. And she would talk to Mom too. But once again the words went dry in her throat

171

and Mom's face refused to appear. She couldn't toss restlessly because of the sleeping Opal. She was afraid that Mom's big black bird would descend with its smothering wings and envelop her. She lay there wakefully, gradually realizing that the dark bird had in fact taken flight. Lara knew at last that the big black bird she feared was no longer there. But neither was Mom.

13

It had not been as difficult as she'd imagined to avoid Gowd Gadrey for two whole days at school.

Lara told Pearl on the drive to the bus stop, "He knows he's not getting the silver dollar! He didn't even try to speak to me yesterday." The younger girl looked startled at this news. "Don't be so sure, Lara. I don't trust him." But Lara said firmly, "I've changed my mind for good this time. Don't worry about it, Pearl."

Today he was already standing at the bus stop. But he merely nodded a polite greeting. Nor did he speak to them on the bus. In fact it wasn't until they were walking through the school gate that he came close to Lara, saying, "Don't forget I want to see you later."

Something in her glance must have alerted him to some sort of change in her. He repeated what he'd said in a louder voice, only satisfied when she nodded agreement.

"Catch me if you can," she thought with a shiver, as she sped towards the library, safe in the knowledge that she would not see Gowd Gadrey until the end of the school day. Again she felt a kind of elation when she thought of the safe hiding place of Mom's silver coin. She hadn't told Pearl as she hadn't told anyone else, all too aware of Gowd's arm-bending tricks. After Mom's letter she felt she could stand up to almost anything

Gowd Gadrey could dish out. Nevertheless, her stomach was churning uneasily at the thought of the afternoon ahead.

The day passed swiftly and easily. There was no sign of Gadrey. Stan Redmond came into the library, though. He seemed to be watching her, she thought, as she wheeled a cart-load of books past the table where he sat. Yes, he was watching all right, for he nodded his head in a kind of greeting. But she passed by as if she hadn't seen. She knew he wasn't really one of Gowd's group as she knew that what Garnet had said the other afternoon at the station was right — that Stan liked her. But she felt she couldn't afford to trust anyone at this school. He might say something to Gowd. He might be frightened of him like so many of the others who hung around him.

"Let Gowd come in here and try to get me," Lara thought angrily. "I'll scream bloody murder. Tell Mrs. Magill everything. Only let him try." Stan only stayed a few minutes. Lara saw him thumbing through a magazine, before he got up abruptly and left. She wished she could trust Stan — talk to him.

That afternoon at the bus stop she searched for Pearl. She tried to look cool and calm for she was all too aware of Pearl's anxious eyes when they caught sight of the pale-faced boy. He nodded at both of them. "You've got something for me, haven't you?" he said heavily as he went by.

"See," Pearl exploded, "I could tell it was too good to be true. He'll . . ." Lara talked to Pearl in low tones in the bus about what they should do when they got off and he demanded his spoil.

If they both opposed him really strongly, she suggested to the surprised Pearl, maybe he'd give the whole idea away. "Bullies are like that, Pearl — all soft and mushy inside when it comes to it," Lara said, trying to convince herself. "We'll just speak really strongly and not give in." Pearl wasn't so sure.

"He'll break your arm, I bet, if he gets mad at you," she said. "I think we should run like mad to the Toymakers and wait there until Dad gets worried and comes to find us."

"I think we've got to face him," Lara said, bravely, clenching her hands on her lap so that Pearl would not see they were clammy and trembling. "Dad could come today. But then there's tomorrow, you see, Pearl. And Gowd'll be about to-morrow and tomorrow. You've got to face your fear, really." She used Mom's words to try and give her courage. Pearl's nervous little face and surreptitious glances down the back of the bus where Gadrey was working diligently, arranging his books in his backpack, made her feel edgy and nervous.

"I don't want to face Gowd Gadrey when he's mad. No way!" Pearl whispered fervently to her. Scared as she was, Lara just wanted the whole confrontation with Gowd to be over now. She had really changed her mind about him. She believed now that once he knew he would not get the dollar and that she could resist him, he'd punish her in some way. But then he'd lose interest and leave her alone. It was facing up to the possible punishment that was the difficult thing to do.

"Why are you doing this, Lara? It's crazy," Pearl whispered as they approached the open countryside where the inevitable corner meant leaving the safety of the bus.

"A day or so ago Gowd Gadrey knew he had me. But not today. I still have Mom's silver dollar — well — I know it's safe. And last night — it kind of helped me change my mind about Gowd." She knew she couldn't really convince Pearl.

"You've gone out of your mind," she said stubbornly, turning to the window and staring out. Lara had seen Pearl in this kind of mood before. But she knew that she had set her own course. In a way, it was nothing to do with Pearl at all.

"Nearly there," Pearl said nervously. "We could stay on the bus, Lara. Go on to Bula and then hitch-hike back," she suggested. But Lara shook her head. "I've got to do this, Pearl. You stay on if you want."

She was glad, though, when the younger girl gathered her things and scrambled down the bus stairs almost on top of her. When they passed by the Toymakers, Gowd was close behind them.

"He's kind of strolling and looking around on purpose. Trying to look cool," Pearl retorted, after a stolen glance behind them.

"Don't look back," Lara said, "and don't let him see you're worried."

"But I am," Pearl said grimly.

It was well along the dirt road and not far from the fire trail turn-off that Gowd usually took, that he gained on them.

"Didn't see you at school yesterday. And I had a meeting after school. Didn't see you today either, Lara," he called.

She put her head down and they walked on.

"I didn't look too hard though, 'cause I knew I'd see you and little Pearl here, anyway."

Lara could hear Pearl's loud gasping breaths, but she didn't break her pace as they forged down the road close together.

"Where's the coin then, worm? You didn't forget it now, did you?" he asked.

She stopped then and turned to face him. He started a moment when he saw the blazing eyes of the white-faced girl. "No, I didn't forget it. But I've changed my mind. You're not getting the silver dollar. It was my mother's and now it's mine. You're not having it and that's that!" Her voice rang out clearly so that even Pearl, impressed by its conviction, gazed defiantly at the boy.

"And that's that, is it?" he mimicked, but Lara could see the surprise in his pale eyes.

"So you can just leave me alone, C'mon, Pearl." And she turned to go. But he darted in front of them and Pearl's gasp of terror spurred him on. "I'll leave you alone," he said in that smooth tone of voice that always struck terror into her soul, "once I get what you promised."

She gazed back resolutely. She wouldn't give in. Not now. Not ever. "I promised nothing," she blazed.

Again his face showed a flicker of uncertainty. He could not quite grasp the change in Lara. Where was the girl he could make go down on her knees for him? He knew that his power over her seemed somehow to have diminished. He would have to make her frightened and submissive again by sheer brute force, if there was no other way, he thought.

"The worm's turned, has it?" he sneered. "Well, we'll see about that."

"You're the only worm here," she said, standing her ground, inviting his full wrath now.

He leapt at her in a rage, wrenching her arm up behind her back, rendering her powerless.

"Pearl," she gasped at the burning pain of it. "Oh, Pearl." When Pearl darted in, wielded her school bag, Gadrey kicked it out of her hands so easily she retreated, dancing to the edge of the road. "Stop it!" she screamed. "You great big bully. Stop it!" But he had turned his full attention to his intended victim.

"I want the silver dollar. Say you'll give it. Go on, say it!" he said, bending over her.

Lara was silent. She bit her lip to stop crying out that yes, she would give it. She felt the salt taste of blood on her lip where her teeth had cut into the skin but still she didn't reply. The idea of being brave had been easy on the bus. But as Gadrey forced her down on her knees in the roadway, she knew she probably couldn't be brave for long.

"Say you'll give it!" he urged again, giving her arm an extra little twist so that a cry was forced from her lips.

"Oooooooh!"

"Say it then," he repeated.

"Say it, Lara, say it," Pearl sobbed at her.

Lara could see the small pebbles scattered on the roadway and the red earth. She could hear her own gasping breath. But as her face went down to touch the roadway and the pain in her arm and shoulder seemed insurmountable, she heard a vibration in the earth. It was a familiar sound, a wonderful sound. It was an approaching car. Pearl saw the vehicle, a bright yellow through the trees, and gave a sudden cry of relief. Gadrey heard it too, a few seconds later. He released Lara, springing back into the shadows of the forest.

"Run!" Pearl screamed, and they did as the car came towards them. They fled down the afternoon road almost into the path of the oncoming car. The driver, an angry stranger, blasted the horn and swore at them as he swerved to avoid them, frowning in confusion when he heard the fervent words from Pearl's lips that sounded something like: "Thank you, oh, thank you, mister."

From the corner of her eye Lara had seen Gowd slip into the shadow of the forest. At the next corner Pearl stopped dead. Up high above them on the forest path was the heaving panting boy. He looked down on the two of them contemptuously.

"I'll get you, Ritchie vermin! I'll get you, worm!" he called and then he was gone.

Lara had to comfort Pearl then for she was in a panic of indecision. "Let's run back to the road, Lara. If we go on he'll be there hiding . . ."

"No Pearl. Let's go on home. He won't come back."

"How do you know?" she sobbed. "I'm scared of him."

"I just know he won't. So let's not waste time. C'mon, Pearl, let's run." So they ran until they could run no further. And then they walked, speaking in gasping breaths to one another. "You see, he's cleared off."

"I'm telling Dad," Pearl panted as they came up the driveway at a gallop.

"It's no use," Lara said, stopping and bending double for the stitch in her side. "You said yourself Gadrey's clever and that he'll fool Dad like he has everyone else."

"I'm telling him anyway. I'm fed up with that Gadrey," Pearl said. "I think Dad should know."

She strode off across the field to where her parents were working by the dam. Lara, red in the face, and nursing her arm, sank down on the back step. From the side of the house she heard the cries of the kids and could see them leaping about with great energy on the sagging trampoline. "La-ra," they called, "come and play," but she was too worn out for the moment to raise herself from the step. She sat watching Pearl's determined stride across the field.

She saw Dad wipe the sweat from his brow and lean on his shovel as he listened to Pearl's story. She saw Gladwyn glance across at her once or twice and then talk once more to Pearl, whose head was nodding violently.

Dad threw down the spade and came across to Lara almost at once. He spoke shortly to her. "You're okay, aren't you?" She nodded.

"You should've told us," he said. "You don't have to put up

with that, Lara." And he walked by her into the house, his face dark with anger.

"Where you going, Dad?" she asked, terrified at the answer she already knew.

"Going to see Bill Gadrey right now and talking to him about his son, Gowd."

"Oh, please don't, Dad. There'll only be more trouble at school."

"And I'm going to see the principal tomorrow at school." Dad sounded really angry and she could hear him rummaging for a clean shirt inside. Then she heard his heavy steps to the front door and the sound of the truck starting up. And then he was gone.

Pearl joined her on the verandah. "Dad believes our story, Lara. It'll be okay — I think." But she still looked worried.

"What did your mother . . ."

"She says we're both idiots for not speaking up before. She's pretty mad about it."

Lara didn't reply. But she remembered the evening after her first day at school when Pearl had spoken up for her about the Gadrey boy's taunts. And she remembered all too well Gladwyn's terse reply: *"She can look after herself."* But she was relieved they both knew at last how bad it was. And maybe Dad could do something.

When Pearl went to feed the horses, Lara accompanied her as usual. She kept glancing up at the darkening sky, where storm clouds were gathering, and then away over the creek and up the hill.

"If you want to go for a walk up there, Lara, I can finish this okay." Lara flashed a smile at Pearl, wondering if the girl who had become such a good friend now, as well as her half-sister, knew about the dog. She had never tried to intrude on Lara's late afternoon expeditions, sensing her need to be alone.

Lara wanted to see the dog more than anything else at this moment. She was exultant at the idea that her Mom's silver coin was safe. Even the worry of Dad's visit to the Gadrey's and what might happen after that did not cloud the fact that she had finally faced up to Gowd Gadrey. She had fought for the thing she knew she had no right to surrender. She wanted to be with the dog in her hour of small triumph.

"Ripper of a storm coming," Pearl warned, as she darted away over the field. Lara felt more lighthearted than she had in a long while. She moved up through the tall grasses to the place where the dog always appeared, calling for it, not too loudly on account of the small children playing by the dam near their Mom. It wasn't until she reached the top that Thunderwith appeared, as always bounding joyously towards her.

"No, Thunderwith. No walk today. Look around, dog — a ripper of a storm coming. All right then, dog, we'll walk halfway down the hill and sit on that old log there."

She sat beside it then, fondling its head and staring across the paddocks to the forest. "Today something good happened, Thunderwith," she said. "Something very good. I guess you know, don't you?" And then she hugged the dog gladly to her. "It's going to be different from now on. I just know it! Feel it in my bones!"

She felt the dog stiffen and heard it growl about the same time as she saw the figure among the trees at the side of the hill. Not any of the family, either — not the kids and too thin for Dad. But a man was there, she was sure. She started to her feet, calling nervously, "Who's that?" But there was no need for any answer. She recognized Gowd Gadrey as soon as he stepped out of the trees. He had a large canvas bag slung over one shoulder and something else over the other. It looked like a rifle, she thought in fright. He was coming towards them. She waited for the ugly words that she knew would come, comforted by the fact that Thunderwith was by her side. But Gadrey didn't address her at all.

"Rover," he called sternly, as he came. "Here sir, to heel, Rover." Lara looked around, waiting for a dog to appear, one that would certainly be larger and fiercer than Thunderwith. But when Gadrey spoke in that curt commanding tone, the boy was looking straight at Thunderwith. And when he repeated his stern words, Thunderwith left her side and slunk forward towards the boy, who had almost reached them.

"Thunderwith!" she called in turn, her voice ringing out strongly, amazed at the dog's strange behavior. "Stay, Thunderwith."

"Thunderwith!" the boy exclaimed, "Thunderwith! What's this Thunderwith garbage?" He sneered at her. "This dog's ours, and it's called Rover." And with that he kicked at it with his great heavy boot. "I said heel, dog."

She watched amazed as the dog, her proud and beautiful beast, slunk grovelling on its belly, beside the boy.

"It's not your dog. It's my dog. My own dog. It was sent to be my . . ." But Lara stopped short, knowing she'd already said too much. Gowd threw back his head and laughed, an ugly humorless sound.

"It was sent to you? By parcel post, I s'pose. What sort of nonsense is this?" he asked. "Rover's a broken-down farm dog. No good any more for working. Hardly worth feeding. Dad only does it out of softheartedness. It stays up here out of the way of the other dogs. They'd make mincemeat of a pathetic thing like this around the farm. It'll only feed from Dad's hand, like it was trained to do. Won't wander far from that old shed over there, where it lives. I've told Dad this sort of dog should be put down. Useless sort of thing it is." And again he lifted his foot. She couldn't bear to see her dog cowering there, accepting the cruelty and power of the boy who stood over it just as he had stood over her, pale and threatening.

"Thunderwith," she demanded, and the dog raised its pleading eyes but not its body, which was still lying submissively at Gowd's feet.

"Stay, Rover. You'll do as you are told. Stay!" Gowd's voice became louder. He placed his boot on the dog's neck, and it whimpered now. "It's my dog and it'll do as it's told," Gowd said triumphantly. He kicked the dog in the flanks, then said, "Get home. Go on, you cur of a thing! I'll deal with you later. Go!" The dog looked back at Lara but it sprang away from Gadrey's foot and kept moving.

The idiot of a boy had kicked her dog! This creature had spoken contemptuously to her proud beast! Lara knew that in the fury she felt surge through her was the strength to push him to the ground. Gowd Gadrey felt the force of this fury as she leapt forward towards him, ready to strike. He ducked quickly out of the way, steadying himself to face the onslaught that he knew would follow.

"You!" she burst out, her eyes flashing dangerously, "You . . ." He had raised one arm ready for her but she swung away from him suddenly, her eyes on the dog. She called again in a loud urgent voice to its retreating back. "Thunderwith. Come back here, boy. Now!"

They both saw the dog pause, confused for a moment.

"Get!" The harsh voice began again. "Get home, Rover."

"Thunderwith!" There was such a wild insistence in Lara's voice as it rang out across the hill that the dog stopped in its tracks. It turned back towards her and its dark eyes held such an entreaty. "Oh, Thunderwith," she called. "Come on, come on, boy!" And she opened her arms instinctively, aware by the look in those dark and knowing eyes that nothing would stop the dog now. "Thunderwith!" It was a strong, glad call and the dog bounded joyously towards her.

"Run, boy, run," she called, and for the second time that day she was fleeing the enemy. But this time it was with the dog at her side. They began their flight up the hill, leaping fallen logs and clumps of grass effortlessly.

"Ritchie vermin," screeched Gadrey after them.

"You're nothing," she screamed back at the boy still at the foot of the hill. Her voice was bitter with vengeance and loud with triumph now that the dog was hers again. "Nothing and nobody to me!" She could have cried at the relief of these words, for she felt released from fear of him at last.

She ran fast, confident of the dog beside her, unmindful of Gowd Gadrey's yell of fury: "Ro-o-ver." It seemed to echo in the hills all around them, as he called repeatedly.

But the dog did not falter. Its bounding form was close to hers as they breasted the hill together. There were black massed clouds up ahead. Lara had the feeling that she and Thunderwith were running headlong into a storm and that when they reached the top of the hill, they would leap straight into it. Leap to safety, cradled by its welcome fury.

It must have been a moment before they reached the crest of the hill that she heard the crack of thunder quite loud, very close. As she went down in a tangle of arms and legs, hers and the dog's, she realized it was not thunder she'd heard at all. It was a gunshot! She'd been shot! Oh, Dad! Daddy! Dad! Oh, Pearl! Help!! Help me! Gowd Gadrey has shot me! He must have! Daddy! She didn't know where the bullet had hit. Just that at the same moment as the crack of thunder, the crack of the rifle, she had fallen heavily to the ground. She waited for an explosion of pain in her back or in one of her arms or her legs. But she was still breathing: she was still alive. Surely the pain would envelop her any minute! Eat at her consciousness, cloud her vision.

"Oh, Thunderwith, I've been shot!" she panted, clutching at the dog and seeing the dark swirl of cloud rotate above her, as sky and ground seemed to swing wildly round her head. But still no pain.

She was numb, then she was calm. And yet she'd been shot by the merciless boy with the rifle who hated her so much. No pain, only the steel-gray lowering cloud, only a peculiar rasping sound close by her ear, a sound she recognized eventually was coming from the dog's throat.

The dog lay quite still beside her. Gradually, as the clouds stilled above her and the landscape righted itself, she understood the strange stentorious breathing from the dog's throat were sounds of great distress. "Thunderwith!"

It took Lara seconds to realize exactly what had happened when that fateful shot, that terrible clap of thunder, had rung out. Gowd Gadrey hadn't shot her at all! That was why she had felt no pain, there *was* no wound. No wound to her at all!

Gowd Gadrey had shot her dog! Her beautiful magic Thunderwith. And she'd fallen over him when he had sunk down on the earth.

"No!" she cried in the anguish of this realization. "Noooo!"

She knelt over him feverishly, searching the thick fur for where the bullet might have entered, so that she could staunch the flow of blood with her hands, as Gladwyn that day had staunched the flow of blood from her wound. She found the place, for the dog's side was wet and dark blood seeped from it.

"Noooo!" Her cry again echoed in the hills as Gowd Gadrey's had minutes earlier. The boy had disappeared into the shadow of the forest, leaving her alone with the panting, faltering dog. "No. No. No. No!" She stuttered the useless word, taking the head of the dog in her hands and gazing into its glazed eyes.

"Don't die, my darling. Please, please don't die. I'll go and get Dad. He'll fix it. I know he will. Only don't die. I'll get Gladwyn. She'll know what to do. I'll get them. Yes, they'll know." And then looking up at the dark sky, she whispered: "Oh, please God, don't let my darling dog die. Oh, please, not that! Not that!"

She should go, dart down the hill and find them. Leave the dog for a few minutes. But somehow she couldn't leave its side, recognizing death as instinctively as she had known the great life force that the coming of the dog had offered her.

She stayed. She took the dog's head on her lap, caressing it and crooning into its ear. "Oh, my darling dog. My darling."

She waited. And she heard what she recognized as the last sighing breath. She knew it had gone as the startled wallabies and kangaroos went, evaporating into the bush like wraiths, quickly, silently, mysteriously, at the sound of footfall.

"Oh, my darling," she cried, not willing him to live any more as she had done so uselessly with her mother. "Thunderwith, my darling." She stroked the dear head and then crooned incoherently, hearing a strange babble from her own mouth but not really aware of what it was she was saying.

An hour must have gone by in this way. For the last light had left the sky and the scudding clouds had made it quite dark, with only intermittent cold flashes of moonlight. Lara had little sense of time and place now as she sat, face to the wind, the dog across her knee.

It seemed impossible to Lara, too cruel to contemplate, and yet she knew finally that even as she was alive and warm and breathing, Thunderwith, her magic dog, her true friend, was dead. She sobbed aloud at the realization of it.

With the darkness came a kind of stillness inside her, despite the rush of wind around that heralded the storm finally breaking.

"A storm for the stormdog," she thought, somehow briefly comforted in the thick bunched clouds above her, in the brilliant flashes of lightning and the first drops of cold, cold rain. She'd stay here forever with the dog. Never move from this place. Never! She tilted her head back and, face to face with the wild sky, felt the full impact of the deluge.

How long she received the pounding of the rain on her face in this way she didn't know but, eventually exhausted, she crouched over the dog once more, rocking to and fro. Then a violent paroxysm of longing, sorrow, and futility seized her swaying body and she lifted her head to the sky once more and uttered the word, calling on the help she had wanted all the difficult months she had been at the farm. It was not so much a word as a terrible cry from the heart.

"Mother!" she screamed. The wind tore the word from her throat and carried it off and away across the fields and into the dark forest. "Mo-o-o-ther!" she called again so that her throat swelled with the sound and rasped with pain at the intensity of that prolonged cry. It seemed that every fiber of her strength went into the word issuing from her blue cold lips.

And again, "Mo-o-ther!" Her voice rose up louder than any summer-shrieking cicada shrill.

"Mother, oh, Mother," a lamentation, an incantation. Over and over again she chanted the name.

The cries she uttered seemed to echo in Lara's ears so that the whole hillside was alive with the storm and with her mother. In every flailing branch and errant twig, in the scattered rocks and the humped trees, in the wild wind and now as she lent over the inert body beside her, in the dog, too. The cry seemed to rise up above the noise of the storm. For Larry, long returned from his errand and searching the hills for his daughter, heard it and made for her straight away. Gladwyn might have heard it, too, as she pulled the windows shut against the storm. She ran out of the house to see the glimmer of Larry's flashlight, moving in a direct line to where the cry had come from.

Lara had sunk down from her crouching position, arm still cradled round the dog. And now the word was a whisper and a prayer. "Oh, mothermothermother." She felt she could chant it like this forever. But when the flashlight beam fell on her, she looked up, startled to see her father.

"Lara, for God's sake, are you hurt? What's happened?" he began.

"No, no, no," she sobbed. "It's him, it's the dog. It's Thunderwith. You see, he was real after all. He was flesh and blood real, like Mom. Not a dream, not magic at all. He's been shot. Thunderwith's been shot." Her father didn't fully understand her words but, sensing her distress, sat down beside her. "Lara," he said, his strong arm around her, "who killed Rover? Why are you sitting here with the Gadrey's dog? Who shot it?"

"I killed it." She was laughing and crying now. "I might as well have. I made it my friend and he hates me, so he killed it. The dog was my friend. My only friend. I thought Mom sent Thunderwith to be my friend, but it was a trick, too."

"Lara, Lara," he said more urgently. "Who shot the dog? Who shot it?"

"It doesn't matter," she murmured, her hands beginning a feverish caress of the rain-wet body. "Thunderwith's dead, so it doesn't matter."

Her father kept repeating the question slowly, slowly, until she made him understand in between her bouts of sobbing. Finally he was able to piece it all together. "Gowd Gadrey chased us both up the hill. Here, a few hours ago, before the storm. He had a rifle. I thought he'd shot me, Dad." For the first time she turned to him, seeing his face in the dim light. "I wish he'd shot me."

"No, Lara, no," he said, gathering her in his arms again. "Don't talk like that. Don't ever talk like that." And she cried once more, leaning against his shoulder, but still not comforted.

Eventually they heard the sound of voices at the bottom of

the hill and then Pearl's shrill voice: "Dad! Lara! You okay?"

"It's okay. Go home, love. Tell your Mom I've found her. We'll be home soon." But Lara couldn't bring herself to leave the place on the hill. She cried and clung to Larry and it took him some time to calm her.

The wind and rain had eased by now but still they sat by the dog. When Dad reached for Lara's hands and held them in his own large rough ones, she poured out the whole story of Thunderwith to him. How the dog had come to her in a storm; how it had been her only friend and comfort during the long difficult months of his absence; how she had walked in the hills with it, sharing her thoughts and her confused feelings; how they'd found the wonderful cave with the painting of the dog that had confirmed his magic. And then how Gowd Gadrey had finally claimed her dingo dog.

He listened silently to her faltering voice.

". . . So you see, Dad, because I needed Thunderwith so badly, he's dead now. And it's my fault. It must be. Thunderwith died instead of me. Died because I thought he was magic."

"Thunderwith was magic and special to you, Lara. That's all that matters, love."

She began to shiver violently now and when rain began to fall again her father lifted the dog from where it lay.

"Dad, what . . . ?"

Larry spoke gently but insistently to his daughter. "I'm taking Thunderwith down the hill now, love. Taking him home. We'll wrap him in some sacking. I've got some real nice stuff in the shed. And then tomorrow when we can see, we'll bury your dog Thunderwith in a real nice bush grave. Come on, love. We're going home."

Lara allowed herself then to be led down the hill, Larry in front carrying the burden of Thunderwith in his arms. As they came across the tree bridge and through the reeds and into the field where the edges of the dam gleamed whitely like a moon landscape, she thought, "I shall never come this way again. Never." And a little shiver of certainty passed over her.

187

"I'm leaving here," she thought, glancing at Dad's strong square shoulders in front of her now and feeling a terrible pain in her chest, "because everything's all finished now."

And the thought that had persisted all these months and had terrified her so much, of the home somewhere far away from all she knew, suddenly held no terror for her any longer.

She would leave here. She would go to the home. "But I won't be alone any more." The thought of this shocked her but the words kept recurring in her brain. "I won't be alone. I won't ever be alone again."

It seemed to Lara that through the dreadful events that had happened on the hill this evening, she had finally summoned her mother. Cheryl had come out of the storm. And Cheryl was here now, beside her daughter.

Gladwyn ran out of the house to meet them. Larry said a few quick words to her while Lara stood, her hair streaming wetly down her white face, feeling nothing. Nothing at all.

Gladwyn left them alone then and they continued to the shed where they wrapped the dog and set it down on the wooden floor. From somewhere nearby she could hear the roar of the chip heater and water running into the bath, as she watched her father's gentle hands.

"See," Larry said, "your dog's right here beside you. He'll like it in the old shed until tomorrow. He lived in Gadrey's shed back of our farm, you know — when he was their dog." He glanced up at her.

"Look, love, I want you to have a big hot bath now. Gladwyn's heated the water for you and you must be chilled to the bone. Now come on, otherwise you'll be too sick to help in the morning. Do you want to eat anything? You've missed supper, you know."

She shook her head. "No, Dad."

As they passed her bed on the verandah, he asked "Do you want to sleep indoors tonight?" But she said "No, I'd rather stay here." The thought of a door closing on Thunderwith tonight was unthinkable.

Until the mention of hot water she hadn't realized how wet

and cold she was, and tired too. When she came from the bath-house she found a mug of Gladwyn's sweet strong-smelling tea and a night light by her bed. Someone small lay curled up and asleep in her bed. It was Opal, and as Lara slid in beside the small form, her eyes opened a moment and she smiled drowsily. " 'Lo, Lara," she whispered and then drifted back to sleep. Lara, warm and comforted by the nearness of the small child, gazed, as she had so many nights before, up into the night sky, where ragged stars showed through briefly between the travelling clouds. Dad came out to sit by her silently. As she drifted towards an exhausted sleep she saw him move qui-etly indoors again. That was when she saw an image of Cheryl's face, clear and bright and close.

"I'm leaving here, Mom," she whispered. She felt strong enough at last to leave the place that no longer seemed to matter to her, the place that had been so bittersweet for her, that had given so unexpectedly and then taken so cruelly.

She was sure she felt the strength of her mother's love all around her, though with Thunderwith going something also seemed to have finally died inside her. And there were tears involved as she whispered, "It's okay, Mom, I can do it now."

14

In the morning when she went inside, Lara sensed a change of atmosphere in the house. Gladwyn was awkward, almost apologetic in her manner, although she didn't speak directly to Lara. Lara's breakfast plate was placed in front of her and a mug of tea, the only sustenance she could face, was poured for her. Pearl seemed nervous, too, lingering around Lara's chair as if about to speak and then swooping over to the sink to busy herself with the plates there. Only Dad and the smaller kids were the same.

"Aren't you going to eat that, Lara?" Opal asked, always hungry, eyeing the untouched plate.

"Lara and I have got to bury her dog, Thunderwith," Dad told them, after breakfast was finished.

"I didn't know Lara had a dog," Pearl said, surprised, turning from the sink, towel in hand. But Garnet said importantly: "I did. It was Gadrey's dog, wasn't it, Dad? I watched her on the hill with Gadrey's dog lots of times. The one they call Rover, that looks like a dingo. Only Opal and I heard Lara calling it 'Thunderwith.' 'Here, Thunderwith!' plenty of times. It's out in the shed now, isn't it? It's dead."

Gladwyn said, "Hush your mouth, Garnet, for goodness' sake," glancing at Lara's grim set face.

Dad said: "Yes, it's dead all right. But Lara and me are going to bury it somewhere real nice."

"Will Mr. Gadrey be mad?" Opal asked when they all went out to watch Dad gently lift the wrapped dog into the wheelbarrow for its journey across the fields.

"It's Lara's dog as well, you know, Opal. It sort of became Lara's dog when she came here to live with us. So Bill Gadrey won't be mad at us if we bury it here, at Willy Nilly. Now, how about you kids let Lara and me do this alone."

But Lara said, "Let them come, Dad, if they want to," and so they took Thunderwith over the creek and to the foot of the hill where Lara had first seen him. And there, where she'd left Mom's silver dollar in the earth for such a brief time, they dug a deep wide hole and buried Thunderwith in the shade of the fat pinkish branches of the large tree. "Under the old Angophora tree," Larry said, standing back. "Magnificent resting place. My favorite tree on this place, too."

She helped Dad heave a large stone from the creek while the other kids carried smaller ones which they arranged lovingly in a pattern to mark the place. Garnet, always near Lara, took her hand and kissed her cheek, and Lara squeezed the warm little hand that was placed in hers, but without the usual feeling. She felt remote. Remote from all of them. Dad of the kindly eyes and the silent children gathered around the foot of the tree to say good-bye to her dog. They would soon have to say good-bye to her, too.

"It looks real pretty, Lara," Pearl said, quietly.

"Yeah," Opal sighed sadly, and Jasper in Pearl's arms put his head on her shoulder as if he were about to cry.

"I had a lovebird that died once," Garnet said, "and we buried it too, didn't we, Pearl?"

They returned to the house and soon the little girls, who'd sat by Lara for a while on the sagging bed on the verandah, were fidgety. Eventually Jasper came and took Opal to one of the tree trunks close by, to inspect a bright green cicada emerging from its dull shell. And that drew Garnet away, leaving only Pearl. When she was called inside to do some chore for her mother, Lara was relieved. She didn't want to talk, really. She wanted to be alone for a bit, and there was no thought now of going over the creek and up the hill again.

The strange calm feeling from last night persisted as Lara sat on the verandah, released from school and chores. It was over, here at Willy Nilly. All over. It was like a curtain coming down on a play, she thought, feeling quite matter-of-fact. That was all. She didn't belong here any more, if she had ever really belonged at all. She'd felt it so strongly last night and she felt it still. With the death of Thunderwith had come a release of sorts. She was released from the farm and the forest and the surrounding bushland she'd come to know so well. She was released from Gladwyn's contempt and the struggle to win her approval, much less her affection. She was released from *trying*.

She'd tried so hard to fit in and she'd never really succeeded. Never would, while there was Gladwyn's indifference to contend with. She didn't like to think about Dad and the kids. But they were Gladwyn's in a way that she could never be Gladwyn's. And so she must relinquish them, too. She wasn't scared of the home any longer. It didn't seem to matter.

When Dad came in from the fields for a while to sit with her she told him. There was no use delaying. Everywhere around here reminded her of things she didn't want to think about any more. She needed a fresh start.

"Dad, I want to leave Willy Nilly Farm. I want to go back to the city. I've got to leave here. I — it feels all wrong to stay now."

He was silent for a moment but she had seen a flash of alarm in his eyes. Then he spoke quietly, "But where would you go, Lara?"

"I'll stay in a home for a while until I work out what I want to do," she said flatly and unemotionally. Then, watching his troubled face, she burst out, "It's not your fault or anything, Dad! Honest to God! But please believe me, I've just got to go now."

"Why don't you wait a little while, Lara? You're feeling so upset — and maybe confused about — well, why don't you just give yourself some time to work things out here? Let things settle. Things'll be different, you'll see. I know it's been hard for you, but it's been hard for Gladwyn too. There's things I can't explain but if you'll give her, give us both, a chance, darling, then . . ."

"Gladwyn'll be the same," Lara said quietly. "She can't help it, Dad. We'll all be the same really. I've never belonged here, and I don't belong now. Let me go, Dad. You've got to."

"What about your sisters and baby brother?" he asked then, and she stared hard at her feet, dusty from their walk across the field. But she didn't want to think about them at all.

"You were all okay before I came here and you'll be okay when I go," she said stolidly.

It was funny, there wasn't even a tremble in her voice when she spoke and yet she knew the hardest thing in the world would be to say good-bye to the kids, to the family. But something made her certain that this was the right thing, the only thing left to do.

"I can't explain it, Dad. I just know I've got to go, that's all."

He said he wouldn't stop her if she really wanted to go but asked her to wait just a few weeks. To think about it some more. "Maybe go and stay with the Robinsons for a while, just to sort things out."

"I have sorted things out, Dad," she told him quietly, and he knew she was resolved.

His eyes looked so sad that she would have liked to throw herself into his arms and let his love wash over her like Mom's high tide and carry her safely to somewhere else. But there was a kind of torpor still hanging over her and she could respond neither to his sadness nor to his kindness.

"You'll wait a while longer?" he persisted, but it was a question.

"Okay, Dad, if you want."

"And in the meantime, I can make some inquiries about places where you could go in Sydney," and then, pathetically, "or maybe Newcastle. It's closer."

"Thanks," she said, and then because she couldn't bear to see the look in his eyes for another minute, she said: "I'm going for a walk now, Dad. I'll come and help you later."

She didn't head for the familiar path across the fields for she knew the tree would be a blaze of beautiful pink branches she couldn't bear to look at ever again. And the stone mound beneath would pretend to cover all that had been the dog, her dog. And she couldn't bear to look at that, either.

She walked out the front gate, gathering Garnet and then Opal from the wet trampoline where they had bounced ceaselessly for an hour at least. They went down the driveway, not avoiding the deep puddles in the broken surface of the dirt, but mindful of the leeches in the dripping foliage by the edges.

"Ha, you got one, Lara!" Garnet called, triumphantly, but she flicked it expertly, watching the slender thread of its body twirl uselessly under the force of the stick she held.

"You're not scared. No way! Are you, Lara? You're not scared of anything anymore?" Garnet said admiringly.

"No, I'm not scared anymore," Lara agreed.

"But you're real sad about the dog," Opal observed. "Aren't you, Lara?"

"Yes."

"Me too," Garnet sighed. "I'm very, very sad."

Though they lingered, gathering some of the white gravelly stones that looked like pieces of marble along the way and collecting twigs and leaves, too, Lara was surprised how quickly they reached the Old Creek Road, the point where they had agreed to turn for home once again.

When Lara went back to school in the next few days as Dad had asked her to do, she was surprised at how much the same it all seemed. She felt as if she'd been away for weeks and months, not just a few days. Dad first took her to see the principal. He was kind to Lara, but clearly upset at what he had learned about Gowd Gadrey.

"One of our best class officers. And such a fine sportsman — I wouldn't have thought this possible. Can't understand it really . . . Of course, I've spoken at length to his father and he seems to think it best if Gowd goes to an aunt and uncle up the coast for a while. The boy's agreed. He seems terribly upset."

"We're terribly upset, too," Dad said quietly. And the principal had nodded his head vigorously. "Of course. Of course. I do understand. Shocking business."

After the terrible incident with the dog, and with his son present, Bill Gadrey and Dad had discussed the whole dreadful thing. Gowd had insisted it had all been an accident. That he'd gone out rabbit shooting as he sometimes did (yes, he took out his rifle on occasions without his father's knowledge); that he'd run into Lara, acting a bit strange on the hill and calling out at him something about the dog; that Lara had infuriated him with her claims of owning their dog, and then hurled insults at him when he had tried to send it home. They'd both got really angry, he said, and then when she'd run off with the dog, he'd meant to fire over her head just to frighten her, which was, he admitted, a stupid thing to do. And then as he'd aimed the gun and fired he'd stumbled on a tree root and the shot had found a mark with the dog — unintentionally. He was sorry. He was terribly sorry. He hadn't meant for it to happen that way. Not at all.

He seemed chastened and upset, glancing away whenever Larry tried to meet his gaze. When Larry reminded him of the unpleasant incident on the road just hours before the gun incident, the boy insisted that the girls had dramatized it. He only admitted to teasing them a bit. "Nothing too heavy though, sir. I was just having a bit of fun. They must've taken it to heart."

"Well, the gun can hardly be described as fun," Larry said, grimly. It added up to a serious charge against Gowd, no matter what he said in his defense.

After further long talks with Larry and his son, Bill Gadrey had decided to send Gowd away from Palm Grove High School altogether. Upstate, to finish out the school year with relatives in Coffs Harbour. Bill Gadrey, quite shaken by the whole sorry turn of events, was extremely grateful that Larry hadn't taken the matter further, as he might have done. The fact that Lara might have been killed by that shot from Gowd's rifle played on Bill Gadrey's mind. He'd been over to see them at Willy Nilly Farm several times since, worrying and lingering until Dad or Gladwyn reassured him once again.

"If there's anything I can do for you, Lara, anything at all," he said, his faced creased in a frown of concern. "I don't know what got into that boy. I've been thinking and thinking it over. And I've had talks with him about it, too. Maybe his mother's death when he was just a little fella? And then that hell of a school in the city where he was so unhappy. And then me not being able to give him too much time. He's spent too long alone, I think. I don't know why he'd set on you like that — all that stuff at the school and now this."

"I don't know," he mused another time, his face frowning in puzzlement. "He's always liked sort of having power, you know, over younger kids, or even the animals round the farm, even when he was just a little fellow. It worried me a bit then. But at school when he got this class officer thing, I thought it would do him a lot of good. You know, he had the power he always seemed to need to make him feel — important, I s'pose. Must have gone to his head." The man was obviously nonplussed by his son's behavior. "I'm just hoping my sister can talk some sense into him. Hope it's not too late for that."

He had looked so miserable Lara could almost have comforted him, except this awful numbness that seemed to have crept inside her being stopped any real action she might have made.

"It's all right now, really, Mr. Gadrey," she'd said in that strange flat voice, the one that she spoke in all the time now.

"Heard the news? That GG, the horse, the Great Gowd has gone for good?" Reg asked Dieuwer and Shelley. They'd seen Lara and her Dad go into the principal's office and now were waiting for her to reappear.

"Yep, I heard," Dieuwer said. "And he's finishing the school year somewhere else, thank God."

Reg told them that Henk Rangers of the Wallingat had told

his Mom that Gowd had gone onto Ritchie property with a rifle. And that he'd shot the old dog Rover stone dead."

"So?" Shelley said. "Maybe it was sick or something. We had to put a dog down once."

"I know who's sick. It's that creep Gowd. Talk about a bully," Dieuwer said. "He threatened Lara with the gun, you know. Henk said he tripped and shot the dog by mistake. But I don't know about that . . ."

"Jeez!" Shelley exclaimed. "They must've had a real fight! But it's not fair they're sending Gowd away just for that. A lot of kids'll miss Gowd around here. He's coaching the Junior Soccer team for one. And he's one of our best swimmers. And he's really nice to all those new kids . . ."

"Except one," Dieuwer commented. "He was downright cruel to Lara. You know that. And you know he's picked on Pearl ever since he had that fight with her Dad, too."

"Yeah, but it takes two to tango, my Mom says. A bit their fault too. That Pearl can be a real little bitch sometimes. She's got a big mouth. And lots of the kids say Lara's stuck-up. Hard to get to know."

"You know that's not true, Shelley," Dieuwer said.

"Yeah, but kids get that feeling about Lara, though. She sort of looks stuck-up if you get what I mean."

"Bull!" Reg said.

"Anyway, I for one, will miss Gowd. And I'm going to write to him, too. Poor thing. Banished like that by his own Dad. And all because of an accident. I mean, I know he can act tough sometimes, even very tough. But anyone who knows Gowd really well'd know he couldn't possibly do something like that on purpose . . ."

"Hey, here's Lara," Reg said, but Shelley was already on her way to pass on the news about Gowd to the others.

"We got the National Parks and Wildlife stuff," Reg told Lara as she passed them. "Wanna see it?"

"Are you okay, Lara?" Dieuwer asked. She wanted very much to put her arm around the white-faced girl, but Lara seemed so remote. "I'm fine, thanks," she said, automatically, "I'd like to see those things, Reg. Maybe later. In the library."

She noticed Stan Redmond nearby waiting about as if he wanted to speak to her too. But Lara didn't want to speak to him. Nor to any of them. She fled to her refuge in the library. There were books to be unpacked and covered and shelved and for a while Lara was too busy with them to think. But Stan found her there at the desk and spoke to her. "I heard about the dog, Lara. And the accident." He looked at her with a serious, worried expression. "Gowd did an awful thing. And I'm sorry, I should've . . ." His voice drifted off and she nodded at him, busying herself with the books. "Look, if there's anything I can do to help, Lara."

She knew Stan was trying to be kind, had sensed his attempts at friendship all these months. But she couldn't answer him any more than she could properly answer anyone else. And it just didn't seem to matter any more. It was too late.

Then Joslyn found her. "We heard about your dog, Lara. God, it's awful! You must feel dreadful, you poor thing." For a moment Joslyn's kind face, filled with sympathy, made Lara want to put her head on the woman's shoulder and weep and weep. But the bleak feeling took over once again and she nodded, dry-eyed.

"Thanks, Joslyn," and turned away. Then Joslyn put her hand on Lara's arm. "Neil wants to see you, Lara. You know he's finished the storytelling here for Mrs. Magill. He's going away soon for quite a while. But he's got something of yours, Lara. You know, what you gave him in the library to keep safe? Will you come and see Neil at our place, Lara? Tomorrow?"

Lara knew she would have to see Neil, the person who had been such a friend, before she left this place. The only person who had really understood about her magic dog. She nodded at Joslyn, "Yes, of course I'll come to your place." But somehow there was still no warmth or pleasure in her voice.

"Know what I think about your dog, Lara? He wasn't just special to you because you loved him. It was much more than that."

Neil had listened silently to her whole story as they sat on the front verandah of Joslyn's weatherboard house looking out across the ocean. She had told the story as if it were about other people, another animal, not Gowd and Lara, not Thunderwith. That was the only way she could get through it. She had told it coldly, without emotion.

"Something I wanted to tell you, Lara. From a long time back," the old man went on, "when you first told me about your dingo dog, your Thunderwith, I thought maybe I'd be telling you this someday. Not like this with your terrible sadness . . . but now seems kind of the right time . . . I told you the other day in the library that my totem is the dingo, didn't I? Well, listen to this, Lara. I reckon it's your totem, too. The dingo dog's your totem, Lara, for sure. That's what I think. That dingo dog'll always be for you and you'll be for it."

It was hard to listen to his familiar kindly voice without experiencing the rush of feelings she'd been so long without. She knew that Thunderwith was part of her, absolutely part of who she was and always would be, as Neil said. But there was only his memory now, wasn't there? It didn't lift this great square ugly heavy weight from her heart. Nothing ever would, she thought. Nothing ever could.

A silence had fallen. They both gazed out across the verandah rail from where they sat in Joslyn's creaking canvas chairs. It was such a sight, the spine of rocks plunging out into the water and the vague outline of other beaches somewhere far off across the waer. There was a sense of being on the edge of the world, she thought, sitting poised here. But it was no longer her world.

She knew there was something else she'd wanted to say to Neil before she left him forever. And now the time was slipping away. Dad would be here soon to pick her up. What was it she had wanted to tell him? Or was it something she felt Neil could tell her? Something she needed to know before she went away from here?

And then it did come to her: "When Thunderwith went — it's pretty strange, Neil, but I felt like — well, I felt like my Mom came back to me. I can't explain it, really, but I can feel her close to me again. She's with me now. She was kind of lost before."

The old man sat silent again for a very long time.

"*You* were lost for a while, Lara. But she was there all the time, I reckon. She sent the dog to you, to look out for you all those long hard months when you couldn't see her. She sent Thunderwith just as you thought, she sent something real to be with you. And then when the dog died, she had to let you know real quick that she'd come to stay by you forever," the old man said. "That's why you can feel her close to you. Just like I can feel all my mother-aunts and my Dad and my old Grandpa. They're all part of who you are."

"But did Thunderwith have to *go* for me to know that?" Lara asked, feeling the graveness of the sea seeping into her very being.

"You needed your mother real bad when that dog went away forever. That's all. That's why she came close. She would have come sooner or later, Lara, because she's never been far away. And that dog hasn't gone far away either. He'll come back when you stop being angry that he's left you. Like your mother. You needed her very badly and you let her spirit come near again."

She couldn't quite understand all that Neil had told her. She knew she would have to think about it later when she was alone. But somehow it seemed that a shred of comfort had penetrated the cold armor of her feelings as he spoke. Then, when she told him her plans to leave and go to the home, Neil sat silently, lost in thought again.

"You know, Lara, I thought a lot about that cave you and the dog found," he said eventually. "And the painting of the dog. Big handsome dingo dog. Thunderwith. And how you felt when you saw it."

She felt the ache of something deep in her throat at the way Neil said *Thunderwith*, kind of lovingly, as if it was a lullaby. But she summoned back the numbness and the deadness inside of her. She had to.

"Do you remember what you said?" The old man didn't wait for an answer. "I think you were right about it. I think it *was* meant for you, that big beautiful painting. It was a sign for you. It was no accident you found that cave, saw that painting, had that feeling you did. It was what your Mom wanted you to know: that you'd come home. Only she couldn't tell you directly. So she told you through the dog that you had. You're home, Lara. Right here. You'd better think about that. Think real hard."

And then he said no more.

Joslyn brought them afternoon tea. And she told Lara that Neil would be making one last visit to the school before he left for his storytelling trip all around New South Wales. "So many good-byes," Joslyn said, heavily.

Then Neil went inside to fetch the precious jar with Mom's silver dollar inside it. When it was back in her hands, Lara realized that she had saved something really special. Not the dollar, that gleamed and clinked in the glass jar, but a dream she and Mom had shared. At the sight of the silver coin, and with Neil's words on her mind, the numbness she had felt all this time seemed almost to melt away.

But in the truck going back to Willy Nilly with her Dad, there it was again. The cold hand on her heart. And really she was glad of it, because while it was there, she would be able to leave as she had planned. She knew if she began talking to Dad about what Neil had said, looking up at his firm jaw and all those frown lines around his eyes, she mightn't be able to go through with it after all. That if he pleaded again with her, she might weaken.

There was no doubt that, despite her heaviness of heart, the thought of going was getting more difficult for Lara every day that passed. But when she'd stop to think of Gladwyn, who had been remarkably quiet since the death of the dog, she knew what she'd known the night on the hill. That it was time for her to move on. No, she wouldn't stop to think about Neil's last comment about the cave . . . it would make her uneasy. She'd think about it later. When she was living somewhere else, far away.

When she and Dad reached the farm, Gladwyn was alone at the washing line. Lara could hear the others somewhere over by the creek and their excited cries at some new discovery. But she didn't have the heart to join them. Dad changed into his working boots and was gone off across the field in no time. Lara began to help Gladwyn, automatically taking down and folding the familiar garments, shorts and T-shirts, some of them her own.

She dumped them on the big dining table inside where Gladwyn was sorting them into neat piles for the drawers, and turned to go outside. But Gladwyn suddenly spoke to her.

"Lara," and she looked back, surprised, for Gladwyn rarely used her name.

"I want to talk to you a moment while the rest of the kids aren't here." Lara turned to look at her again inquiringly. There was no way Gladwyn could hurt her any more, she thought. That period of time was over, but at Lara's wish now.

She could see that it was hard for Gladwyn, because she was folding and refolding a small pair of shorts, Jasper's favorite swimsuit, and there were never wasted movements like that when Gladwyn worked at anything. Lara watched fascinated as Gladwyn's work-worn hand smoothed the faded material again and again.

"Larry tells me you want to leave here. You want to go to a home." The words rushed out, awkwardly.

Lara nodded, waiting for Gladwyn's approval. It was, after all, what she'd always wanted. But Gladwyn spoke heavily, her voice filled with strange new emotion.

"I'm not pretending I'm going to ask you this on my account alone," she said, speaking so softly that Lara had to strain to hear. "You've got to understand that I don't like to see Larry — your father — so upset. He doesn't want you to go to the home, that's for sure." And then her face flushed darkly, as she said, "And I don't want you to go, either."

Gladwyn might well have slapped Lara across the face, she recoiled in such surprise at these totally unexpected, unrecognizable words. It couldn't be true that Gladwyn, who hated her so bitterly, actually wanted her to stay. It just couldn't. Lara could only stare in surprise, completely dumbfounded by the impact of the woman's words.

But Gladwyn, who had finally put the re-folded garment down on the table and rested her hands helplessly on the chair-back, plunged on. "I want to say something else to you, Lara, too." She looked up at the girl now, unflinchingly. "I know I'm partly responsible for your unhappiness here. I've made it hard for you, there's no doubt about that. I didn't want you to come. I fought Larry. But he insisted on it. Your coming to live here was hard for me, you know. Very hard. And I just want you to know why. Maybe then you'll understand a bit better that sometimes . . ." She paused, looking up and out the door where the plastic strips fluttered slightly, and beyond. ". . . People can't help . . . can't change all that easily."

Lara would like to have turned and run away from Gladwyn and her unexpected words. She didn't want to stay and listen to this. They were all too shocking, these strange revelations. But somehow she couldn't move a muscle. She stood trans-fixed, feeling the blood draining from her face, as Gladwyn forged on.

"You see, I hated you and — and feared you long before I met you. And your mother, too. I hated what happened to Larry before I met him. What reduced him to a broken man. He couldn't get over the fact that she — Cheryl, your Mom, left him. Went off with some musician to Melbourne. He tried to find her. He tried to find you. He pined for his little girl, Lara. When I first met him I couldn't stand to see the way he suffered. And then I watched him change, especially when our children came along. This might be hard for you to understand but I find it very difficult to — to show my feelings, to show love." She spoke these last words so softly that again Lara had to strain to hear her.

"I've seen you with the kids and with your Dad. You, you can love so easily, Lara. Give it and receive it because that's what you've been used to all your life. For me, it's been differ-ent.

"Larry was the first thing in my life since my childhood that I found I could love. And then there were the children. And with each one, it became easier and easier. They were mine and they were not going to be taken away. Although even now, I fear this could happen. I didn't like seeing the love they gave to you, the stranger who was my husband's daughter."

Lara couldn't remember Gladwyn ever talking for so long without stopping in the whole time she'd been there. But obviously she was still not finished.

"I don't want you to go to a home, Lara, because it will make Larry so sad. But also because it'll make me sad too. You see, I spent a large part of my earlier life in foster homes, Lara. My mother, for a whole lot of reasons when she came to Australia alone, found she just couldn't support me. There was a series of foster homes and then, when she finally disappeared, an orphanage. I don't have very good memories of what happened to me there. It made me very afraid of ever getting attached to anyone. Every time I did it seemed the person I loved disappeared from my life. Things might have changed now in those places, but it won't be good for you, Lara. Believe me, it won't be. I wouldn't want you to go into a home when you have your own family," she said, bravely. "I wouldn't want you to leave here, where you really belong."

Lara gripped the back of the chair near her, too. What Gladwyn was saying made her feel shaky and weak.

"I — I —" she faltered, close to tears, not knowing what to say, her mind was in such a whirl. So many confused feelings assailed her.

"I haven't finished," Gladwyn went on, grimly. "There's something else I want to tell you that I've been wanting to tell you for a long time, and didn't have the courage to."

She looked steadily at the young girl and then said, "You've got guts, Lara. A heap of courage. And that's the truth. That's what I wanted to tell you and didn't know how. You've got guts, the way you saved Opal in that fire, it was brave. And the way you drove that car through the storm when I was cut so badly, that was a miracle. You're a very brave person."

Tears sprang into Lara's eyes at the words of praise from Gladwyn's lips. They were surely the miracle, she thought.

And then Gladwyn began to falter, looking down uneasily again at the patched shorts in front of her. "And so I just want to ask you . . ." Lara was horrified when Gladwyn's voice broke and a teardrop, yes she was sure, it was unmistakable, a teardrop, stained the pale yellow fabric in front of her on the table. She was crying, but still she managed to say in a choked voice, "Please, I want you to stay here with us where you belong. You're one of us. And we need you, Lara."

The young girl leapt around the table to put her arm awkwardly around Gladwyn's fine taut shoulders. She patted her as she would have done Jasper, and whispered: "Oh, Gladwyn, please, oh, don't — don't cry. Oh, please don't cry." But the woman's tears, which mingled now with her own, were nevertheless important and beautiful to Lara. They swept away all the resolve of the last few days. They lifted the awful torpor that had descended on her. They made her feel alive and vibrant again. They hurt, but she was glad to feel such pain.

When Larry came into the room, he found his wife and daughter seated at the table talking so intently that they didn't even look up for a moment. When Gladwyn realized he was there, she said at once, betraying her emotion, in the loudness and eagerness of her tone, "Lara has something to tell you, Larry. Something very important."

15

"Well, what do you think?" Larry asked, stepping back from the picture he'd just hung on the wall in the brand new room. Lara and Pearl nodded approval at this final touch. The small painting of a rock pool, its edge broken with a lacy foam and a larger wave poised to follow. It had been placed next to the drawing Neil had given to Lara when he'd come back to Palm Grove High to say good-bye to everyone. A drawing of a platypus dreaming on a pinkish piece of real bark.

Neil had given her a thick notebook, too. It had a wonderful hand-painted border on the front cover. Neil had put all the animals from his stories in that border: black cockatoos, frogs, bats, goannas, kangaroos, emus, brolgas, crows, fish. All of them. But right in the center of the notebook he'd drawn a finely detailed dingo, its head held alert and high.

"It's a real beauty," Lara had said to him, accepting the gift with tears in her eyes.

"I've been talking a lot with Mrs. Gilbert about you, Lara," he told her. "She's very pleased you've decided to stay at Palm Grove High. And she tells me that you write real pretty stories. Well, I figure maybe one day soon, you'd want to put down a special story. And if you do, then you'll maybe want to put it somewhere special. And this old book will be sitting waiting for you to tell it."

Lara was grateful that the friendly Joslyn would still be coming to the school and that she'd have news of Neil Symon, storyteller, from time to time. But she knew it would never be quite the same again after he'd left.

Lara and Pearl stood on the threshold of their new room. It was unpainted but sweet with the smell of freshly sawn timber. The room was large enough for two beds, a tiny dresser, a cupboard and a desk. Best of all, Dad had added a small verandah out the front so that it looked like a little bush cabin.

"It's nice to be able to sit out of doors," he'd told them. "You can look right across the dam and up into the forest from here."

"Have to get you some chairs, though," Gladwyn observed, "or maybe you can take those canvas ones from out front."

Dad, with the help of Bill Gadrey and Henk Rangers, had labored to finish the room for days on end, finding extra hours away from farm toil, so that it would be well and truly finished before the winter came on. It was as important to Dad as it was to Lara. Part of the new beginning here at Willy Nilly Farm. A fresh start for her without going away. A fresh start for everyone.

Gladwyn had allowed them to choose bits and pieces of furniture from the house ready for the day it would be completed. And Arlie had brought them a gift of a large woollen rug she'd finished on the front verandah one day where Jasper and Louis had played together. "We're really happy to see you settled in the Wallingat," she said, tying off the last green thread. "No place like it in the world."

"You can say that again," Pearl had enthused.

And Lara said, "No place like it in the world, Pearl." And then they'd all laughed.

"Just a few finishing touches," Dad called from somewhere up on the roof where he had built a look-out big enough for one. "It'll be ready for you tomorrow, I promise."

The two girls looked with satisfaction at the lovely timber room that was at last their own. Their beds had been transferred only this morning across the clearing to where the room stood by itself, like a little house in the woods. "Fantastic," Pearl enthused as she sank onto her bed, and then throwing her feet up and propping her head against the wall. "Wow! Come and look at this, Lara! We can see everything from our bed! The whole world out there!"

"It's great, Dad," Lara agreed, smiling at him. "Our own place."

"You can sleep here tonight, Gladwyn says she's going to cook up a feast. A celebration of your new living quarters. Could be rain tonight, too," he said, glancing outside the door. "Still, that'll really test the roof, I guess." And he went outside to check the placement of the corrugated iron roof whose sheets had been fastened securely against any storm that might blow in from the sea or come scudding over the mountains.

"Why's Pearl having a room with Lara? All by theirselves?" Opal began again. "It's not fair." But the practical Garnet defended them at once.

"More room for us, silly, in the house. Dad says when we're grown up he'll make another room just for us, won't you, Dad?"

"Mmm, that's right," Dad said absently, but he was not really listening. He glanced at his watch for the second time. "Bill's really late today. Said he'd be here at eleven, and give me a hand with the new windmill. And I'd like him to see the room now that we've got your furniture in it." Almost at once Jasper came running across the clearing yelling to them excitedly: "Gadwey, Gadwey. He's here," and they saw the truck spin into the yard.

"Tell him to come on over," Dad called, after Garnet and Opal took off to greet the man who often carried jellybeans in his back pocket. But he didn't come over. And presently the two small girls came back hand in hand, looking mysteriously important.

"Mom said you gotta come over the house right away, all of you," Garnet said. And then she looked at Opal and Opal looked at her and they burst out laughing. "For a surprise."

They all went across the clearing to the house and when Dad drew aside the plastic strips, there stood Bill Gadrery right by the door, blocking his way. Behind him they could see Glad-wyn at the table.

"Where's Lara?" she asked.

"C'mon, Lara," Garnet said, shoving her forward as Opal gave little excited squeals, much like the little pig in the story Pearl had been reading her every night.

Lara stepped wonderingly into the dimly lit room, with Jasper clinging behind her. The others crowded in after them.

Bill Gadrey stepped aside so that Lara could see something that had been hidden behind him. Something on the floor was covered with a scrap of striped towelling. There were more shrieks of excitement, this time from Garnet, when the towelling began to move.

"Guess what it is, Lara? Guess what?" Opal began.

"Shut your mouth, Opal," Garnet broke in and then, not able to contain herself: "*Can* you guess, Lara?"

Then Bill Gadrey knelt down to fling the stripes aside, revealing the plumpest, dearest little puppy Lara thought she had ever seen. It looked up at her with its bright alert eyes. But she could see it was trembling in fear.

"It's for you, Lara," Garnet announced, as if there could be some doubt about the matter.

"When Rov — Thunderwith went, I remembered the Grants of Mt. George," Mr. Gadrey was telling her proudly, "where we'd got Thunderwith in the first place. They breed good working dogs, the Grants. I went out there not long after the — er, the accident, just on a hunch. And you wouldn't believe it, the mother was in pup. I tell you, it was a real miracle to me. I told the Grants how badly I wanted one of the pups and so they said I could have one. This female was the only one left. Three others have already been spoken for. I've been waiting for weeks for this little one to be old enough to leave the mother. And now it is. Pretty dog, isn't she? It's for you, Lara."

"Oh, you darling thing," Lara said, falling to her knees to stroke the small frightened head ever so gently.

"Thunderwith," Dad said, softly, for you could see the dog would one day look exactly like the handsome dog from the hill. But Lara shook her head. "No, Dad, not Thunderwith," she said. "There'll never be another Thunderwith. But you're a little beauty, you are."

"And it just diddled on the floor," Opal said, hopping around excitedly, "it did, it did!"

"You could call it Diddles," Gladwyn said and the kids shrieked at this unexpected humor from her.

"Diddles dumpling," Garnet crooned.

"Diddles," Jasper copied.

Lara gathered the small thing in her arms and eager hands reached to pat it. "Careful, Jasper," Gladwyn said, "don't pinch the puppy."

"What will you call her?" Pearl asked.

"She's so glad to see you," Dad remarked watching the puppy nestle down in Lara's arms.

"I know," Lara said at once, an expression of real pleasure flitting across her face as she glanced at Gladwyn. "I'll call it Gladheart. That's it," and she looked down at the puppy, already closing tired eyes, "you're Gladheart of the Wallingat."

"Sounds like a fancy storybook name for a farm dog," Bill Gadrey said, "but it's kind of nice. And if that's what you want . . . it's your dog, Lara."

"Gladheart. Got a real ring to it," Dad said.

"Gladwyn-Gladheart," Opal chanted, "Gladwyn-Gladheart! Glad, glad Gladheart."

"Hush your mouth, child," Gladwyn said, but they took no notice of the half-hearted admonishment and went out onto the verandah to chant their song.

"Thanks, Mr. Gadrey, it's — well, it's —" Lara couldn't think of words to express how happy his gift of the puppy had made her. But she could see by the look on his face that it made him extremely happy, too.

She went to sit outside on the long seat that stood where her bed had been. The little dog lay almost asleep in her arms and the kids gathered at either side of her.

"You could leave the puppy in the house with us nights, and we'll look after it," Opal suggested.

210

"Or it could sleep right on my bed, just while it's small," Garnet added, hopefully. But Lara shook her head.

"I think Gladheart better stay by me." And then when their faces fell, she said, "But you and Jasper can look after her all day while we're at school."

"Gladheart, you're the luckiest dog in the forest. You get to come to Willy Nilly Farm. And you get to be with all of us," Garnet said to the dog, who was sleeping soundly now.

"This is the best farm in the world, bar none," Opal said, "Isn't it, Lara?"

"The best!" Lara said. "You'd better believe it!"

"I do," said Garnet. "I really do."

"Me, me," Jasper said, climbing on to Garnet's knee to get closer to the newcomer. "Won't pinch Diddles," he said. "Noooo. Won't squeeze Diddles either."

"Diddles," Opal shrieked. "Ha! He calls it Diddles."

Before they got into their beds every night in the new room, Lara would sit at the crudely fashioned desk and write in Neil's book. Dad had made the desk in one afternoon, a slab of smoothed pine that rested on stumps of rough-hewn wood, put in the corner of their room. Neil's thick white notebook had become a kind of diary. In the few weeks that she had owned it, she'd filled page after page.

Her final visit to the cave had been described in loving detail; how she'd asked Neil's advice about going there and how Neil had said she should take someone, take her Dad with her there for the last visit. Dad had been thrilled by the hidden cave with its magic drawing of the proud dingo. But it wasn't just to show Dad the drawing that they'd trekked all that way through the bush. Lara had brought Mom's silver dollar with her.

"Take it out of the jar," Dad had whispered (somehow the feeling inside the cave made them want to talk only in hushed tones), "and you can bury it down much deeper, love."

They'd left Mom's silver dollar buried down deep in the sand, right up in front of the Thunderwith drawing.

"They're together. For good," Lara said, raising her head

and looking at the dog, so lovely in the bright beam of her torch. She didn't say good-bye as she left the cave but she knew, as Dad did too, that they would never come back again.

Yes, she'd recorded that important visit in Neil's thick notebook as she'd recorded all that she was feeling about the changes here at the place she could so confidently now call home. She'd written lots about Gladwyn, too. How Gladwyn after their long talk had reverted to being her quiet self for the most part. But how things were so different between them now and everyone, down to young Jasper, was aware of it. There was an air of light-heartedness in the household now that there had never been before. Lara was sure. And one day, one day soon, Lara felt, she might even be able to throw her arms around the woman she had learned to understand a bit more and increasingly to love. She had written about this as she made her first forest visit to Angophora tree where brave Thunderwith lay.

She'd gone alone one day and sat for quite some time, close to the stone mound that the children had helped make, against the great pink trunk, thinking about what Neil had said to her. It was hot, and though blowflies buzzed nearby and birds called harshly, she felt quite still and calm. Her own Green Cathedral, she thought, right here at Willy Nilly under the great Angophora tree.

She closed her eyes. She remembered the first day the dog had come bounding towards her, springing from the top of the hill and the storm as though it had come out of the earth itself. The dog from the earth, the tree from the earth, Lara thought, against the great trunk on the earth. Lara and the dog. She was lulled by the thought of it. For a moment she felt part of the earth and the tree and the dog and the creek and all the smells and sounds and even the silences of the bush around her. She was so still that she felt she could merge into the landscape, become the tree she leaned against, there in the warm sun. What had Neil said so many times about the heartbeat of the old earth?

But gradually the brittle shrillness of a new cicada song intruded. Her ears vibrated with their swelling sound and she

212

opened her eyes, remembering with a shock a detail she had long since forgotten. It was like a line of poetry that had suddenly flashed into her mind as the cicada song gathered its momentum and it took her back to that first day. Only, of course, it wasn't from a poem at all.

She had chanted it the day Thunderwith became hers. The words had come out of her mouth like a poem as she welcomed the beautiful creature into her life. She remembered them vividly now: *With thunder you'll come and with thunder you'll go.* That's what she said as she'd embraced the dog for the first time.

It amazed Lara to think that in reciting these words that first day, she'd had already known something she in fact hadn't known. For the dog had come in the thunder of the storm, hadn't it? And had left in the thunder of a single gunshot. She closed her eyes again. Thunderwith had gone and yet its memory was here sharply, clearly, because she was still here. She was sorry Neil wasn't around any more to talk to about this. But there was his precious notebook to write in, wasn't there?

She'd gone straight back to the house and written snatches of things untidily all over the page. For the moment she just wanted to capture some of her feelings as she'd sat over there by the creek and the Angophora and the dog.

"*I am the dog,*" she'd written in a firm clear hand. "And so the dog goes on and on." That might be the beginning of a poem one day. A poem that might be as mysterious and beautiful as the ones Mom used to read to her.

The puppy, who was called Diddles by the little kids but Gladheart insistently by Lara and Pearl, had been moved from the basket between their beds in the new room permanently on to Lara's bed. When it woke and whimpered as it still did sometimes, in the middle of the night, she could comfort it. Once she'd settled it down, patting and soothing it, Lara would often lie awake a while, gazing out across the fields, beyond where the trees in a line flanked the creek's edge in their dense loveliness.

Tonight she thought about her visit to the Angophora tree and her story. It was a lustrous night out there. Just a hint of rain in the low bank of clouds far away up the hill. The bright moon, unimpeded, lit the dam edge and tree trunks so that they shone whitely and boldly. A tiny breeze made the trees sway and their soothing sound washed in over her. She thought of Mom as she often did now. But not in the blaming way she used to think about her, as she lay alone on her verandah bed. Not a bit like that. She still felt a heavy sadness when she thought of her mother, but it was different. She knew Mom was here now. Somewhere, forever, very close by.

The puppy whimpered a moment and she stroked it gently, watching it settled in a little nest of the blanket, against the warmth of her leg. She felt very peaceful in the new room with the little dog beside her and with Pearl fast asleep in her bed not far away. She stared up into the hills where the dark clouds formed a backdrop for the grand old trees that had been there so long. How she loved it up there, where she could look back down on Willy Nilly Farm, or into the heart of the palm forest, or way over the back of beyond to the Bulahdelah Mountains. Her mountains now, too, she thought, remembering the secret of the cave.

"I'll take you up there tomorrow, Gladheart," she whispered to the sleeping puppy, "over the log bridge and past the big pink tree. We'll go for a long, long walk up the hill. And the kids and Pearl can come with me this time. And maybe I'll tell all of you a story, little dog, about another beautiful beast. A true story about a dog called Thunderwith."